S0-BYA-657

"You don't have much of a choice, Harry," Bolan said

"Here's the deal. Give me the location of the drop and you can take the money, go as far as you can and take your chances."

Sweat was pouring down Tipping's red face. He looked from the cash to Bolan and back to the money. The numbers were clicking away in his head as he worked the odds.

Take the money and run, gambling that DiFranco was going to be so involved with this guy with the gun that he would forget about Harry Tipping until it was too late.

Or DiFranco might figure out what was going on and send out his icemen the minute he realized.

"What the hell," Tipping replied. "I don't have much else going for me. You've got a deal."

Other titles available in this series:

Ambush
Blood Strike
Killpoint
Vendetta
Stalk Line
Omega Game
Shock Tactic
Showdown
Precision Kill
Jungle Law
Dead Center
Tooth and Claw
Thermal Strike
Day of the Vulture
Flames of Wrath
High Aggression
Code of Bushido
Terror Spin
Judgment in Stone
Rage for Justice
Rebels and Hostiles
Ultimate Game
Blood Feud
Renegade Force
Retribution
Initiation
Cloud of Death
Termination Point
Hellfire Strike
Code of Conflict
Vengeance
Executive Action
Killsport
Conflagration
Storm Front

War Season
Evil Alliance
Scorched Earth
Deception
Destiny's Hour
Power of the Lance
A Dying Evil
Deep Treachery
War Load
Sworn Enemies
Dark Truth
Breakaway
Blood and Sand
Caged
Sleepers
Strike and Retrieve
Age of War
Line of Control
Breached
Retaliation
Pressure Point
Silent Running
Stolen Arrows
Zero Option
Predator Paradise
Circle of Deception
Devil's Bargain
False Front
Lethal Tribute
Season of Slaughter
Point of Betrayal
Ballistic Force
Renegade
Survival Reflex
Path to War

Don Pendleton's Mack

Bolan®

Blood Dynasty

A GOLD EAGLE BOOK FROM

WORLDWIDE®

TORONTO • NEW YORK • LONDON
AMSTERDAM • PARIS • SYDNEY • HAMBURG
STOCKHOLM • ATHENS • TOKYO • MILAN
MADRID • WARSAW • BUDAPEST • AUCKLAND

First edition July 2006

ISBN-13: 978-0-373-61512-4
ISBN-10:   0-373-61512-4

Special thanks and acknowledgment to
Mike Linaker for his contribution to this work.

BLOOD DYNASTY

It is time for a new generation of leadership, to cope with new problems and new opportunities. For there is a new world to be run.
—John F. Kennedy,
1917–1963

When the Mob changes guard, nothing changes. The same old illegal activities that bring misery to people prevail. But I keep coming back to even the score as best I can.
—Mack Bolan

PROLOGUE

Walter Kershaw had been a federal agent for almost eight years, and part of the Witness Protection Program for three of those years. During the past few weeks, his team had been assigned to the ongoing protection of witnesses involved in the investigation into the criminal activities of Arkady Suvarov, head of one of the largest and most influential Russian *mafiya* organizations.

Suvarov was under indictment, charged with a catalog of crimes that seemed to get longer and more complicated every time Kershaw checked—murder, conspiracy to commit murder, blackmail, drug dealing, the procurement of young women for a variety of illegal purposes, prostitution and pornography being the most lucrative. There was also money laundering and the transporting of stolen motor vehicles. From what Kershaw had been able to work out, if it was illegal and made money, Arkady Suvarov would have a finger in the pie. The man was powerful, had friends in high places and was incredibly wealthy. Even now, languishing behind the walls of a secure federal facility, the Russian's name still had the power to terrify people. His influence extended beyond high walls and electronic surveillance.

The gathering of witnesses had been slow. The fact that the Russian was in prison did nothing to ease their concerns. Suvarov had a large organization, and all it took was a simple instruction for someone to move on a suspected witness. During the first few weeks of the federal investigation, a number had died. As the fear began to spread, individuals who at first had only been too eager to talk started to lose their memories. They denied any knowledge of Arkady Suvarov—this despite the information they had been willing to pass along days before. There was a rapid exodus of people allied to the Suvarov organization who might have been able to provide the federal investigators with evidence. As more bodies showed up, silence descended and the name of Arkady Suvarov became taboo.

The message was simple: point the finger at Suvarov and see how long you stay alive.

Despite the implicit threats, there were a number of people more than willing to risk reprisals. They came forward and were immediately placed in protective custody. The machinery swung into action and the ready witnesses were spirited away, relocated and spread across the country in safehouses. It was accepted from the start that the Suvarov investigation was going to be a long one. Suvarov himself had been arrested and jailed, his pleas of innocence duly recorded and his demands for bail refused. Arkady Suvarov was too big a catch. The federal prosecutor had no intention of allowing Suvarov the chance of freedom and possible flight, so he was shut away while the case against him was prepared.

Initial depositions were taken from the first of the witnesses. There was more to be done from that point. Every piece of information noted had to be thoroughly investigated, corroborated, pinned down so that the defense would have no chance to tear it to shreds. It all took time. And that meant the witnesses were forced to stay hidden.

Three weeks into the investigation the first of the protected witnesses was gunned down as he was escorted to a local hospital where he was to undergo a check for a possible stomach ulcer. He had been killed by a single rifle shot to the back of the head. The bullet had penetrated his skull, expanding on impact and had mushroomed into his brain. Despite all the efforts of the on-hand medical teams, he had been pronounced dead.

Just under a week later the second killing took place. The scenario was similar to the first in that this witness was being escorted to court to advance his original testimony. He was shot down as he walked out of the safehouse where he was being looked after by federal agents. One shot to the head, and the man was dead within a few minutes.

In the aftermath of this second murder the authorities became almost paranoid in their protection of the remaining witnesses. They were all relocated to alternate accommodations. The problem adding to the concerns of the protection squads had to do with the expertise of the shooter. Both sniping sites had been discovered to be a long distance away. It was indicative of a highly professional shooter, a sniper of uncanny accuracy. It made the task of protection that much harder. It made the teams nervous.

The first two deaths were kept from the other witnesses. If the story had gotten out and had reached the widely dispersed witnesses, they might have backed out.

Two weeks later the third shooting took place— the location Cleveland, where the WPP had its witness based. The killing had added complications and concerns because, more importantly for the Justice Department, one of their own was also killed.

Federal Agent Walter Kershaw.

He was shot within seconds of the witness's death. There was nothing his partner could do for him except call in the hit and try to keep his fellow agent alive until medical help arrived.

CHAPTER ONE

New York City

"Fact," Leo Turrin said. "One federal agent and three witnesses already dead. The witnesses were all under federal protection, each of them involved in the case being built against Arkady Suvarov, Russian crime boss. Walter Kershaw was on assignment protecting one of the witnesses."

Turrin took a laptop from its carrying case and placed it on the table between himself and Bolan. "You should find that interesting," he said, turning on the computer. "It's everything I have on all the players."

Bolan reached out and swung the laptop around so he could see the screen.

"Just give me the condensed version for starters, Leo."

"As you know," the former undercover mafioso said, "the Russian *mafiya* started to make its presence known in the late '80s, making Brighton Beach its turf. There were skirmishes among the various groups while they jockeyed for position. In the end the toughest bosses reached the top of the heap and carved up the district between them. They were all after the usual things—power, money, the usual strutting stuff these people have to do to maintain their credibility. The problem is, people get hurt in the process, and I'm talking about the innocent who always seem to get caught in the cross fire. Hell, Mack, I don't need to tell *you* how it works."

No, Bolan thought, I know how it works. The good get dragged down by the undertow. They walk in at the wrong time and catch the back draft. They have no quarrel with the combatants but they still get hurt. Killed. Maimed. Physically and mentally scarred by what they get trapped in. No one cares enough to see what they need or how they feel. The rush is always toward the perpetrators. They have their own care package—people who clean up after them, doctors who patch them up and lawyers who have the clout to spring them from custody.

"Witnesses getting hit suggests a sellout in the Witness Protection Program," Bolan said.

"I'm working on that right now. It has to be done quietly so we don't scare off the son of a bitch, which is why I'd like you on my team, Mack. No one else, except Hal Brognola, knows I'm talking to you and that's how I want it to stay. I'll give you all the backup I can. Feed you whatever information you need. You deal with me and no one else. Except Hal and Stony Man. This thing is getting out of hand. The Suvarovs are playing games with us, still orchestrating murder and keeping the businesses going. We have a good chance to bring down Arkady Suvarov and his organization, but every time we get close to building our case witnesses are being killed right under our noses. We need to break the Suvarov hold before we end up with another Mob empire. We need his organization splintering, Mack, kicked every which way, his establishments put out of action. And I need to find out who on my team is feeding information to the Mob."

"We keep it in the family?" Bolan smiled. "Just like we did before."

Turrin stood, heading for the cabin's kitchen.

"There's big heat coming down on Justice over this whole shooting match. We're catching six kinds of hell, and we don't know which way to turn. Mack, I need someone out there with street savvy, someone who has the smell in his nostrils and doesn't have to duck and cover every time someone shouts he's stepping over the line. Christ, Mack, they're moving that line every damn day. How do they expect us to put these mobsters behind bars when they tie our hands and gag us at every turn?"

Bolan leaned back and caught Turrin's eye. "Come on, Leo, don't be so coy. What is it you really want?"

"Well, I was thinking on the lines of Mack the Bastard."

"Is that politically correct, Leo?" Bolan asked, a smile tugging at his lips.

"Hell, no. Which is why I want you on the prowl."

"How long can Suvarov be kept in custody?"

"Good question. There are big dealings going on all the time. There was enough evidence against Suvarov to have him arrested. Justice has been building its case for months, using every angle available to pin something on Suvarov. They finally got him on an accessory to murder. One of his boys had actually walked into a restaurant and shot a rival. He was caught red-handed by a couple of cops who were on the scene. They collared him and he panicked, saying he wasn't going to take the rap for the murder. He'd been ordered by his boss, Arkady Suvarov, because the dead guy had been trying to move in on one of the Suvarov operations.

"The hit man really pointed the finger, giving names and dates and a heap of other stuff implicating the Suvarov Mob. Whatever he said must have reached the ears of one of Suvarov's allies because by the time a warrant had been issued, Arkady Suvarov, against character, had decided he was getting out of the country. Agents caught him just as he was boarding a flight out of LaGuardia. The guy resisted arrest. He punched out two agents, breaking one guy's cheekbone. So he was arrested and taken into custody. Before the dust had even settled his lawyers were screaming blue murder and demanding he should be released. Justice dug in its heels. Hauling Suvarov off to jail showed he wasn't as untouchable as he'd been telling everyone. They asked for time to prepare their case, saying they needed to get their witnesses together, and they demanded that bail be refused because Suvarov had already shown he had no intention of staying around for any trial."

"And they got it?"

"Damn right they did. The judge presiding at the arraignment made no concessions toward Suvarov. He made it clear whose side he was on, and he stipulated Suvarov should be kept in a federal lockup until trial time."

"And that was when the witnesses started to come forward?"

"Things were looking up—until the witnesses started getting hit."

Bolan nodded.

"Time to do some homework," he said.

Turrin watched as Bolan hunched over the laptop and start to look at the extensive files. He pushed to his feet, reaching over to pick up some paper files and drop them beside the laptop.

"Some other stuff I hadn't managed to put on the computer."

"Thanks, Leo."

"I'll make coffee," Turrin said. "I think we're going to need it."

AT 2:00 A.M. Bolan sat upright, pushing the laptop aside and reaching for the coffeepot. It was cold. He stood, working the kinks out of his spine as he made his way to the kitchen area. He spent a few minutes brewing a fresh pot, then returned to where he'd been working and sat. As he filled two mugs, the aroma of hot coffee stirred Turrin from his sleep. He sat up, blinking his eyes and peered across at Bolan.

"Have I...?"

Bolan grinned. "Like a baby."

Turrin picked up his mug and took a swallow. "Hell, Mack, what did you do? Pour water into the coffee jar?"

"Thought you liked it strong?"

"I want to drink it, not etch stainless steel." Turrin glanced at the computer. "You up to speed?"

"I get the main picture. These people have it all tied up, Leo. And they're greedy. They want it all."

Turrin shrugged. "Maybe it's a spin-off from the old Communist way of life. They had so little under that regime that freedom has hit them hard, so they're grabbing at every damn thing they can."

"In the end all they are is a bunch of lowlifes who don't give a damn for anyone who gets in their way."

"Mack, I'd give my pension to have you stand up in court and take them on."

Bolan smiled.

"I'm no politician, Leo. I see things in black and white. They come here and take advantage of our system, and when they get caught they start quoting human rights violations. They hire the best lawyers to play with the legal loopholes and scream bloody murder when they don't get what they want. When was the last time you heard anyone doing that for the victims?"

"It's the world we live in. Hell, Mack, I didn't create it. All I do is try to make it work."

"The way I read these reports, Walt Kershaw was in the wrong place at the wrong time?"

"Yeah," Turrin acknowledged. "The guy was just doing his job protecting one of the witnesses. He caught one of the bullets that took down Malinkov.

"Malinkov was one of Suvarov's money men. He handled millions in cash transactions. The money came in from all of Suvarov's enterprises—gambling, prostitution, drugs, black market videos and music CDs, stolen cars. The guy traveled all over the Eastern seaboard doing weekly runs to pick up the money, delivering merchandise, arranging pickups and drop-offs."

"What turned him?"

"His name came up in an investigation. It seems Suvarov got word and decided there had to be something going on. Like Malinkov actually *was* working with the Feds. So the nod was given to off Malinkov. The guy must have had some friends left in the Mob, though. He was tipped off and got out just ahead of the hit team. His girlfriend wasn't so lucky. She ended up in the East River. What they did to her with a knife was not very pleasant. Malinkov turned himself in two days later. He said he'd tell them everything he knew about Suvarov and his organization if they kept him alive."

Bolan came across the N.Y.P.D. Crime Scene report file, which had included photographs of the dead girl. The face of death wasn't new to Mack Bolan. He had seen it many times before, maybe too often. Yet even now, in these stark and graphic images, he recognized the evil hand of the soulless monsters who had perpetrated this atrocity, and he felt pity for the victim. The woman, in her late twenties, had been attractive before the butchers had done their terrible work as they attempted to extract any information she might have had on Malinkov's whereabouts. Whatever dreams she might have had for her future had been extinguished along with her life.

"That was the work of Tibor Kureshenko. Our people recognized his handiwork. He runs Suvarov's enforcement squad and does any dirty work that's asked of him. This is one mean guy, Mack. He's been up on charges more than a dozen times—assault, intimidation, twice on suspicion of murder, but nothing ever sticks to this guy. He's been bailed out more times than Perry Mason won cases. The term 'arrogant bully' covers his better qualities.

"Someone is working to clear the way for Suvarov's release," Turrin continued. "His legal advisers visit him every few days. They're working hard to prove his innocence. Gathering evidence is hard enough. If all the protected witnesses are taken out, we'll have even less. The prosecution needs witnesses and time to build their case against this guy. They need to have it sewn up tight before it reaches court, because if it isn't, Suvarov's lawyers will find the weak spots and home in on them."

Bolan brought up a series of photographs and their accompanying biographies on the monitor. "Vasily Suvarov. Do we assume the son's running the organization while his father is out of the loop?"

Turrin nodded. "We guess he's the one. He's nowhere as strong as his old man. More of a playboy. He'll need help, and he'll get it from this guy, Nikolai Petrovsky, a long-time member of the Suvarov clan. He's Arkady's adviser and sounding board. He's well respected and has a lot of influence within the Mob. He has legal background, so he has a cautious approach. His hands on the reins keep things on an even course."

Petrovsky's image showed a dapper, well-groomed man in his forties. Nothing was out of place. His neat, tidy hair was slicked back.

"And this is the daughter?" Bolan studied the image.

Valentina Suvarov was younger than her thirty-three-year-old brother. She had the same bone structure, the family resemblance. On her it looked better. The woman had thick dark hair, big soulful eyes and a mouth that looked soft yet with a sensuous hint in its subtle curves. Looking at her photograph, Bolan sensed something alive and intelligent about Valentina Suvarov. She stared directly into the camera lens, her expression challenging, as if she was asking the viewer to take her on. The implicit boldness was slightly disturbing.

"Daddy's little girl. The baby of the family."

"Some baby, Leo."

"Suvarov is extremely protective of her. They're very close."

"Is she in the Family business?"

Turrin shrugged.

"No idea. We haven't found any connections. She has to know what daddy does for a living. She has her own apartment in New York, a condo in Miami, but still spends a lot of time at the family mansion."

Bolan had already viewed the long-distance footage of the Suvarov enclave, a sprawling mansion in the Hamptons. The place was protected 24/7 by Suvarov's own people.

"So it's Vasily and this guy Petrovsky who handle the day-to-day affairs?" Bolan queried. "Your information says Suvarov still has connections back home in Russia."

"He has his roots in Mother Russia. A lot of his drug supplies come in via the Afghanistan trade. Suvarov runs a near-duplicate operation in the old hometown as he does in New York, and makes a lot of money from Russia and Europe. Suvarov is nothing if not expansive."

"The guy likes to travel," Bolan observed. "He has a house in the South of France, a big place on his own island off Puerto Rico and owns property on three continents. He has an oceangoing boat, his own private jet. The guy's wealthy and likes to flaunt it."

"He owns people, as well. We've tapped into that with this mole we have in the department."

"According to the New York CSI reports, all the assassinations were carried out by the same shooter. Handmade bullets, no prints, clean shots from a distance. That suggests a professional shooter."

"Police located the points of origin, marks where the shooter set up, but not a damn thing else. There were indications of a two-man team, but that's it."

"My guess is that this team does regular work for Suvarov. Could be worthwhile looking back over previous hits linked to Suvarov. Anything on the rifle used?"

"The FBI report has pinned it down as custom built. No manufactured items. Someone special has built that rifle from scratch. They're trying to get a make on the guy who put it together. He's a craftsman. They might find something. If they do, we could get a lead on the shooters. They have confirmed the ammunition is the same from each shooting. Identical grooving."

Bolan sat back, toying with his coffee mug.

Turrin produced a manila envelope from one of his paper files and slid out more photographs, images of young women with vacant expressions on their faces, clustered together in the hold of a ship.

"Just one of Suvarov's human cargoes on its way to the U.S. The Coast Guard intercepted it off the coast of Florida two weeks ago. Twenty-five females. If they hadn't been discovered, they would have been working the streets within a week. They were young women from Eastern

Europe, and the majority of them couldn't even speak English. Suvarov's teams picked them up and transported them halfway across the globe.

"Mack, we know this is one of Suvarov's deals. We *know*, but we can't offer solid proof. So this time Suvarov loses his merchandise and the money they would earn, but he stays in the clear. As clear as a guy can be when he's locked up."

Turrin offered more photographs. "These are the people involved in the transportation ring. They deny any links with Suvarov, but they understand we know the truth, and that's what hurts." Turrin slammed the photographs onto the table. "It gets to me sometimes, Mack. We get so damned close. Up close and personal. And these bastards smile and walk away with their lawyers. Back on the streets in hours and using their cell phones to set up the next deal before they step inside their cars."

"It all sounds so familiar, Leo. So old-fashioned methods might work for us. Okay. Can you get everything on the shootings sent over to Stony Man? Let Aaron run some of his own checks. Have him pass the information on the hit team to Cowboy Kissinger. He might turn something up on the rifle. We don't have anything to lose."

"And you? What are you going to do?"

"I'm going hunting, Leo. My way."

Brighton Beach

BOLAN'S SECOND DAY watching Vasily Suvarov was uneventful. The younger Suvarov had a varied agenda. The first day he had traveled in from the family mansion into the city and had spent most of the morning at the Golden Troika, the Suvarov organization's largest nightclub. Turrin's data had the club down as the center of Suvarov enterprises. The Justice Department had the suspicion but not the proof. Suvarov's legal team had already established that Justice Department agents were harassing the club's manager and patrons without cause. There were restrictions on any form of search and seizure.

Turrin's own suspicion of a leak within the department had been confirmed when he had quietly slipped details into the system that told of a possible upcoming raid that wouldn't be broadcast. The information was purely a decoy, and Turrin was rewarded by a call from Suvarov's legal team warning that any such raid would be in violation of the restraints. Turrin had talked his way out of the matter by claiming it was an old assignment detail that had been wrongly issued. There was no such planned raid.

Turrin thought the call was interesting.

Suvarov's lawyer was a smart man. He would

use the law to his client's advantage, employing every legal loophole and trick in his arsenal. The little Fed wasn't fazed by that. It came with the job.

What he was pleased about was the definite proof that there was a mole within the department. His hoax message had reached Suvarov within two hours of it being issued. All Turrin had to do now was locate the source of the leak.

Bolan had been told about the subterfuge, and Turrin added that following his discussion with the lawyer, David Garland, one of the legal team, had made the trip out to see Arkady Suvarov at the federal facility in New Jersey.

"Letting him know firsthand what's going on, no doubt."

"Looks like you stirred the pot," Bolan said. "Let's see if I can keep it going."

Which put him on Vasily Suvarov's trail yet again. Suvarov's visit to the nightclub on the first day had been followed by a run into New York City. He had spent the afternoon shopping, visiting a number of exclusive clothing stores. On his return to the mansion the trunk of the big BMW had been loaded with the results of his excursion. Bolan had followed the BMW all the way out to the Suvarov estate in the Hamptons until Vasily had retreated behind the gates of the estate. There had been a number of visitors during the early evening. Bolan identified a couple of minor Suvarov employees from Turrin's extensive and detailed photographic files. There was also a group of young women, arriving in open sports cars. Bolan's stakeout lasted until midnight when the majority of the visitors departed.

Day two and Bolan followed Vasily to Greenwich Village. He watched as Vasily went inside an apartment building. He stayed for the morning. The car he had arrived in remained at the curb, his bodyguards keeping watch. Just before noon Vasily left the building with an attractive dark-haired young woman on his arm. They climbed inside the waiting limousine and it pulled away. Bolan followed at a discreet distance. If Vasily's people were professional, they might spot him. He wasn't too concerned about that. If he was seen, it would have to become part of his strategy. As it was, he tailed the limo to a midtown restaurant where Vasily and the woman went inside for lunch. They stayed for almost two hours.

Bolan called it a day. If nothing else, he had established that Vasily Suvarov *was* more a playboy than a hardworking mobster. Two days and he had done little of consequence. Nothing that justified his suggested position as head of the Suvarov clan in the absence of his father. It gave Bolan food for thought.

If Vasily wasn't running the organization, who was?

His first choice was Nikolai Petrovsky, Arkady Suvarov's right-hand man. Petrovsky would understand the business as well as his boss. Much of the decision-making that came from Arkady Suvarov would be based on advice offered by Petrovsky. The man's legal background would be used to vet any moves Suvarov was considering. His expertise would be needed more than ever.

Bolan mulled over the possibilities as he drove back to the city. If he was correct and Petrovsky was the real power, then Vasily was purely there as a figurehead, someone to show the world that the Suvarov organization was still up and running.

THE FOLLOWING MORNING Bolan drove out to New Jersey. It was time, he had decided, to shake up the Suvarov Mob. It was too complacent, too secure in the knowledge that it was invulnerable to attack. It was time to rock the boat.

Turrin's people had tagged a stolen-car ring in New Jersey that was run by the Suvarovs. Stolen vehicles were brought to an isolated warehouse in an old industrial park, and by the time they left the facility for resale, little remained of the original vehicle. It was a lucrative business. The cars were loaded onto semi-rigs and shipped out of state. Quick sales with no questions asked, and the Suvarovs were making good money.

Gregori Lebowski was in charge of the business. Beneath his urbane charm he had a reputation for violence that was only exceeded by his ability to treat everyone around him with total disdain. Lebowski was followed everywhere by his second cousin, Tasha Lebowski, who was his bodyguard and the only man Gregori trusted after Arkady Suvarov. Tasha had a low tolerance for most things, and had a reputation for unrestrained violence when it came to relationships with women.

It was barely noon when Bolan parked his car in the shadow of a derelict industrial building. From where he was sitting he could see the site where the car ring worked its magic. The Executioner was rigged for battle. He was dressed in black pants, roll-neck sweater and a leather jacket that was zipped over the shoulder rig holding his Beretta 93-R. In the trunk he had heavy-duty weapons supplied by Stony Man: a 12-gauge Mossberg shotgun, its 9-shot magazine topped off by a Side-Saddle attachment that held six extra shells, and an M-4 carbine fitted with an underslung M-203 grenade launcher. Bolan had a number of incendiary rounds for that.

He sat and studied the place for a while, spotting a semi-rig already fully loaded with modified cars. Using a pair of powerful binoculars, he was able to study the comings and goings of the employees. He spotted Gregori twice, his shadow Tasha always at his heels. Gregori obviously worked on the principle of keeping his people in line by yelling and waving his hands around most of the time.

Bolan had noticed the sky starting to cloud over, the light turning gray, and he wasn't surprised when it started to rain. It was chilly and it fell across the backwater location in shimmering waves.

He opened the trunk and armed himself, making sure both shotguns, carbine and grenade launcher, were fully loaded. He pulled a thin black ski mask over his head, adjusting its fit, then started the car and swung the nose around so it pointed at the building. Pushing his foot down on the gas pedal, Bolan cut around the perimeter road and prepared to fire the opening shots in the war against Arkady Suvarov and his organization.

The sound of the approaching vehicle drew the attention of the man who was about to climb into the cab of the semi. He had a long trip ahead of him, which would terminate in St. Louis where he would collect payment in cash. Always cash. It was *that* kind of deal.

He turned at the sound of the engine and saw a dark-colored, late-model Dodge sedan heading in his direction. The falling rain streaked the windshield and made it difficult to identify the driver. It was only when the car swung around, placing the driver's door feet away, that he made out the black ski mask the driver was wearing. Even as he registered the fact, the window powered down and the truck driver found himself staring into the muzzle of a shotgun.

"What do you think…?"

"You have a choice," Bolan advised the man. "Walk away and don't get involved. Stay and the pay is the same for anyone getting in my way. It's not open for debate."

The Mossberg moved a fraction, settling directly on the target's chest.

"Okay, I'm gone," the driver said.

He walked around the car and away, moving quickly across the rough ground. He didn't look back. Not even when he heard the thump of an explosion, followed by a succession of bangs. That would be the gas tanks of the cars loaded on the truck. He knew that if he turned he would see his vehicle and its load in flames. Let Gregori deal with it. The guy was always throwing his weight around, telling everyone what a big man he was and how he made millions for Arkady Suvarov.

Okay, you loudmouth bastard. Talk your way out of what's coming your way.

THE LOUD EXPLOSIONS brought men racing out of the building. They milled around in confusion, staring at the thousands of dollars going up in flames. Smoke was billowing from the fiery mass, curling into the rainy sky.

By the time Gregori Lebowski leaned out the door, staring with disbelief at the burning vehicles, Bolan had already moved to the far end of the building, swinging his car out of sight. He braked and went EVA, entering the workshop by its partly open rear doors, granting him easy access into the building. The soldier paused in the shadows, letting his eyes adjust to the gloom. He had the M-4 slung across his chest, the Mossberg in his hands, ready for use. He could hear raised voices as Lebowski's crew rushed outside to look at the blazing vehicles.

Bolan eased his way through the workshop. It was an untidy mess of automobiles, body parts and equipment. The sharp odor of auto paint filled the air along with the acrid tang of welding and cutting smoke. Somewhere a radio blared out music. Bolan passed a dusty Cadillac with its engine running, tools spread out around the vehicle.

He spotted Gregori Lebowski as the man stepped from the open door and turned back inside, pulling a cell phone from his pocket. He was muttering angrily as he punched in numbers. He had almost finished when he caught sight of Bolan's dark-clad figure, the Mossberg held in plain sight.

"Are you the bastard who...?"

"Closure time, Lebowski," Bolan said. "The Suvarovs are going out of business."

"Who the hell says that?"

"Work it out. People want you out of the game so they can move in."

That was just added to increase the man's confusion.

Bolan touched the shotgun's trigger, the charge ripping into the polished side panel of a sleek late-model Lincoln, tearing ragged holes in the metal. Lebowski recoiled from the blast as he felt the edges of the charge tug at his clothing.

The moment he triggered the Mossberg, Bolan

let it hang from the shoulder strap. He backed away, swinging the M-4/M-203 combo into action. He had already loaded an incendiary round into the breech. He fired it directly at the rear of the Lincoln, dropping the charge in through the window. The shell detonated, filling the luxury vehicle's interior with white-hot flame that blossomed into a fiery incandescent ball. The ensuing explosion offered Bolan enough cover so he was able to move back the way he'd entered. As he went, he reloaded, fired and reloaded again. He directed the rounds at the most available of the vehicles he passed. By the time he reached the rear doors there were five cars already burning fiercely. Bolan dropped his last canister among an untidy stand of metal paint and solvent drums stacked against one wall.

As he emerged into the downpour, Bolan caught a glimpse of a dark-coated figure coming around the end of the building. The fleeting glimpse he had of the man's face allowed him identification.

Tasha Lebowski.

Gregori's cousin.

Tasha had an autopistol in his right hand. He opened fire, laying down a volley of shots that hammered into the wall over Bolan's head.

Splinters from the crumbling brickwork peppered the back of his jacket. As the shots rang out, Bolan dived behind his car and moved quickly along its length. Crouching, he grabbed the slung shotgun. Tasha's cursing revealed his position, and it was no hardship for Bolan to pinpoint his man.

As Tasha paused, searching for Bolan, the black-clad figure rose from behind the car and leaned across the low roof. He pulled the trigger and Tasha took the 12-gauge charge through the back of his skull. The devastating force took his head apart and blew his face off in a bloody discharge. The gangster fell facedown into the rain-softened ground, his body jerking in reaction to the fatal hit.

Bolan jacked a high-explosive into the M-203 and lobbed the round through the building's rear doors. He ducked behind the car as the charge went off, spreading more destruction to the stored vehicles inside. Metal debris clattered against the car's bodywork. The soldier yanked open the door and threw the M-4 and shotgun inside.

He started the engine, dropped into gear and raced away from the building, aware of men shouting in the background, panic and anger mingled as they surveyed the intruder's handiwork. As he sped across the uneven terrain, Bolan dragged off the ski mask, a crooked smile edging his lips as he envisaged Lebowski shouting down his cell phone at the Suvarovs.

"EASY FOR YOU TO SAY, sitting there in your comfortable office. Come out here and see the fucking mess that bastard made. Every car we had burned up. The transport truck, too. The building's on fire. This is going to cost a fortune to reclaim."

Nikolai Petrovsky made soothing sounds that might have worked on lesser men. All they did was enrage Lebowski even further.

"Fuck your 'calm down.' Nikolai, I'm standing in the rain, with my merchandise up in smoke. My cousin Tasha is dead. His head is so mangled even his mother wouldn't recognize him. We need to find out who did this to us. The way that son of a bitch was talking, it sounds like we have someone out there who wants to take us over. We should get our people out and about. Find out who it is and hit them back."

"I'll take that suggestion under advisement, Gregori. Look, if there's nothing you can do out there, call it a day. Send your team home. Tell them to stay out of sight. Don't do anything until we can get this worked out. You hear me?"

"I hear you. Hey, Nikolai, one thing."

"What?"

"This doesn't come out of *my* salary."

CHAPTER TWO

Bolan was back in the New York apartment Leo Turrin had appropriated for him from the Justice Department. A number of the safehouses were located around the city, available at a moment's notice when required.

The communication system was useful, allowing Bolan to link up with Stony Man as well as Turrin. The secure telephone provided vocal contact. He wasn't expecting to spend a great deal of time in the place but during his visits the contact availability would prove invaluable.

On his return from New Jersey he stripped out of his clothes and had a shower. With that out of the way and dressed in fresh clothing, he put coffee on to percolate and sat to make contact with Leo Turrin.

"Been a busy boy have we?"

"Had to start somewhere."

"New Jersey P.D. is all smiles according to our local guy. He put in an appearance after the main event and asked around. Seems the cops aren't anticipating an early breakthrough in the case."

"Shame on them. No complaints from the owners of the establishment?"

"What owners? By the time the first unit arrived there was no sign of anyone. It appears Mr. Lebowski and his crew fled the scene. I think the Suvarovs have cut their losses and decided to handle this themselves. They know damn well there would be awkward questions to answer if they involved the cops."

"Leo, I'm really cut up by hearing that."

"So where next?"

"I want to keep up the pressure. Make them start to question what's happening. Anything you can pass along?"

"Something dropped on my desk a little while ago. I don't know if it's going to be much help, so I'll let you decide. As soon as we finish here, I'll send it in an e-mail attachment."

BOLAN WAS on his second mug of coffee when he heard the incoming mail wav. coming from the computer. He crossed to check it out, opening the e-mail from Turrin.

This guy, Frank McKay, is a freelance journalist. He's been running a long-term investigation into the Russian Mob for almost a year now. According to background, the guy is either totally fearless or a naive idiot. He's openly admitted to being threatened by the Mob if he doesn't quit. But he won't. He just keeps on digging. Justice has talked to him a couple of times, but he isn't saying anything. Claims to have insider information but isn't going to reveal anything. Might be worthwhile talking to the guy. His biog is in the attachment.

He opened the file. It contained personal details on Frank McKay: images that identified him; the make and type of vehicle he drove, with the license plate number; his address. Bolan read through the data a couple of times, familiarizing himself with McKay. When he was satisfied he had it all burned in his memory, he deleted the file and the e-mail.

Bolan sat back, a fresh mug of coffee in his hand, and considered his next move. Turrin's details on McKay intrigued him. If it was as the information said, and McKay did have some insider knowledge, he might prove useful—if Bolan could get him to talk. That might not be such an easy task. Journalists were of a breed reluctant to reveal sources or to divulge anything they knew unless they considered it profitable. On the other hand, if Bolan could extract even a small amount of information capable of giving him some insight into the Suvarovs, then it was worth a small amount of effort.

Bolan had put on civilian dress, as he termed it, and now shrugged into a shoulder rig holding his Beretta 93-R, covering it with a zippered leather jacket. A couple of extra magazines were stored in an inside pocket. He placed his blacksuit and other necessary equipment in a carryall. He took along one of the cell phones that had come from Stony Man along with the car. Leaving the apartment, Bolan made his way down to the parking garage beneath the building. He stowed the bag in the trunk. Glancing at his watch, he decided he would be able to make it across town to McKay's house in a half hour.

IT WAS JUST OVER thirty minutes later when Bolan eased the Dodge into a curb space a couple doors down from McKay's apartment building. The journalist lived on a quiet, tree-lined street just off

Queens. Bolan spotted the man's dark green SUV parked nearby.

Bolan used his cell phone to call McKay's number. He heard the phone ring out.

"Yeah?"

"Frank McKay?"

"That's me. Look, I don't have a great deal of time right now."

"My name's Matt Cooper. I want to talk to you about the Suvarov organization."

"What do you mean 'talk'?"

"I understand you're doing an exposé on the Suvarovs. I have an interest in them, as well."

"I don't know who you are, pal, but I haven't got time to waste on you."

"McKay, the Suvarovs are my business, too. I just need a little—"

"Mister, could you afford my hourly rate? I doubt you can."

"This isn't about money, McKay. It's about closing the Suvarov Mob down. Putting their operations out of business."

"Look, pal, let's put this in perspective. *My* job is to put the Suvarovs over the front pages. Expose them on national television. You know how long I've been working this deal? What it's taken to get where I am?"

"I want some help."

"Yeah, sure. You and half the country's news agencies."

"You think I'm the competition?"

"Hold it right there, Cooper. I don't give a rat's ass who you are. I do know one thing. You're not getting anything from me. Right now I have my own job to do. *My* job, pal. What I'm good at."

The phone slammed into its receiver. Bolan cut the connection. He leaned back, considering his next move. Appealing to McKay wasn't going to do it for him. He was going to have to confront the man and—

That was when the door to McKay's building opened and the man himself ran out, camera bag over his shoulder. The journalist opened the door of the big dark green SUV parked at the curb, threw the bag inside and climbed in behind the wheel. He fired up the engine and took off very fast.

"I don't think you're going to pick up a bucket of chicken, Mr. McKay," Bolan muttered as he pulled away from the curb and fell in behind the SUV.

BOLAN FOLLOWED McKay across town, staying well behind the journalist. It soon became apparent the man was heading for the interstate; the signs for Interstate 95 kept showing up along the route. Bolan settled back in the Dodge's comfortable seat as he followed the SUV onto the busy highway, noting that they were heading in a southerly direction. He was intrigued now as to where McKay might be heading.

The rain increased during the first hour of the run. Bolan stayed a couple of vehicles back. He flicked on the radio and tuned to a music station, keeping the volume at a low level, and set the climate control to a cool temperature.

They bypassed Philadelphia, McKay maintaining a steady speed. The weather improved after the third hour, and Bolan saw McKay start to ease over to the exit lane. The signs were for Baltimore and, as they got closer, Bolan sensed their journey was coming to a close. The SUV slowed and took the off-ramp indicating Baltimore Docks. Bolan was aware of the vast size of the various complexes: shipping and rail, with facilities for containers and cargo from global suppliers as well as U.S. base companies. The sprawling sites covered acres of land.

Exiting the ramp, Bolan kept the SUV in sight as McKay drove with confident ease. The man seemed to know exactly where he was going, and his direct action confirmed Bolan's suspicions that the journalist was on to something.

Fifteen minutes later Bolan was tailing McKay down a service road that led into an area housing companies involved in catering to the needs of the various aspects of dock activities. It was late afternoon, the service roads still active with company vehicles pulling in and out of freight yards, forklifts ferrying spare parts back and forth.

Bolan saw McKay drive up behind a sleek Plymouth of indeterminate age. Almost immediately a man climbed out of the vehicle and walked to the SUV. He leaned in at the driver's window and began an earnest discussion with the journalist.

There was something about the Plymouth's driver that stirred recognition in Bolan's memory. He took a closer look and later he made the connection.

The man talking to McKay was Morey Jacklin.

According to the information in Turrin's files, Jacklin worked for the Suvarov organization. He was no big wheel, more like a lower-level hood. Jacklin was a street guy. A wheeler-dealer who carried information in his head, knew everyone and was always just one step short of grabbing the big deal. He was a dreamer, along with his other attributes. He would never actually achieve the big-time because his fantasies were larger than his capabilities, so he would stay down.

Jacklin, lean and compact, dressed sharp and cool. He seemed to be doing all the talking, his slim hands moving all the time to emphasize his words. All Bolan could see of McKay was his head leaning out from the window. Finally, Jacklin stepped back, head bobbing as he reached his conclusion. He turned, walked back to his Plymouth and climbed in, pulling away and taking the first turn, taillights winking briefly as he vanished from sight.

Bolan turned his attention to McKay. The journalist sat at the wheel of his vehicle for a time before he fired up the engine and moved off. The soldier allowed him plenty of distance before he followed.

They drove through to the fringes of the docks, McKay sure of where he was going—away from the main sprawl of the massive sites to a quiet backwater where smaller companies operated. Here McKay pulled his SUV into a narrow service road just short of a small dock site. He parked after reversing into the shadows of rusting containers, climbed out, camera bag over his shoulder, and checked around to get his bearings.

The light was starting to fade. Bolan had parked his own vehicle and was catfooting behind McKay, keeping the man in sight while staying concealed himself. He was curious to see what the man was up to and what Morey Jacklin had fed him.

McKay crouched beside a rusting old truck that had weeds sprouting around it. He took out his camera and spent time checking it. He kept glancing at his watch, plainly expecting something or someone to show up.

When it did, Bolan realized immediately that it wouldn't be what McKay was hoping for.

A two-man team, both carrying suppressed autopistols, was closing in on McKay from his blind side. They moved with confidence, clearly knowing exactly where they would find him.

Bolan moved in fast, aware that the hit team wouldn't waste much time. Once they had their target under their guns they would strike quickly. McKay would be a dead man without even understanding what was happening.

The journalist, leaning against the side of the old truck, had to have picked up a slight sound from one of the approaching men. He turned, light catching his face and revealing the uncertain expression as he spotted the two men and, more significantly, the weapons they were carrying.

"What is this? Where's Jacklin? He was supposed to be coming back."

"On his way home," one of the men said. "Don't waste our time, McKay, we have a shipment to escort back to New York."

"Jacklin..."

The speaker said something to his partner in Russian and laughed. The language served as a warning to McKay. He turned to run, stumbled and went down on one knee. It saved his life as one of the hit men pulled the trigger, sending a bullet harmlessly over the journalist's head.

"Fuck..." McKay yelled.

Bolan, already closing, knew that a second shot wouldn't miss. He brought the Beretta into target acquisition and put a 3-round burst into the guy who had already taken his shot at McKay. The 9 mm slugs cored in through the back of the Russian's skull, kicking him to his knees, then facedown on the ground. Blood began to pump from the massive wounds.

The second hood turned fast, swinging his weapon into play, and fired on the move. His bullet winged by Bolan's face. Then the Beretta jacked out three more 9 mm shots. The Russian stepped back as they plowed into his chest. He made a feeble attempt to return fire, but his motor skills were already leaving him. He toppled backward and when he struck the ground the back of his skull cracked hard against the concrete.

Bolan moved in to clear the discarded weapons from the downed Russians. He glanced across at McKay. The journalist was slumped against the side of the truck, staring at the pair of dead men who only seconds ago had been doing their best to deprive him of his own life.

"Still don't have time to talk, McKay?"

The journalist picked up the phrase he'd used himself only hours earlier.

"Cooper? You're the guy I spoke to back in town. I…what the hell is going on here?"

"Haven't you worked it, McKay? This was a setup. All for your benefit. To get you out here so they could shut you up once and for all."

McKay looked startled, then skeptical.

"You mean kill me?"

"It's starting to sink in."

"Why now? I've been a pain in their butt all this time.…"

"Arkady Suvarov is in jail. His Mob being investigated in-depth. They're being pushed against the wall with nowhere to run. And they have you, McKay, picking away at them. Turning over every stone you can find for any scrap of evidence. The last thing they need right now. So they use the one solution open to them that will get you out of their hair. If this had gone down like they'd planned, you'd be coming in with tomorrow's tide."

McKay let out the breath he'd been holding.

"Morey. That son of a bitch." McKay forced a laugh. "I must have been pushing buttons too close to home. Made them jumpy."

"I can see why they don't like you."

McKay feigned hurt feelings.

"What? You saying I deserve this? A bullet in the back of my head? Am I that much of a wiener?"

"You really need an answer? McKay, you might as well paint a red spot on your forehead and shout, 'Come get me.'"

"If those Russians think this is going to make me quit, they're wrong. Damn it, Cooper, I'm not throwing away eight months' work. Hey, I could write you in. Kind of a new angle. Do an exclusive." He looked Bolan up and down. "Just who are you, anyway? Some undercover cop? Government agent? Covert operator?"

"*I* don't have time for this," Bolan growled, making his feelings known. "McKay, I'm fighting a war here. Not looking for journalistic awards. The Suvarovs are killing people. They deal in death and misery to earn their money. You want to write your story? Go ahead. But don't get in my way if you're not going to help, mister."

"Me help *you?*"

Bolan paused, turning slightly, his tall figure still poised for sudden movement. Those blue eyes fixed McKay with an icy stare.

"Okay, I'm a jerk." McKay stepped forward. "I get wrapped up in what I'm doing. Sometimes I forget it's all going on out there. What the hell, Cooper, I'm no angel. But I'm no asshole, either." He managed a self-deprecating grin. "Not all the time."

Bolan recognized the apology and cut the journalist some slack. He lowered the Beretta, letting his features soften.

"Trouble with being on a roll is we all get out of the loop."

He held out a big hand and gripped McKay's.

"Let's talk. Tell me what Jacklin set you up for."

THE DOCKS WERE in shadow, security lights high on steel poles throwing diffused light over the area. Thin rain was drifting in across the harbor. At this time—close to eight o'clock—there was little movement other than the activity around the freighter rolling gently on the swell, its bulk tugging at the ropes securing it to the dock.

Bolan and McKay, crouched in the shadow of a dockside crane, pressed close to the steel structure.

"The way those guys were talking, it sounds like the pickup is genuine," Bolan said. "The freighter is here. Correct dock. And name."

He glanced at his watch. It was time for the pickup to take place, according to the information Jacklin had given McKay.

"You still want me to get out of here?" McKay asked.

Bolan nodded.

"If this goes hard, I don't want you around if I get into a firefight."

McKay shrugged deeper into his coat. "Yeah? Well, tough. I don't walk away just because things get hard.

"I expect our respective interpretations of hard are different."

"You're serious about this."

"McKay, these people will cut your heart out and let you take a picture while it's still beating."

"You mean, I'm stepping in too deep?"

"Just do me a favor and take a back seat."

"That's expecting lot on our short acquaintance."

"If this goes down and hard, I'm not going to have time to be looking out for your comfort. Make your own choice."

McKay considered Bolan's words. He was still able to conjure up the images of the earlier clash with the Suvarov hit team. The journalist held up his hands in surrender.

"Maybe you can cut me some slack later and give me something I can use."

"I know where to find you," Bolan said.

McKay grinned. "Hope you meant that in a friendly way."

"Trust me, McKay, I never hurt a friend." Bolan considered his next option before deciding to go ahead. "You got a notepad?"

"Would a journalist be without one?"

McKay handed over a pad from his pocket and a ballpoint pen. He watched Bolan write down a number and name.

"In case you get an aberration and decide I'm a worthy case for information." Bolan handed the pad back. "That's a friend. Anything you tell him will be safe. Now get out of here, McKay."

McKay retreated, vanishing in the shadows. Now that he was alone, Bolan felt better. The responsibility for a civilian was something he could do without.

Movement on the dock caught his eye. A light-colored panel truck rolled along the dock, coming to a stop in line with one of the open access hatches in the side of the freighter. Three men climbed out, opened the truck's rear doors, then went to the open hatch. Figures appeared inside the hold, and heavy cases were passed out to the panel truck crew and stored inside the vehicle. Bolan counted at least twenty cases. When the loading had been completed, the access hatch was closed. The rear doors of the panel truck were secured and the three-man crew returned to the cab. The truck rolled away from the freighter, along the dock, and vanished from sight around the side of the end warehouse. That would take it to the service road and the main highway.

Bolan was already on the move, angling back the way he and McKay had entered. He emerged close to the end of the service road. From there the panel truck would pick up the access road that led away from the dock area. He had already chosen his spot, just around a bend in the road where the truck would need to slow down. As he moved, he pulled a black ski mask from one of his pockets and tugged it on.

He broke out of the shadows and waited. Moments later he picked up the low murmur of the panel truck's engine as it approached, heard it drop in register as it cruised around the bend. Bolan let it draw level with him, then stepped into view alongside the driver's door. He reached out and caught hold of the door handle, opening it and yanking the door wide. Before anyone inside could react, he had the 93-R's muzzle jammed hard against the driver's head, climbing on to the step and bracing himself against the frame.

"Stop now, or I pull the trigger."

He emphasized his demand by jamming the muzzle of the Beretta hard against the driver's skull. The guy got the message, let go of the gas pedal and rode the brake until the truck came to a dead stop.

"You two. Hands where I can see them. If this 9 mm goes off, you'll all catch it."

The other crewmen knew they had no choice. Neither made any overt moves. They showed their hands.

"Wise. Whatever Suvarov is paying you isn't any good if you're dead." Bolan stepped back, his weapon still covering the occupants of the truck.

"All out, single file. Driver first. This side of the truck and lie facedown. Let's go. *Let's go.*"

Bolan watched as the three men exited the vehicle. They were taking things slowly, not wanting to do anything that might alarm their captor. Not until the last guy stepped down. His actions had been less obvious, and Bolan had made sure to watch him closely. As the man stepped onto the road, he turned his body slightly, from the waist, so that his left side was hidden from Bolan's view. Shielded by the man in front, he was able to slip his right hand under his jacket, fingers curling around the butt of the autopistol resting in a hip holster. He began to slide the weapon clear and as he stepped forward, away from the man in front, he pulled the pistol and began to raise it.

Bolan's attention hadn't faltered, and he was more than ready as the dull black pistol came into view. The soldier moved instinctively, sweeping the Beretta around and cracking it down across the man's gun hand. The blow was delivered with maximum force. Bone snapped, drawing a yell of pain from the would-be killer. As the pistol fell from numb fingers, Bolan kicked it under the truck.

"Not smart, pal. Now stand over there with your buddies." Bolan turned, following the three with the Beretta as they moved. "Any more surprises under those coats? Let's see them. Now." Two more handguns appeared. "Lose them in the shrubbery. Now, all of you, facedown on the ground. Hands clasped at the backs of your heads."

"You broke my fuckin' wrist," the guy who had tried to draw his gun protested.

"Do I look as if I care? Down."

"You know who we are?" one of the men asked.

"The guys lying facedown in the dirt? If you feel like telling me I'm making a big mistake and you work for the Suvarovs, don't bother. I can live with my mistakes and I never did get excited about cheap hoods, so stay quiet."

Broken Wrist twisted his head around.

"You won't look so tough when we come after you."

"Coming from a jerk who can't pull his gun without getting his arm broken, I doubt I have much to worry about."

Bolan turned quickly and climbed into the panel truck. He dropped it into Drive and stepped on the gas. The truck picked up speed, leaving the stranded Suvarov crew unable to do a thing except watch his taillights vanish.

Bolan returned to where he had left his vehicle. He transferred his duffel bags to the panel truck. Moving on again, he picked up Interstate 95 and headed for New York. The Interstate was quiet, so as he drove he put in a call to Turrin.

He recounted what had happened, including his run-in with McKay.

"So you got out of Dodge alive again, huh?"

"Leo, keep the faith."

"What happened with McKay?"

"I hauled his ass out of the fire tonight. The rest is up to him. He isn't the type to quit. He's going to go right on with his investigation into the Suvarovs. Next time I might not be around to play bodyguard. One more thing. I gave him one of your contact numbers in case he decides to pass anything along. It's no guarantee, but we don't have anything to lose."

"Okay. So where are you now?"

"Behind the wheel of the Suvarov panel truck, carrying a load of illegal weapons and ammo— MP-5s, SIG P-226s. There's enough here to equip a small army."

"Some haul. You want me to have it bagged and tagged and put in storage?"

"Uh-uh, not yet. I might need to show it to someone as a gesture of intent."

"I won't pursue that. Oh, I had a message from Kissinger. He's working a hunch he might know who uses that sniper rifle. I'll let you know what he finds."

"Okay. Listen, I had to ditch the Dodge. I'll need fresh wheels when I get back to town."

"I'll arrange it."

"Talk to you later."

CHAPTER THREE

The following day, near noon, Bolan located Morey Jacklin in a small restaurant in Brighton Beach. The information in Turrin's files had indicated that Jacklin ate there most days.

Bolan made his way across to Jacklin's table, pulling out one of the vacant chairs so he could sit. Jacklin didn't notice immediately. He was too busy eating. When he realized he was no longer alone, he glanced up, his fork partway to his mouth. He took a slow look around the restaurant, then back to his uninvited guest.

"So all the other tables are full?"

"I'm only interested in this one, Morey."

"Morey already? I never had a relationship grow so fast. So when do you want to marry my sister?"

"I'd have to meet her first."

"Picky now. Don't insult me. She's beautiful."

Bolan leaned forward.

"The word is you're the man who can fix me a deal."

Jacklin's attitude changed instantly. He placed his fork back on the table, fixing Bolan with a hard stare.

"Deal? What deal?"

"The Suvarovs are short some merchandise. For a consideration, I might be able to arrange a return."

Jacklin's eyes glittered. His interest had piqued and Bolan could almost hear his brain working.

"You lost me, pal. Suvarov? Merchandise? I think you picked the wrong table."

"Morey, don't screw with me. You set up the meet with McKay in Baltimore. You put him on the spot. Let him walk right into it. I've got you right there. Identification of your car. What you were wearing. All neat and tidy, Morey."

Jacklin tried to bluff it out. He stared into Bolan's eyes, and the ice-cold expression he recognized convinced him this man wasn't fooling.

"I didn't know they were going to kill him. Believe me. I figured they'd give him his lumps. Beat him up. Break a couple of limbs to convince him he should leave things alone. By the time I found out, it was too late. Hell, I wasn't even there. All I was told to do was to arrange the setup, get McKay on the spot, then leave. That's what I did. Then I took my car and went home."

"The weapons?"

"The shipment was genuine. I had to send him somewhere a real deal was going down. If he smelled it was a fake, he would have bailed before it happened. McKay might be an asshole, but he isn't stupid."

"I think I'm being played."

Bolan started to stand. After a moment's hesitation Morey waved him back into his seat.

"Hey, wait. Maybe we can talk." He waited until Bolan had taken his seat again. "Look at it from my side of the fence. You walk in off the street. I don't know you from Adam. Then you come out with some wild offer. Jesus, what am I supposed to think?"

"So now that you've had a minute to think, we got room to talk?"

"Maybe," Jacklin conceded. "Let's say I *might* know what you're talkin' about. How would I know you actually got the goods?"

"You take my word."

Jacklin laughed.

"A panel truck was hijacked off a Suvarov crew

last night leaving Boston docks. The truck was carrying a load of weapons and ammunition. Pistols and SMGs."

Bolan let it rest there and Jacklin absorbed the information. He reached for the wine bottle and poured some into a spare glass, pushing it across to Bolan.

"Enjoy," he said. "I need to make a call. Stay around."

He stood and walked out of the dining area, pulling a cell phone from his pocket as he went.

Bolan waited, ignoring the wine.

"I need to see the merchandise," Jacklin said when he returned.

"A sample?"

"Uh-uh. The full shipment."

"Morey, if I do that, you'll bring along another one of Suvarov's hit teams to cancel *my* ticket. You walk away with the merchandise and all I get is dead."

Jacklin sighed in frustration.

"This is too much like hard work. So how do we work it? And what the hell do I call you?"

"Smith will do for now."

"You figure this is going to become long-term? Smith, this has the smell of a scam."

"Morey, I'd be crazy to try to scam the Suvarovs."

"You talk crazy enough."

"How's this, then. We get out of here right now. I take you to see the goods, then you call your boss and we close the deal."

Jacklin hesitated.

"Those are my terms, Morey."

"Okay. I don't have any choice, do I?"

They left the restaurant and walked to where Bolan had left his car. Once they were on the move, Bolan handed Jacklin a ski mask and told him to put it on. Jacklin wasn't happy but he did as he was told.

"Morey, it goes on back-to-front."

"Even I figured that."

He dragged on the hood and slumped down in his seat, arms folded across his chest. He said very little during the rest of the forty-minute journey.

Turrin had arranged for Bolan to use a deserted warehouse by the river. Bolan pulled up at the big doors, opened them and drove inside. He returned to close the doors, then leaned in Jacklin's window.

"You can take the hood off now, Morey," Bolan said.

Ample light shone in through the high windows to illuminate the interior. Jacklin stared around the warehouse. It was empty except for the panel truck in the center of the floor. The truck was the one stolen from the Suvarovs. Jacklin recognized the license plate and description. The information had been passed out to every Suvarov contact once the hijack had been confirmed.

"Don't screw around," Jacklin said. "You guys pulled the friggin' heist yourselves and now you want to sell back to the Suvarovs."

"Believe what you want, Morey," Bolan said. "All I want is to get this cargo off my hands."

"They're not going to believe that *you* didn't steal this truck."

"I just want to return it," Bolan said. "For a consideration."

"Oh, yeah. That sounds like another word for blackmail. And you don't want to be doing that to the Suvarovs."

"Let me worry about that."

Bolan opened the panel truck and allowed Jacklin to look inside. It didn't take him long to verify it carried the weapons that had been stolen. Jacklin stepped back from the panel truck.

"They look okay."

"Come on, Morey, you know what you've just seen. Can we deal?"

"I guess." Jacklin took out his cell phone and tapped a number. "Yeah, it's me. Confirmed. It's the real stuff. No shit? I'll ask him."

"Ask me what?"

"He wants a face-to-face."

"You can show him my photograph."

Jacklin wasn't sure how to take that. He looked shocked that someone could actually make fun of his employer. It wasn't done. Either this guy was stupid, or he was tougher than he appeared.

"Look, you want this deal to go through?"

"Yeah."

"Then you get to meet Mr. Suvarov. He likes to handle deals personally."

Bolan allowed a few seconds to go by before he answered. He was getting exactly what he wanted, but he wasn't going to appear too eager. So he made Jacklin wait.

IT WASN'T TURNING OUT to be one of Vasily Suvarov's better weeks. His handling of the McKay hit had gone wrong and to add insult to injury the consignment of guns being used as bait had been hijacked. And now someone was negotiating with Morey Jacklin to sell the weapons back to the Suvarovs.

Their own damn guns.

He was trying to visualize Valentina's response when he told her what had happened. She would hold him responsible. He knew that. The fact that it hadn't been his fault would make no difference. The same thing could have happened to her under similar circumstances. The events at the dock had come out of nowhere. It couldn't have been anticipated. What he had to do now was to find out how the information had gotten out. Had someone talked? Sold out the Suvarovs? The latter made him angry.

Was it possible they had a traitor in their ranks? Someone willing to defy the family for money?

He thought, then, about the people under Justice Department protection. The ones who had turned to save their own skins. They had betrayed the Family. Maybe not for money, but their acts were still nothing more than betrayal. They had forfeited the Family for the opportunistic embrace of the federal government. They were no different than one who would sell out for cash. In Vasily's eyes they were to be pitied. Weak, vainglorious fools who would not profit from their dark acts. The Suvarovs had their own way of rewarding those who had betrayed them.

Vasily pushed to his feet and wandered through the apartment. He found himself in the kitchen where he boiled water and made himself a mug of instant coffee. He opened the drapes and stood looking out across the city.

On impulse he crossed to where he had left his cell phone and picked it up. He hated having to do this but putting off the evil hour would only make things worse. He punched in a number, which was answered after three rings.

"It's me, Vasily."

"Something is wrong?"

He smiled. Trust Valentina to go straight for the jugular.

"McKay was being protected. Our people were killed and McKay got away. And the panel truck was hit as it left the dock," he said.

He held the phone and listened to the silence.

"What have you done about it?"

"I spoke to Jacklin. He's had contact with someone who has the weapons. He wants to make a deal. I set things in motion, but I wanted to bring you up to date."

"So now I know."

Valentina hung up, leaving Vasily with nothing but the dial tone. He hesitated for a moment, then made his decision and punched in a number. When it was answered, he gave orders, barely taking breath until he had finished. He put down the phone and headed for the bathroom where he showered, then dressed. Thirty minutes later he was being driven to the Suvarov headquarters in Little Odessa, to the Golden Troika.

He received a call on his way in from Morey

Jacklin. He spoke to Vasily, then handed his phone to the man who was offering to deal for the guns.

"How do I know you're not pulling something?"

"Morey already told you the guns are here. You've lost something. I can get it back to you. A simple business transaction, Mr. Suvarov. You should understand that."

Vasily's mind was in overdrive. He was out of his depth, but he didn't want this man to know that.

"How do we do this?" he asked.

"I'll meet with you at the club."

"Yes."

"Shall we say an hour?"

"Very well." Vasily paused. "Who are you?"

"Just the man who is about to do you a favor."

THE MOMENT HE ARRIVED at the club Vasily went straight upstairs to Valentina's office. He went in without knocking, and found her in conversation with Nikolai Petrovsky. The man was leaning against the edge of Valentina's desk and they were sharing something that was providing both some amusement. Vasily felt his cheeks burn. Were they talking about him?

"Are you in the right place, little brother?" Valentina asked. "I don't believe this is the Lost and Found department."

He ignored her remark. "I have the man coming who may be able to help us get the consignment back."

Valentina glanced at Petrovsky, then back to her brother.

"Tell me all about it."

"I'm not joking," Vasily said. "I received the call on the way in. This man said he could arrange a deal for us to get our guns back."

"For a fee, of course," Petrovsky said.

"I don't think he works for a charity organization."

"Jokes, too." Valentina leaned forward. "Whatever next, brother?"

"At least I've got the guns back."

"True. But you did lose them in the first place, so don't expect a parade down Fifth Avenue."

"Vasily, who is this man?" Petrovsky asked.

"At this time, just a voice on the phone. But you'll be able to see for yourself very shortly. He's coming here to make the deal."

"Here? He's either extremely confident or totally arrogant," Petrovsky stated.

"We'll use father's office. We can watch through the one-way mirror." Valentina stood. She walked by her brother without a word until she reached the door. "Vasily, please do not screw this up. If there's a chance this is a good deal, we need to make it. Understand?"

"Do you think I am stupid?"

Her lack of a reply implied more than any comment.

Vasily called one of his waiting men. "We'll be having a visitor. When he arrives, bring him to my father's office." The man nodded and left.

Vasily made his way to the office his father had used for so many years. It was large, and simply furnished. Arkady Suvarov wasn't a man who needed to advertise his authority. He *was* the authority. Inside, Vasily closed the double doors and crossed to stand at the window. It overlooked the street and the beach beyond. The water looked gray, chilly. Vasily remained at the window for a while before he turned to where his father's desk sat, the big, padded leather swivel chair behind it. He could visualize his father, his powerful bulk relaxed in the chair as he conducted some matter of business. He wished Arkady Suvarov was back behind that desk, in charge, running the organization as he had for so many years. His father made the task look easy. He had total command of the business and the people who worked for him. Whether they were here in America or back in Russia, Arkady Suvarov held full, unchallenged control. Vasily knew he would never match his father in any way. It just wasn't within him. Valentina, on the other hand, possessed exactly the qualities her father admired. She was hard and ruthless. She commanded respect, and she used her calculating mind to her advantage.

Vasily admired her for that.

At the same time he was envious of her abilities.

Most of all he hated her for what she was and how she treated him. He was also frightened of her—too frightened to do very much about the situation.

BOLAN SAT ACROSS THE DESK from Vasily Suvarov. He waited for the man to speak, watching, noting the edge of nervous strain showing in his expression.

"You really want to do this?" Vasily asked.

"Sit and stare at each other for the rest of the day? Not really."

"Play games with us, I mean."

"I'm serious. I have something you want. You pay me, and I'll hand over the merchandise. A simple trade-off."

"And how much are you expecting me to pay to get my own goods back?"

"I'm not greedy, Mr. Suvarov. I also know money isn't a worry where you are concerned, so let's agree on a figure, say $90,000."

"We already paid—"

"That isn't my problem. I'm negotiating the safe return of lost property. I have my own expenses to cover."

"How do I know I can trust you?" Vasily asked. "Maybe you were the one who took the guns in the first place."

Bolan ignored the suggestion. "I made my offer. Now it's up to you. One way or the other, I come out okay on this. You don't buy them, no problem. Once the word gets out they're up for grabs, all I have to do is take the best deal offered."

"You didn't answer my question about maybe being the one who did the hijack."

Bolan didn't miss a beat. "That's right, I didn't."

"You realize I could have you taken captive right now? Have my people work on you until you told me—"

"Of course you could. But don't waste your time. You think I didn't consider something like that? If I don't call my backup from an outside phone when I leave, *he* calls Vash Kukor's people."

"Kukor died in the hospital last week."

"I know, but his organization didn't die with him and they're a restless bunch and Oleg Kirov wants to be the main man. He's just waiting his chance to move on you. If they get their hands on those guns, they're going to have a big advantage."

Vasily wasn't sure how to react to Bolan's calm indifference. It threw him off balance.

"I need to know...."

Bolan pushed to his feet. "That's it, Suvarov. I came in here to fix a deal, but all I'm getting is the runaround. The clock is ticking. You want the merchandise? Don't want it? Just tell me so I can get on with the rest of my life. I'm not getting any younger."

Vasily cleared his throat. He stared over Bolan's shoulder in the direction of the mirror, wishing he could see Valentina.

At that precise moment the phone on his desk rang, the shrill sound jerking him back to the moment. He gave a weak smile and reached to pick it up.

"Say yes, Vasily," Valentina said. Her voice was flat, cold. He knew she was angry with him. "Before he walks out. Let us get our hands on the damn weapons first. We can worry about this man later. Now do it."

The line went dead. Vasily squeezed the receiver. There were times when he could have cheerfully... Then he carefully placed the receiver back on its cradle and turned to face Bolan.

"You have your deal," Vasily said. "Tell me when we can take delivery."

"Tomorrow evening. I'll call later this afternoon and you can tell me where. Have the money ready. Cash only, Suvarov. I don't take checks. And *you* bring the money. If I don't see you at the meet, the deal is off."

BOLAN FOLLOWED THE ESCORT through the club on his way to the front door. As he crossed the floor, a door opened and a woman appeared. She was young, dark-haired and beautiful. Bolan recognized her as Valentina Suvarov. The images he had seen on Turrin's computer file failed to do her justice. She was dressed in a slim-fitting light dress that ended just above her knees. He couldn't fail to be aware of her shapely figure. As he walked past her she caught his eye, held his gaze for a moment, then lowered her eyes shyly. There was a hint of delicate perfume as he drew breath. Then she turned, and he heard the light tap of her heels as she retreated to the far side of the club.

Outside Bolan saw one of the security men holding the door of the SUV Turrin had supplied him with. The Executioner slipped behind the wheel and the door was closed for him. He fired up the engine and drove away from the club, constantly checking his mirror to see whether Suvarov was having him tailed. After several miles, he finally realized he was in the clear.

The Suvarovs were in a bind. Their expensive consignment of weapons had been hijacked. Bolan showing up and offering to get them back didn't solve the problem. Someone had stolen them, and they would want to find out who and why. And at this moment in the game Bolan was the only connection they had to the stolen weapons. Simply agreeing to trade wasn't an end to it. In the mind-set of the criminal, Suvarov would want more than just his guns. He would want revenge and his financial investment returned. That meant not trusting Bolan.

So why had they let him walk free and clear?

He considered that and came to the conclusion he hadn't been set free, only released on probation until they were able to arrange something of their own. He didn't have to think too hard to work out how that might happen.

They wanted their weapons back. To get them they would need to play Bolan's game. Once they had sight of the shipment all bets would be off and Bolan's life expectancy would click down to zero.

They had him down as a risk-taker, someone willing to take on the Suvarov Mob because he saw an opportunity to make some money. He gave them full marks for their reading of his current role. What they didn't realize was that this time they were up against a master of the game.

He would play his assumed role right to the line, then once the cards were dealt he would turn over his hand and show his true colors.

He was stringing them along, playing on their reputation as hard-liners. His strategy was to play them at their own game, show them their ranks could be penetrated, that the Suvarovs were far from invulnerable. And then he'd crush them.

BOLAN FOUND HIS SPOT and waited for the inevitable to happen. While he waited he considered the possible outcome and the actions that dictated those results.

He doubted that Vasily Suvarov would actually show. He would send in his soldiers to handle Bolan and to retrieve the weapons, establishing his position by removing a possible threat to the Family honor.

The Suvarovs, in common with every other Mob Bolan had ever known, were hung up on the conceptual myth of "honor." They wore it like an emblem, flaunting it at every opportunity.

Honor.

The selfless pride they imagined gave them

credence, washed them clean of every vile activity they indulged in. It removed the stains of blood and violence and the smell of corruption. It was pure delusion, a mantle they wore to blind themselves to the fact that in the stark glare of day they were simply nothing more than gangsters who preyed on the weak and the gullible.

Vasily Suvarov, with all his expensive clothes, his sleek cars and rich lifestyle, was a hood who considered himself smart and full of guile.

Bolan knew better. He had spent too much of his time rooting out these soulless monsters, had seen them at their worst and held them beneath contempt for what they did.

The exchange had been fixed for mid-evening in a secluded spot in the Wawayanda Swamp area, an isolated section with wooded stretches and quiet back roads off the main track.

Bolan arrived well in advance, parking in the clearing he had been told about just off the back road, going EVA and losing himself in the dense undergrowth, prepared to await his visitors.

The weapons were in the rear of the SUV he was using this time out, covered by a tarp. He could see the vehicle from his place of concealment, sitting there as bait.

He had been in position for more than an hour

when he heard an engine and a car nosed into view. He wasn't surprised when it turned out to be the Plymouth that Morey Jacklin drove. Jacklin climbed out and stood scanning the area. He spotted Bolan's SUV. He didn't cross over to check it out, just stood there nervously and waited. Every little sound caused him to look around, eyes staring into the undergrowth.

Bolan moved forward silently, coming up behind Jacklin.

"Morey, don't turn around. Stay exactly where you are."

"What's going on?"

"Tell *me* what's going on, Morey."

"You were told."

"I was told Vasily would be here for the exchange. Where is he, Morey? And what are you doing here?"

"He said he wanted me to come, as well."

"Why?"

"Because he gives the orders and I take them."

"You think that's the way it's going tonight?"

Jacklin was sweating. He tried to cover it by giving a nervous shrug and running a hand across his forehead.

"Warm night, huh?"

"Could turn out that way for some," Bolan replied quietly.

He was on his guard now. Something in Jacklin's manner warned him the whole thing had been turned sour. The situation, edgy at best, had racked up a notch. And Jacklin was starting to fidget. He reached up to scratch a cheek, cleared his throat and started to throw too casual glances in the direction of the road.

"Hey, maybe I..."

"What?"

Jacklin shook his head. A moment later his attention was taken as the sound of an approaching engine broke the stillness beyond the clearing.

"Looks like he made it."

"Still feeling the heat?" Bolan asked.

"I don't understand—"

"Sure you do," Bolan said, and moved in fast to step right up behind Jacklin, the muzzle of his Beretta nudging the man's spine. "A 9 mm at this close range would take your spine apart. If you came out alive, you'd spend the rest of your life in a bed. Understand *that,* Morey?"

There was no other answer Jacklin could give. He nodded.

"Jesus, man, don't fuckin' shoot me."

"Give me a reason why I shouldn't. That isn't Vasily out there. This is a setup. Just like the one you set for McKay. Right?"

"I…"

"The finger is on the trigger, Morey. Make sure it's what I want to hear."

Jacklin watched the dark sedan roll around the curve in the dirt road just beyond the clearing and come to a stop.

"They said to keep you talking until they got here."

"Why, Morey? I was already *supposed* to be expecting company. Why did they write in a part for you?"

Jacklin moved, tensing, and Bolan wondered if the man was going to attempt to break away.

"You know what I think, Morey? I think you're supposed to go down with me tonight. They get rid of us both."

"Me? What the fuck for?"

"Maybe Vasily thinks you were in on the heist back at the Baltimore docks. Think about it. McKay gets off. The guns get hijacked. The next day you call and say you've met a guy who can sell him back the guns. Big coincidence. So he figures you sold him out."

"That's crazy."

"Looks to me like we've both been screwed, Morey."

Jacklin watched as the car doors were opened

and two men stepped out. They were dark shapes behind the glare of the headlight beams that came on abruptly, but the outlines of the shotguns they carried showed clearly enough.

There was a brief pause before one of the men spoke. "Jacklin, we can get you both whether you move or not."

The voice was hard, the accent Russian.

"No. Vasily wanted to make sure he stayed."

One of the men laughed. "You dumb, or what? Tonight we get rid of both of you."

"That Russian fuck. He did this to me?" Jacklin yelled.

The lead man stepped forward, the shotgun rising to hip level.

Jacklin let out a howl of terror as he envisaged what might be about to happen.

Dropping to a crouch behind his semihostage, Bolan caught hold of Jacklin's coat and dragged him to the ground. The move caught Jacklin unaware. He fell with a solid thump, a choking gasp of expelled air indicating how hard he had hit.

Bolan rolled to the opposite side, coming up on one knee, the 93-R already on track. As he pulled the trigger he heard the solid boom of the first shotgun. He felt the air ripple close by as the charge went wide, the shooter having already committed himself to his shot at targets no longer there.

Bolan's triburst went straight to target. The 9 mm slugs punched into the shooter's chest and flipped him backward. He struck the nose of the parked car, his weapon angling skyward, discharging its second shot at the stars. The guy grunted, losing his grip on reality as Bolan hit him a second time, this time slightly raising the muzzle of the Beretta so that the follow-up trio of slugs cored into the guy's throat. He spit blood, gagging as he doubled over the hood of the car.

His partner moved away from the vehicle, firing as he went. Jacklin uttered a cry of pain as he caught a stray shot across his left side. He had been trying to get to his feet, but the hot fire of the wound altered his perspective and he decided that hugging the dirt wasn't such a bad idea after all.

Bolan pushed to his feet, turning his eyes away from the direct beams of light coming from the car. He had seen the second shooter make his break, following his progress as he sprinted across the open clearing and closed on the guy.

The shooter cleared the back of the vehicle, its rear lights catching him in a red glow and outlining him perfectly. Bolan saw the shotgun angle around and threw himself to the ground, below the shooter's line. The shotgun boomed and the side windows of the car blew out in glittering fragments. The brief muzzle-flash erupting from the barrel was enough to give Bolan his target area. He had the Beretta two-handed and squared the muzzle on the bulk of the man behind the shotgun. His finger stroked the trigger, and the 93-R chugged out a triburst. A second burst brought down his target. The wide-shouldered Russian dropped to ground hard and lay still.

Bolan made the body check quickly, moving the discarded shotguns well out of reach. The two men were both carrying auto pistols, which he lobbed into the shadows, well clear of the downed men. The Russians looked dead, but the Executioner had known the dead to suddenly come back to life and gun down a careless enemy.

Behind him he could hear Jacklin moaning, thrashing about in the dirt. Bolan reloaded and kept his Beretta handy as he walked back to stand over Jacklin.

"Those bastards shot me."

"It's what they do, Morey."

"Some help you are."

"Are you forgetting you brought me here for that pair to use as target practice?"

Bolan crouched beside Jacklin, the Beretta in plain sight.

"What? You going to finish the job?" Jacklin was almost sobbing. "What the hell. I'm dead anyway. Once Vasily Suvarov finds out I got his boys killed, my ass won't be worth a nickel."

"You're no more use to me, Morey. I don't have the time to haul deadweight around."

"You got a funny way with words."

"Morey, I get a little pissed when people set me up."

Jacklin looked up from examining the bloody tear in his side. His fingers were red with blood.

"I don't like getting shot by the bastards I'm supposed to be working for."

"Not my problem."

"What if I had something to trade?"

"As if."

"What time you got?"

"Twenty-five after nine."

"I can help you save someone's life. The guy at Justice. The one looking for Suvarov's leak. Right now he has five minutes left."

Bolan's expression became hard. He leaned forward and pressed the Beretta's muzzle against Jacklin's temple.

"What's going down, Morey, and don't waste time on long words."

"A bomb in his office is set for nine-thirty. I

overheard Petrovsky on the phone to some guy. I was outside his office. I shouldn't have been there but I wanted to talk to him about Baltimore."

His explanation was superfluous. Bolan already had his cell phone in his hand, finger working the speed-dial number that would connect him to Leo Turrin. He heard Turrin's own cell phone ringing. It kept ringing for what seemed an eternity.

"Pick up, Leo," Bolan urged softly. *"Pick up."*

Then Turrin's calm, measured voice was asking Bolan what he wanted.

"Don't ask, Leo. Are you in your office?"

"Yeah. Why?"

"Get out. Now. Get as far away as you can and move any people close by. Now, Leo, now."

Turrin didn't say another word. Bolan could hear the sound of him moving, then calling out for everyone to clear the area. His voice carried over the cell phone. For a time the connection faded. The background rose again and this time Bolan could hear the traffic noise around Turrin.

The distant, muffled sound of the explosion reached Bolan's ears, and he caught Turrin's exclamation.

"Who do we have to thank for that?" Turrin asked moments later.

"Petrovsky I've been told."

"Son of a bitch," Turrin said forcibly.

"Hey, don't make it personal. I'll deal with it when the time comes. Anyone hurt there?"

"No. Thanks to you, we got everyone clear. There weren't many around this time of night."

"Good."

"I owe you big-time," Turrin said.

"I'll remind you when my expenses start to show up."

"Yeah." Turrin paused. "Jesus, if you hadn't called…"

"But I did. Leo, go home to Angelina. Give her a hug from me."

"I'll do that. And thanks again, pal."

This time Bolan picked up the slight tremor in Turrin's voice.

"Hey, we're losing blood over here," Jacklin called.

Bolan turned to see the man hunched over, one hand pressed to his side where the fringes of the shotgun blast had clipped him. Bolan could see the bright leakage of blood oozing between Jacklin's fingers. He crossed over and crouched to check the wound, pulling the man's fingers away from the bloody patch soaking his shirt. Bolan pushed aside the fabric and took a look. The flesh had been lacerated by the shot, just over Jacklin's ribs.

"Can you stand?"

Jacklin pushed to his feet, hanging on to Bolan's arm. He allowed himself to be led to the SUV and waited while Bolan pulled the first-aid box from beneath the driver's seat. He opened it and removed what he needed, pulling on a pair of thin latex gloves before he tended Jacklin's wound. The antiseptic he used stung severely and the gangster yelped.

"Jesus, that hurt."

Bolan glanced at him, his expression one of surprised innocence.

"Really?"

"Yeah, really."

"Well…good."

"What the fuck you mean *good?* I've been shot here."

"You seem to have forgotten again that you got *me* out here to get hit by those goons."

"Oh, sure, hold that against me. Hell, why don't you finish the job yourself? Hey, what you looking 'round for?"

"My gun."

Jacklin fell silent and let Bolan complete his work. When he'd finished applying a temporary dressing, the soldier stripped off his gloves, put away the first-aid kit and told Jacklin to get in the

SUV. As they drove away, the gangster cleared his throat.

"Where we going?"

"Somewhere I can have you kept under surveillance."

"Witness protection?"

Bolan nodded.

"Whoa, I don't think so. Let me remind you about the three poor suckers who got themselves canceled out while they were being looked after by your Fed buddies. I'd be safer on the street."

"That can be arranged, too."

"Wait a minute here. Didn't I just save your friend from getting his butt shredded? Doesn't that sort of make us even?"

Bolan glanced across at him.

"What am I thinking, Morey?"

"Probably how you can make me suffer more than I already have."

"You want to cancel what you owe me?"

"Maybe."

"Let's trade, Morey. Your protection, for information I can use against the Suvarovs. Let's face it, I don't think you'll be on their Employee of the Month list this time 'round."

"We agree on something, then."

"Start talking, Morey. I listen well."

"So what is it you want to do?"

"Take their organization apart. Tear it wide open and scatter the pieces."

"I'm your guy then. Anything you need to know about the Suvarovs I can give it to you wholesale."

CHAPTER FOUR

"Who is she?" Chekhov asked.

"I don't know," Berin said. "But I would like to."

"Have you two no respect?" Oleg Kirov said. "We're here to mourn our departed employer, and all you pair can do is ogle some strange woman."

All three of them were still looking across the crowd of mourners attending Vash Kukor's funeral. The young woman stood out among the slowly moving throng. Tall, willowy, she held herself straight, hands held together against her body below the curve of her breasts. She was dressed in severe black, and wore a wide-brimmed black hat. The pale oval of her face was breathtakingly beautiful.

"Thinking about it, I believe Vash would have

appreciated someone as beautiful as that," Kirov added. "He always did have an eye for the ladies."

"Wandering eyes," Chekhov added.

Berin chuckled softly. "To go with his wandering hands."

"One thing for sure," Kirov decided. "She's no Fed."

He was acknowledging the obvious presence of federal agents who were standing on the edges of the crowd, some making notes as they identified the mourners. A couple of agents, standing farther back, were taking the occasional photographs.

"Even today they can't leave us alone."

"You know why?" Chekhov asked. "Because they're busy building their case against Suvarov. We all become suspects. Guilt by association."

Kirov was only half aware of what was being said. His attention was fully on the solitary female.

"There is something familiar about her."

Berin glanced at the young woman again. "You want to know? So go and asked her."

"I will."

Kirov moved away from the others, self-consciously sucking in his slightly paunchy stomach.

"Hey, ask for her telephone number," said Berin.

"And see if she has a younger sister," Chekhov called.

Moving through the milling crowd that was filing past the grave, Kirov approached the young woman. He walked slowly, not wanting to appear too blatant, and he had almost reached her before she seemed to become aware of his presence. She simply turned her head so that she looked him directly in the eye. Before he could speak she held out a slim, perfectly manicured hand. Kirov took it, a faint tingle running through him as the slim fingers, surprisingly strong and cool, curled around his own large hand.

"I am Valentina Suvarov," she said. Her voice was delightfully feminine, soft, with a husky undertone. Kirov tried to pin down her accent. It sounded American yet he detected her Russian roots gently pushing through. It was a delicious combination. "My father is Arkady Suvarov. He asked me to attend today on his behalf. As you know he is being held in a federal facility awaiting trial."

"I know where he is. I also know that he and Vash Kukor weren't exactly on friendly terms."

"In business they were rivals, and I understand there was bad blood between them over various matters. However, that doesn't mean we can't recognize civilized formalities. This is how it would have been back home in Russia."

Kirov inclined his head. He felt almost reluctant when the woman withdrew her hand.

"You father is an honorable man, Miss Suvarov. And I thank you for your courtesy."

The smile she gave him would have melted an iceberg.

"Then we can part as friends and not enemies. I should go now. I have paid my respects."

"That isn't necessary. Not so soon."

"Perhaps we may meet again, Oleg Kirov, under more pleasant circumstances."

Kirov straightened.

"You know who I am?"

"Who would not be aware of Oleg Kirov? The man who now heads the organization that belonged to the late Vash Kukor. My father would expect me to convey his congratulations on your new position. Now you are worthy of even more respect."

"Miss Suvarov, you're embarrassing me."

Her quiet laugh only served to increase his admiration for her.

"Oleg Kirov embarrassed? Never. Now I *will* go." From the small handbag she carried she took a small white card and handed it to him. "Please call me. I would like to speak to you again. Soon."

She turned, walking through the mourners, her long legs carrying her quickly away from him. Even her walk excited Kirov. It was controlled, fluid and extremely sensual. When she was some distance away she turned briefly and saw that he was still standing where she had left him. He held the calling card in one hand, unnoticed, his eyes on her face as she gave him a hint of a smile, then turned away.

Kirov watched her as she reached a parked limousine. She bent to open the rear door, disappearing inside. The door closed behind, the car rolled away and she was gone. The day became suddenly gray and chilly, and Oleg Kirov shivered.

THE MOMENT THE CAR DOOR closed, cloistering her in the luxurious comfort of the rear seat, Valentina dragged the hat from her head and flung it aside.

"God, am I glad that's over. Nikolai, I need a cigarette."

She waited with ill-concealed impatience while the cigarette was lit and placed in her fingers. She took a long drag, pulling the smoke deep into her lungs. Only then did she relax, crossing her long and shapely legs as she slumped back in the seat. Reaching down with her free hand, she smoothed out the creases in her skirt.

"Where would you like to go?" Nikolai Petrovsky asked. He paused for a moment, then added, 'Don't forget we have that meeting with Landsberg at two."

Valentina pretended not to hear, turning to stare out through the tinted window. She could see the straggling line of the other mourners as they began to drift toward their own vehicles.

"Look at them, Nikolai. Those clowns going home thinking what a good, obedient daughter Arkady Suvarov has. A woman who does as she is told and pays her respects to a dead man." She teased the end of the cigarette with her pursed lips, turning to glance across at her companion. "Tell me, Nikolai, do you think I am a *good* girl?"

He smiled. "If I knew the answer to that, I would be a long way to understanding how your mind works."

"Nikolai, I have always believed you understood everything." Her voice lowered to a soft whisper. "Especially about me."

He held up his hands in surrender.

Valentina turned to stare through the window again.

"You see those men out there? *They* do not understand me, Nikolai. Not one of them suspects they are already dead. Give me my chance and I will have them in my grasp, or in graves alongside Kukor."

"I'm certain you will. Now shall we go and complete this deal with Landsberg?"

"There are times, Nikolai, when you seem to take delight in spoiling my simple pleasures." Valentina nodded at him. "Oh, very well, let's do it."

Nikolai instructed the driver where they needed to go. He pressed the button that raised the dark glass panel that isolated them in the rear of the limousine. Neither of them spoke as the vehicle cruised through the cemetery and out onto the highway, merging with the flow of traffic.

"Tell me about our little problem in Moscow," Valentina said, fixing him with a steady look.

Petrovsky held back a smile. He should have known Valentina would get to hear about the problem.

"I was going to discuss it after we dealt with Landsberg. All right. It appears that Denisov has been arranging some deals of his own with one of our suppliers in Afghanistan. The word is he wants to branch out on his own."

"Using our contacts and money to get it up and running."

"So it seems."

Valentina didn't speak for a while. She gazed across Petrovsky's shoulder, watching the scenery and traffic pass by. It was a defining moment for Petrovsky as he saw the vulnerable outer mask dissolve, the face she had worn for her dutiful role as Arkady Suvarov's representative at the funeral of Kukor. All pretense was gone. The soft contours of her beautiful features suddenly sharpened, the flawless skin melding against the bone beneath. Even her eyes changed. The dewy aspect of the young and respectful mourner turned cold and frighteningly savage.

"You will have to start looking for a replacement for the *late* Sergei Denisov," she said coolly.

"I'll deal with it this afternoon."

"Has Denisov any partners in crime?"

Her choice of words amused him. "Three of our people. We know who they are."

"They are to be retired along with Denisov. For the moment we won't replace them. We're not short of people."

"Only those we need to trust."

"Always the cynic, Nikolai."

"I prefer to be thought of as a realist. There is no profit in hoping problems will go away by themselves."

"All they need is a little push in the right direction." Valentina changed the subject abruptly. "Did you find out where Vasily has been since that mess out in New Jersey?"

Mention of Valentina's older brother made Nikolai slightly uncomfortable. His delay in answering earned him a suspicious glance from her. He knew better than to attempt any deception. Before he could speak, Valentina answered her own question.

"He's with that damned woman again. Isn't he, Nikolai? "

He nodded. "We located them this morning. They're at the girl's apartment in the city."

"At a time like this? When we are surrounded by enemies, he can't take a break and keep his pants zippered? Send someone out there. I want him back here as soon as possible. Damn him. He spends his life avoiding any kind of responsibility."

"He's still smarting over the stolen guns and Jacklin."

"Even something as simple as that, he messes up. Can't he do anything except spend money on that woman? I want him back, Nikolai. Have him brought home."

"He won't like it."

"I'm all broken up about that possibility."

"And the woman?"

The expression in her eyes told Petrovsky all he needed to know. He sank back in the seat, taking out his cell phone. He hit one of the speed-dial numbers and waited until it was answered.

"Tibor, that matter we spoke about earlier...

Yes. Go and bring him home. No questions. He comes back. Oh, yes, I asked the same question. I leave that to your discretion."

"You see, Nikolai, it wasn't hard," Valentina said, a gentle smile edging her lips.

"I need to discuss a couple of other items," Petrovsky said. "The hit against the Justice guy running the investigation? Somebody tipped him off. He cleared his office and staff with five minutes to go before the device went off."

"Damn."

"We charred his wallpaper, but he's still alive."

"You said a couple of matters?"

"Jacklin has vanished. He can't be found anywhere. We have more dead people, but Jacklin isn't one of them."

"That little asshole has more lives than a sewer rat."

"More like a guardian angel."

"And we lose the guns, too. Nikolai, the profit margin is taking a beating this week." Valentina blew smoke with a vengeance. "Talking of beating, I can't wait to see my ever-loving brother."

Petrovsky sat back in his seat. "I just love to see filial affection in action. Valentina, if you ever consider adopting me, forget it."

VALENTINA WAS WAITING for him in the club when he arrived. She nodded to the escort and they left the room, closing the door quietly. Vasily made an effort to appear annoyed at the indignity of his return. He was fooling no one, especially Valentina. She ignored him as she continued to scan the papers strewed across the desk. The moment of silence passed and Vasily moved to stand in front of the desk, leaning forward, resting his hands on the top.

"What the hell is going on? Dragging me out of bed like some teenage delinquent. Bringing me here in disgrace. No more, Valentina. This is going to stop," he said, less strength in his tone than the words implied. *"Do you hear me?"* This time his voice rose.

Valentina laid down the paper she was reading. She raised her head and looked him in the eye. She stood, and Vasily was forced to straighten up to maintain eye contact. He was about to raise his hand, finger extended to admonish her, when Valentina hit him. It wasn't a weak, ladylike slap, but a full-on blow that struck his left cheek with enough force to tip him off balance. Vasily stumbled, gripping the edge of the desk with his left hand to keep him on his feet. His face stung from the blow and after a few seconds he tasted blood inside his mouth where the flesh had impacted against his teeth.

"Don't raise your voice to me, Vasily. You can't back up your words with actions. Shall I tell you something? While you have been playing around with that whore of yours, I've been working to keep this organization on its feet. I've been to the funeral of Vash Kukor. Then I dealt with Landsberg and closed our Cayman Islands deal with him. I also arranged for the removal of traitors back home in Moscow, some of our people who have been attempting to set up a splinter group using our money and contacts. Tell me, Vasily, what has been your contribution lately? Oh, I remember. You not only screwed up the simple job of having McKay dealt with, you went on to fix that *deal* to get the guns back and get rid of Morey Jacklin. That was a waste of time, too. Jacklin is in hiding and the guns are gone. We're down more men.

"Tell me, Vasily, what else have you been doing to help? I know. Screwing that piece of gutter trash you picked up a few weeks ago. Tell me, how will Father react when he finds out how you have been neglecting the business? Well?"

Vasily straightened, brushing at his suit jacket. He probed the cut on his cheek with the tip of his tongue. It hurt. He refused to look at Valentina.

She moved around the desk and crossed the expansive office. He could hear her pouring a drink from the well-stocked wet bar. She returned to the desk with a filled glass, sitting again. She leaned back in the big leather executive chair, tilting it back, watching her brother as she took a swallow from the glass. The fine whiskey slid easily down her throat. She had never favored what were delicately called ladies' drinks, preferring the pleasure of fine whiskey. A practice she had learned from her father. Arkady Suvarov had never denied himself the luxuries in life. He could afford to be indulgent and it had pleased him when his daughter had developed her own, individual preferences.

"If I had my way, Vasily, there would have been another name on that list of undesirables. It would solve one of my problems at a stroke."

It took a few seconds for Vasily to absorb the meaning behind her comment. The shock etched itself across his face and he looked directly at his sister.

"You want me dead?"

"Convince me you have something I need that merits keeping you alive. The ability to drop your pants without looking down at your zip hardly qualifies. The fact we have the same father is nothing more than an accident of birth as far as I can see. Have I missed something, Vasily? No? As they say in the best courtroom movies, I rest my case."

Vasily's mind was working at something that had been nagging at him for some time. During the trip from town he had been thinking about it, and now it came surging back, leaving a cold, unsettling sensation in the pit of his stomach.

"Where is Tina?"

Valentina took another drink. Savoring the taste of the whiskey. She didn't miss a single beat.

"Damn, you, Valentina, where is she? What happened to her after I was taken away?"

"Your little virgin maiden?" Valentina gave him a simpering, girly smile. "Don't concern yourself with her. Tibor has made it clear she should stay away for a while. I know you, Vasily. You talk too much. We can't afford to have our business go outside the Family at the present."

"Where is she? What have you done, Valentina? Where is she?"

"Vasily, if I were you I'd be spending my time on more pressing matters. Remind me. Wasn't Sergei Denisov one of your friends?"

Valentina was watching her brother closely as she spoke. She didn't miss the sudden drain of color from his cheeks when she mentioned Denisov.

"You know he is. And why did you say he *was* a friend?"

"How forgetful of me. Denisov is already dead. Along with the other three helping him cheat us. Didn't I explain? *He* was the one trying to create his own organization. He obviously had entrepreneurial skills. Unfortunately going behind our backs and stealing our money wasn't the right way to exploit those talents."

Vasily turned and crossed to the wet bar. He splashed vodka in a glass, spilling much of it. He gulped down half the contents of the tall tumbler, gasping in pain as the raw liquor seeped into the cut inside his mouth. The vodka settled in his stomach with the solidity of molten lead. He squeezed his eyes shut as the waves of nausea rolled up from his stomach and filled his mouth with bile.

"You really have no idea the kind of trouble we are in," Valentina said, her voice reaching him as if it were coming from a vast distance. "All you see is the money and the way people back off when they know you're a Suvarov. You don't look beyond the bright lights, Vasily, and see the darkness—other organizations who want our action, trying to undermine us, to betray us. And we have father locked up with the Feds doing their best to gather proof to keep him there. None of it means a thing to you. As long as you can be the playboy, flashing money and trading on the Family name, nothing else matters."

Vasily spun vodka splashing from his glass. He had been thinking about what his sister had said about having Denisov killed and the realization hit him as an aftershock.

"You had Sergei killed? I can't believe you would do that. He has been with us for years. He was one of us—"

"He was a man who betrayed us. He took our money and used our resources to build his own empire. Do you really believe he was your friend? Friends do not steal from each other."

"He would have…"

Valentina fixed her gaze on him, features set.

"Have what, Vasily? Paid back the money he stole? Returned our merchandise? How would you know that? Unless you knew what he was doing. Is that it, brother? Did you know what he was doing and turned a blind eye because he was your friend?" She rose to her feet, anger boiling now, and without warning she threw the heavy glass tumbler at Vasily. It caught him alongside the head, opening a gash that started to bleed immediately. "You fucking imbecile. You knew. And never said a word because he was your *friend*."

The door opened and Nikolai Petrovsky stepped into the room. He assessed the situation instantly.

"Vasily, go and get that seen to. You're dripping blood all over the carpet. Go now."

Vasily left the room without a word. Closing the door behind him, Petrovsky bent and retrieved the tumbler Valentina had thrown. He held it in his hand, turning it over and over.

"Your father always said you would have made a good baseball pitcher. That right arm of yours is very strong."

Valentina made an angry sound.

"Damn him, Nikolai, he knew about Denisov and kept quiet about it. I can do without that kind of thing so close to home."

"Perhaps the time has come to move Vasily somewhere he can do less harm."

Valentina's anger had subsided as swiftly as it had erupted. She sat again. Petrovsky poured her a fresh drink and placed it in front of her.

"Fine, but what do you suggest? If we take him out of the limelight, who fronts the organization in his place?"

"The one who is carrying him and the organization from the bunker."

"Me?"

"In reality it's what you are already doing.

Vasily has simply been reading the lines you fed him. There's no reason why you shouldn't step in and make yourself known."

"At a time like this?"

"What better time? It happens. In the middle of a conflict commanders have been forced to step in and take over. Valentina, you have to do something and do it quickly. You listen to the talk. You hear what the others have to say. They discuss all kinds of things in front of you because they think you are—"

"A foolish girl who only worries about the latest fashions and who might make the best husband. You have no need to remind me, Nikolai."

"I know you better than any of them. If this organization can be held together, you can do it. You are your father's daughter. A true Suvarov."

"Once I make my bid, there will be no more loose talk in front of me. My usefulness will vanish."

Petrovsky smiled. "Trust me, Valentina, once they get over the shock, they will be eating out of your hand like sheep."

"I prefer to picture them as goats."

"The being-led-to-the-slaughter type goats?"

Her laughter this time was light, and for a moment Petrovsky saw the young woman behind the steel facade.

"Am I so terrible, Nikolai?"

"My feelings on the subject are quite ambivalent, my dear."

"Do something for me, Nikolai."

"You want me to go and talk to Vasily."

"If I go, I'll only end up arguing, or hitting him again. Right now I am so angry with him. I can't make any kind of controlled judgment."

"Let me see what I can do. Valentina, I can understand your feelings. Your brother is a problem we can do without right now. Perhaps he needs to be distanced from us."

"Extremely distanced."

"A word of caution. Vasily lacks your strength of character. If he senses he's being victimized he'll undoubtedly rebel. Like a child being deprived. If that happens, there's no telling what he might do. So we have to be careful not to let him be aware of our intentions."

Valentina raised her hands in mock surrender. "My first instinct was right."

"Oh?"

"I told him I would be better off if he had been dealt with the same as Denisov."

"Your own brother?"

"Now I have shocked you."

Petrovsky shook his head. "The opposite. I'm

impressed. It's the kind of thing Arkady would have done without a second thought a few years ago."

"But now?"

"He would hesitate."

"And whatever else, Vasily *is* his son."

"Yes."

"And they tell me women are the weaker sex."

"Any other man but Vasily. It is the blood that binds. Flesh of my flesh."

"Nikolai, just remove him from my sight. Send him wherever you want. Give him something to make him *feel* he is a man. Now there is a challenge even for you, Nikolai Petrovsky."

"I think I know what to do. I'll send him to Florida and let him work with DiFranco."

Valentina found herself smiling.

"That will make Leon's day. He'll believe we've sent Vasily to spy on him."

"And Vasily will feel he is being pushed out of the way and made to obey Leon's orders."

"Nikolai, I am feeling better already. Let the pair of them watch each other like wolves on the prowl. It will keep them both occupied while we deal with these other matters."

"I'll call DiFranco now to give him the good news. I bet you'll be able to hear him scream all the way from Florida."

"Let him scream. He works for us, Nikolai. He takes our money, he takes our orders. Remind him who bankrolls everything he does down there. Make sure he knows what happened to Denisov when he betrayed us."

"And then?"

"We need to close the matter in Moscow. Now that Denisov has been removed, there'll be unrest. We need to have a meeting to bring that episode to an end and make sure they all know this kind of behavior will not be tolerated."

"I'll arrange the trip."

"Nikolai, make it as soon as possible. When we're in Moscow I'll announce my position as the new head of the Family concern. Let them chew that over. By the time we return, I'm sure the news will have preceded us. I'll be ready to make my position clear."

"There's certain to be opposition."

"I would be surprised if there wasn't, Nikolai. Something needs to be done before we go. We have our loyalists. Tibor is foremost. Advise him and make certain he has his people on standby. And, Nikolai, I want it understood that when I say backup, I mean people who will obey without a moment's hesitation. You understand?"

Nikolai nodded. "A big step."

She smiled. "Very big. But hesitation has never created much profit. Have Tibor set up for a summit meeting at the Isla Blanca villa when we're finished in Moscow. It's somewhere we can have privacy. If I'm going to announce my position as head of the organization, I want the right people there. The ones we can make alliances with and perhaps the ones we need to bring into line. Oleg Kirov. Our West Coast friends from the Tiger Red Yakuza. The Malekov group. His organization is small but it has influence. And he has the ear of Solezin. Any objections can be dealt with in seclusion. I want Tibor to be in charge of security, and it must be in *our* favor."

"Is this how you really want it, Valentina?"

"Yes, this is how I want it. Seeing those idiots out there at Kukor's funeral made me realize what a bunch of old men they are. I think the time has come for new blood to flow through the veins of the organizations. If we do it quickly and do not hold back, we can have them all by the throat before they realize. And when they do, it'll be too late."

Nikolai nodded and turned to leave. He was at the door when Valentina spoke again.

"Arrange for me to go and visit my father. I want him to hear this from me."

He turned and she was seated behind the desk, in the chair previously occupied by Arkady Suvarov. Somehow she seemed to fill the big chair. Her gaze was fixed on the oil painting of her father that hung on the wall opposite, and Petrovsky suddenly had the feeling that *he* would never sit in that chair again.

The king is dead—long live the new King.

The thought excited him and at the same time caused a slight tremor of apprehension. He could understand the excitement, but the concern? He glanced back at Valentina and saw the cold gleam in her beautiful eyes and the slight curve of triumph playing at the edges of her mouth.

And that was when he knew *why* he was concerned.

Federal Correctional Facility, New Jersey

THE VISITING ROOM was large and open, with a scattering of tables with hard benches for prisoners and visitors to sit facing each other. There were a number of visits taking place when Valentina sat to wait for her father. Armed guards stood around the perimeter of the room, watching, ever alert for any forbidden actions.

Valentina sat upright when the door opened and

her father stepped into the room and started across to where she was waiting.

The first thing she noticed was the slow pace of his walk. Arkady Suvarov had always been a man of boundless energy and a zest for life. Now he looked and acted an older man. She was aware of the way his prison denims hung on his wasted frame as he crossed the visitor room and sat facing her over the bare table. He managed a pale imitation of a smile, a pretense at conveying everything was as it should be. She noticed the slightly gaunt look to his features.

Valentina leaned over and kissed him on the cheek.

"This place is killing me," Arkady said with no trace of emotion in his voice.

He spoke in Russian, as they always did during visits, their voices low and secretive.

Valentina laid one of her hands over his. She recalled them as always being large and powerful. Now she could feel the shadow of his bones beneath the mottled skin, the blue veins showing through shiny skin.

"We are doing everything we can to get you out of here," she said.

"They won't let me out now. It was my own doing. I shouldn't have tried to flee the country.

What I did proved to them I was a guilty man and now they have me where they want me."

"No talk like that, Dad."

He looked up at her, his eyes misting for a moment. Valentina had always called him "Dad." Never the formal "father" from the old country, but the more familiar title used by American offspring.

"My little Valentina. But no longer little. Now you are a beautiful woman and so like your mother. I see her every time I look at you."

"I wish she was here for you now."

"Yes." He paused. "I miss her very much."

"We all do."

"Tell me why Vasily is not here. Why he never visits me."

Valentina took a breath. She knew what she needed to say. It had to be brought into the open.

"I have sent him to Miami to work with DiFranco."

"*You* sent him?" Arkady leaned forward. "Explain."

"Dad, Vasily hasn't been running things since you went away. He was just playing at it. He has no control. No dedication. No one has respect for him because he fails to earn it. All he cares about is having a good time and spending money.

When I saw what he was doing, I stepped in. With Nikolai's help I took over. Now *I* sit in your place."

The room seemed to become very quiet around them. In the background the air-conditioner hummed gently. A heavy door closed with a solid thump. Valentina felt her father's hand tense beneath hers as he absorbed what she had just told him. She sat waiting, allowing him time to take it in.

"I should have seen this coming. As you both grew, I watched and I saw you were always the stronger of the two. Perhaps this is all my fault. I always favored Vasily because he was my son. I indulged him—obviously far too much. I made it too easy for him." Arkady stared into her eyes. "Did I betray you, Valentina, by favoring your brother?"

"You always loved me. There was never any doubt about that."

"Then tell me how you became strong. How you were able to step into my shoes."

"I studied the best role model ever. For years I watched and learned. Dad, I watched *you*."

Arkady drew a breath, shaking his head. "Do you understand what you are saying? If you watched as you say, then you must know the things I have done. The terrible decisions I had to make."

"Things you did that made you the strongest. We are the strongest of the Families. If I can do half of what you did, I will achieve a great deal."

"Tell me what has been happening."

"I reached an agreement with Landsberg. He will now handle our cash laundering through his Cayman Island financial organization."

"Good. Now what about Vash Kukor's organization? Who heads it now that he is dead?"

"Oleg Kirov. For now." Valentina smiled. "I introduced myself as your representative when I met him at Kukor's funeral."

"You attended?"

"Of course. It needed to be done. Out of respect, as you would have done. It also gave me the opportunity to see who else was there."

"And Kirov?"

"He is convinced I am your dutiful daughter. I let him believe he has charmed me and he is eager to meet again."

"Be careful of him. Kirov is a great womanizer. Not to be trusted."

"I do not intend to trust him. Just use him to get to his organization so it can be merged with ours."

"Ha! That would be a wise move."

"Dad, I also learned that Sergei Denisov was attempting to create his own organization in

Moscow. He was diverting our money and re-sources to fund this."

"Denisov? Are you sure?"

"Yes."

"Traitors in our own Family. Damn him. Valentina, he must be dealt with."

"The matter has already been settled. Denisov and his accomplices have been removed. Their deaths will warn off anyone else thinking about similar plans."

Her dispassionate reasoning silenced Arkady for a moment. He looked at his daughter and recognized a different person. Someone far stronger and determined than he had ever realized could exist.

"You had them—"

"*Removed?* Of course. It was the only way. Exactly what you would have done yourself."

Arkady straightened. A little of the pressing weight seemed to have been removed from his shoulders. Then, as if even that was a great effort, he shrank back in his seat, taking on the persona of the old man he really was.

"Now at least I know things are in safe hands. *Your* hands, my little Valentina."

"I don't want you worrying," she said 'Let me do that now. With Nikolai helping, we can keep things running smoothly until—"

"Valentina, my darling, please do not humor me. I can see the look in your eyes. The strength in your words. The fire is in your blood and you have control already. Be truthful to at least me. You will not want to relinquish what you have even if I do beat these charges and become a free man again."

"Dad, that is not the way—"

"But yes, Valentina, it *is* the way."

"We're doing everything we can to get your release." She lowered her voice to a whisper. "Have you heard about the federal witnesses being taken care of?"

Arkady nodded. "You did this?"

"We gave the contract to our friends."

"Now I am even more impressed. Do you have any other surprises for me?"

"We do have a problem with someone interfering with our operations. There have been a number of strikes against us."

"From one of the other organizations?"

Valentina shrugged. "We are looking into them at the moment."

"What has happened?"

"Lebowski's New Jersey car ring was wiped out. A big financial loss. And a consignment of new weapons was hijacked in Baltimore just after they came off the ship. We tried to take out the man behind it but *he* killed our people. Morey Jacklin was working against us and helped this man. I have people looking for Jacklin, but at the moment he has eluded us."

"I don't need to tell you what to do."

"I have it under control. Dad, I'm going to Moscow first to settle the Denisov matter. I need to make it clear this kind of thing will not be tolerated."

"A wise move. Make sure they know there is still a Suvarov's hand at the controls."

"I intend to. By the time I return everyone will know."

"Then I can rest easy. Plan for my upcoming retirement."

"Dad, please, don't talk like this.

He patted her hand. When he looked into her face again there was a moistness in his eyes.

"It had to come one day. I'm not a young man any longer, Valentina. If I walk out a free man, then at least I will be able to enjoy some years of peace. At least I hand over to someone I can trust. As long as I am in here, the Feds will keep on with their attempt to have me indicted. It will allow you time to establish your control. Valentina, I give you my blessing and my Family."

WHEN VALENTINA WALKED out of the facility and back to her waiting car, she was barely able to hold back the satisfied smile touching her lips. As much as she loved her father, respected and admired him, she had realized some time ago that he was losing his grip on the organization. She would do what she could to free him, but the control she had over the Family business would never return to Arkady Suvarov. It was her time now. Hers alone.

CHAPTER FIVE

"Mack, I just got word McKay is dead. Somebody was waiting for him when he drove back to his apartment earlier today and drove into him as he was climbing out of his SUV. Crushed him against the door and took him along the street before he went under the wheels. Witnesses said it was no accident the way the driver of the hit-and-run vehicle made sure McKay was under the wheels before he reversed over him, then took off. Big black SUV, tinted windows, no license plates. N.Y.P.D. found it an hour later abandoned in a junkyard. McKay's blood was still on the underside, but the vehicle itself was clean. No prints."

"McKay would have never backed off. I have to give him that."

"For what it's worth, there was a local beat cop

on the scene within a couple of minutes. He did what he could for McKay, but the guy died within a couple of minutes. I don't know how he did it, but McKay gave the cop my number."

"The one I gave him?"

"Yeah. As soon as the cop called, I had McKay's apartment sealed off and got N.Y.P.D. to put men on it. No one in or out until we—meaning you—could check it out first."

"Hell of a way to pay the guy back for losing his life. Searching his apartment."

"I think he wanted that, which was why he gave the cop my number."

"I'm on my way over there soon as we finish talking."

"So hang up, pal, and stop wasting time."

MCKAY'S APARTMENT was neat and functional. After the N.Y.P.D. cop on the door had checked Bolan's Matt Cooper Justice Department ID, the Executioner stepped inside and closed the door. He surveyed the apartment, not sure exactly he was looking for.

The greater part of the living area was given over to McKay's work—a large desk and leather swivel chair. An upscale computer system with a large plasma-screen monitor, notepads and digital photographs were scattered across the surface of the desk. On the wall behind the desk was a large pin-board onto which McKay had stuck photo images and charts. There was even a map, with a location ringed in red. Bolan stood in front of the board, studying the information.

He recognized names and faces he had seen in Turrin's data. They tied up with names Morey Jacklin had given Bolan. And now Frank McKay was adding his signature to the collection.

Only McKay's had more detail and guidance than either of the others.

The location on the map turned out to be an area of rural Kansas. An isolated spot out in the sticks, where there had been farms and ranches, now long abandoned. The area had become a dusty backwater, where little of consequence happened now. Frank McKay had the location of an old farm. Long-distance photographs showed the place in detail—the empty main house and the outhouses, barn and stable, a sagging water tower. According to a property trace McKay had undertaken, the place had been purchased two years previously by an investment company owned, via numerous cutoffs, by a subsidiary of the Suvarov organization.

Beside the images Bolan saw a printout of McKay's summary of his investigation.

Human cargo delivered a couple of times. All young women. What I suspected. Farm is the drop-off point for Suvarov trafficking. This is where kidnap victims are brought for processing. From here they'll be shipped out. Prostitution. Stripping. Porn business.

Photos 1-10 show delivery to farm. Close on a dozen girls. They look dazed, disoriented. Maybe drugged. Clothing and appearance suggests East European. This ties in with earlier research—need to get more detail on this.

Looks like they keep them underground. Probably extended the original cellar to create their lockdown area.

Bolan checked the photos listed and saw the group of girls being herded from a couple of panel trucks. They were under the watchful eye of a number of armed men. In the sequence of shots the girls were moved to what looked like the entrance to an old root cellar—McKay's lockdown. The journalist had managed a couple of close shots of the men herding the prisoners and also shots of terrified girls, lost and alone in strange country, unaware of what was going to happen to them.

Bolan helped himself to material from the pinboard then called Turrin on his cell. He gave a brief summary of what he had found.

"We've had our suspicions about this but never been able to get close. Kansas? These people chose a good spot. Isolated. Not much else around."

"This looks like our next move. By the sound of it, this place needs closing down."

"I get worried when you say closing down."

"Getting cold feet, Leo?"

"No. Just wondering about the cost to the taxpayer."

Bolan chuckled. "Don't I always give good dollar value? I'm just thorough."

"A tornado is thorough."

"Then I'm going to the right state, Leo."

"Do we need to have the quartermaster open the store?"

"Please. Then I need a flight to Kansas and a vehicle waiting."

"Anything else?"

"Get your people over here. I have what I need. You need to pick up McKay's research. Get your guys to break into his computer files. You might strike lucky. McKay did his job well, so we shouldn't let his findings go to waste. The least we can do for him."

Kansas

IT HADN'T BEEN DIFFICULT to find the old Keller property. Bolan had come off the main highway and turned his SUV along the dusty side road that would eventually bring him to the farm. It was close to six o'clock. The Kansas night was cool and silent.

Bolan had dressed for the mission in his blacksuit, wearing a combat harness for his extra ammunition and to hold the fragmentation, smoke and stun grenades he had brought along. Tucked in a sheath on his hip was a Cold Steel Tanto knife with an edge that felt as though it could cut through solid stone. Along with his Beretta and Desert Eagle he had a 9 mm Uzi loaded with a 32-round magazine.

He drove to within a few miles of the farm, then eased the SUV off the road. He picked up the Uzi, hanging it from his shoulder, then locked the vehicle. Turning north, he cut cross-country, aiming for the ridge of low hills that cut across the farm property along its southern boundary.

Bolan took up a steady pace. He had a few miles to go and there was no use tiring himself. He wanted to be in position by dawn, giving himself the chance to check out the area and the farm before he made his strike.

If he could get in close and assess the strength of the Suvarov crew based at the farm, it would help his strategy. Which wasn't overly sophisticated. Bolan intended to get in and create as much chaos as he could. If there were still captives in the lockdown, he wanted them out free and clear. The Suvarov crew was already marked for the Executioner's own personal brand of retribution. He hadn't brought the Uzi along simply for effect.

He was flat on his stomach, looking down on the farm, by the time the sky started to lighten. Bolan had a compact set of field glasses in one his blacksuit slit pockets. He placed the Uzi beside him and used the glasses to scan the area. He took his time, working his way across the property, checking outhouses, barn and the angled doors of the cellar. He didn't fail to notice that the cellar doors were new, the wood still fresh against the weathered boards of the existing buildings. There were a couple of cars parked out by the barn. And a panel truck.

He also noticed there were no guards on patrol. On reflection he decided that was the wisest move. Armed patrols, even out here in this rural area, might attract attention from anyone passing. He accepted that was unlikely, but the possibility existed. The Suvarovs wouldn't want to advertise they were carrying out any sort of illegal activity, so they were keeping it low-profile. If anyone did venture out to the farm, all he or she would see would be a few people going about their daily business. The merchandise would be hidden from sight and sound, down in the cellar.

Just after 7:30 a.m. Bolan saw movement. A man emerged from the house. He wore a white shirt and a shoulder rig holding a pistol. A cell phone was stuck to one ear. Whoever he was having a conversation with had annoyed the guy. He was gesturing with his free arm, plainly angry at something he was being told. As he talked he made his way across to the entrance to the cellar. Reaching it he hauled open one of the doors and made his way down the steps cut from the earth, vanishing into the depths of the lockdown.

Bolan checked the house again, wondering how many there were inside. He moved even while the thought was up and running. Sitting playing guessing games wasn't going to achieve much. He cut along the ridge, working his way around to the rear of the bar and from there he was able to get to the rear porch of the house without problems.

He flattened himself against the back wall, crouching, and unclipped a couple of stun grenades. There was a window just above him. Bolan eased to one side and peered in to see an open living area that also contained the kitchen. Three figures were moving around while a fourth worked over a stove. Bolan pulled the tabs on the grenades. One in each hand, he moved around the house until he was at the rear door, which led directly into the room he had just checked out. Using his foot, Bolan flipped back the screen door, then leaned inside. He released the levers, then tossed both stun grenades inside, immediately pulling back and around the corner, head down and turned away from the structure.

He heard a single yell of alarm, then the crack of the grenades detonating. The harsh sound and the brilliant glare of light would leave the men inside the house crawling around on hands and knees, sight and hearing affected by the grenades.

Bolan returned to the rear of the house, then along the far wall until he located another window. He checked out an empty room. He used the Uzi to shatter the glass before lobbing in a smoke canister. He stayed where he was long enough to see the thick coils of smoke starting to fill the room and drift out through the open door before he continued around the house.

A door crashed open and a half-dressed figure burst out, coughing, waving a gleaming pistol. The guy was cursing wildly. As he hit the ground, head turning back and forth, he saw Bolan's black figure looming in his direction.

"I got the mother..." he yelled, turning the pistol on Bolan.

It was his first and last mistake of the day. Bolan hit him with a burst from the Uzi, the shredding effect of the 9 mm slugs opening his torso and spilling his blood down the front of his white shirt. He fell back against the clapboard wall of the house, his face suddenly pasty-white as he slithered to the ground.

Bolan heard more noise from inside the house. He saw the dark outline of stumbling figures, men suffering the effects of the stun grenades. They pushed at one another as they headed for the exit, hands against numb ears, blinking from stinging eyes. He heard them cursing in English, others in Russian. One in the lead, though deafened, still had clear his sight and he saw Bolan's black-clad figure as he pushed his way out the door. The guy hauled a handgun up from his waist, triggering a shot in Bolan's direction, and received a burst from the Uzi that pushed him to the floor and was a signal for the others behind him to start firing, as well. Bolan tracked the Uzi on the gunners and returned fire, driving them back with a stream of 9 mm rounds that silenced them in bloody seconds.

He angled across the open space, heading for the cellar doors and what ever lay below.

Bolan was only yards from the doors when they flew open, slamming back against the ground. A figure brandishing an AK-47 stormed up the steps, searching for the source of the noise that had attracted him. He found it—Bolan—but for no more than a few seconds. The Uzi stuttered, sending a stream of 9 mm rounds into the guy's torso. He stumbled back, astonishment on his face, and tumbled down the steps, with Bolan close behind.

As the man hit bottom, Bolan stepped over his body, crouching forward as he took in the low-ceilinged tunnel stretching in front of him. It had been originally dug from the raw earth, then strengthened with thick wood beams. The floor was still nothing more than hard-packed dirt. The tunnel ran ahead for around fifteen feet, then widened out. It was lit by dusty bulbs hanging from a cable hooked to nails driven into the beams.

Bolan had almost reached the spot where the tunnel widened when he saw an armed figure rush from his right, stepping into the tunnel section.

The confrontation came with a startling suddenness that caught both men briefly off guard.

There was no room to use weapons, so Bolan hit the guy head-on, spinning him off balance, then followed through with the Uzi, sending a short, hard burst that punched holes in the target's torso. The gangster went down on his knees, still holding his pistol, but having no control over the weapon. It sagged in his loose grip and the guy followed it down, sprawling on his face.

Another gunner came into view, dragging at a handgun that snagged on his belt. Bolan triggered a burst into his chest, driving the man to the floor, his yells of pain echoing along the tunnel before they faded away.

Other gangsters blocked the way ahead, all yelling back and forth. Bolan saw they had emerged from a secondary tunnel that came in from the right. To his left was a similar tunnel, which looked to be clear, and the soldier decided to advance that way, so he headed toward it. Then he saw shadowy figures moving from this tunnel, too, and realized if he didn't deal with the situation he was going to be caught in the middle. He plucked a fragmentation grenade from his harness. One way or the other he needed to clear a path. The main group, four men, saw the grenade and held back as Bolan pulled the pin and raised his arm. They all knew what damage could be done in the confines of the tunnel, and it prevented them from taking further action. They backed into the tunnel behind them.

Out the corner of his eye the soldier spied the shapes emerge from the second passage. An armed gangster held a struggling young woman in front of him as he pushed forward. He was having a hard time because the woman refused to stay submissive. There was a determined expression on her face. When she saw Bolan, hope gleamed in her eyes and she began to struggle even harder.

Bolan made his choice. He tossed the grenade at the four armed gunners as they drew farther back into their tunnel. The grenade had a short fuse. The bomb hit the side of the passage and bounced into the group of moving gangsters. The detonation within the confines of the tunnel was deafening. The close walls of the tunnel contained the explosion. Dust and debris, human and otherwise, blew out of the passage; smoke curled along the ceiling; dirt rained down on Bolan from over his head.

As the grenade went off, the Executioner sank to a crouch, looking back across his shoulder at the other gangster and his human shield.

Even as he turned, the woman came to a dead stop, momentarily catching her captor's attention. Her change of tactic caught him off guard and she used that hesitation to spin and slam a knee up between his legs. There was no fumbling. The woman knew how to deliver such a blow with total effect. The guy let out a high-pitched squeal, slumping back against the wall. The woman reached out and snatched the pistol from his hand. She zeroed in on the *mafiya* hardman and fired twice, putting the pair of slugs into his chest. The force pushed the guy against the wall. He stared up at the woman, stunned at what had happened and angry with himself for letting himself be taken by a female. His final response was to swing his right fist at her. He caught her across the side of the face, knocking her off her feet. Even as she was going down she triggered the pistol again, driving two more slugs into her adversary, directly over his heart. This time was more than enough. The man went down hard.

The thought went through Bolan's mind that there was more to this young woman than his original impression. That consideration would have to be dealt with later.

Bolan scanned the area, anticipating possible attacks from more of the opposition. Nothing. He stepped back, still alert for danger.

The woman got to her feet with surprising speed, one hand pressed to the raw bruise on her face. She caught Bolan's eye and beckoned him to follow her. They left the room and she took him down the dimly lit tunnel passage, which widened into a large roomlike area. There were a number of heavy wooden doors set in the walls. The woman paused at one door, staring at Bolan.

"I hope this is what you are looking for."

She slid back the bolt holding the door secure and pushed the door wide open. Bolan took a look inside and saw she was right. This was what he had been searching for—proof that the Suvarov organization was up to its neck in slavery.

The room was forty feet by twenty feet, poorly lit, but not so that Bolan was unable to see clearly. It had been sectioned off into steel-barred cells, and each one was occupied by a young woman. They all looked exhausted and had the same haunted, hopeless expression in their eyes. Most of them had some degree of bruising on their faces and bare arms.

"This is what they do. They keep the girls here until they move them on. Sometimes girls have died waiting here. The things they do to them…"

She broke off, memories flooding back, and for a moment she was unable to carry on.

Bolan didn't need any further explanation. He had the picture firmly fixed in his mind now. This was nothing more or less than a holding pen. A place where the hostages were confined while Suvarov's people negotiated the next stage of the girls' trade. There was little ahead of them except further imprisonment, more ill-treatment before they were sold to their new employers. Just as Frank McKay had been detailing in his summary investigation.

"Do you understand what they do to these girls?" the woman asked, her regained voice stronger as she insisted Bolan listen to what she had to say.

"I understand," he said.

"Then *do* something."

Bolan managed a smile. "I thought I already did."

"Yes."

"What's your name?"

HER NAME, Bolan learned, was Kira Tedesko. She was twenty-six years old and had been snatched off the streets of Pristina by one of the Suvarov teams as they'd scoured the area for likely subjects. Imprisoned, then drugged, Tedesko's journey to the U.S. had been one long, terrifying nightmare. She had ended up in the lockdown, not knowing where she was or what lay in store, until she had been instructed by the lockdown boss. She had learned very quickly. The instruction session had been accompanied by violence intended to explain to her what lay in store if she put up any resistance. The woman didn't like what had happened, but she'd had the sense not to resist. A couple of days later she'd witnessed the savage treatment meted out to one of the other women who went into total panic and refused to play along. The last image she'd had of the woman was of her broken and bloody body being dragged out of the room. The lockdown boss, Vincent Nash— another name Bolan had seen identified as a Suvarov man—used the example to make it clear to the rest of the captives this would happen to them if they failed to do what they were told.

For Tedesko it was a lesson she'd learned and taken to heart. Not that she'd intended to end up working in some brothel, or worse, one of the clubs that specialized in perversion. She and the other women had been made to watch porno-graphic videos, the implication being that this was something else they could be employed in. Kira had made up her mind she had to escape. Somehow. There was little she could do to overcome the men who ran the lockdown, so any attempt at getting away had to be taken at a time when she was actually out of the place.

She'd spent over a week in the lockdown. During that time she and the other women had received a visit from someone obviously high up in the Suvarov organization. A woman had come into the cell area and taken her time looking over the prisoners, who had been forced to strip. The men were plainly in awe of her as she'd walked up and down the line of holding cells, taking her time as she'd examined the girls. She only had to snap her fingers and the men ran around like scared rabbits. She'd checked out each woman, making suggestions to the lockdown boss on how she should be dressed. How her hair should be styled. Whether it needed its color changed. Where she should be placed.

Tedesko had watched the woman closely. Despite her precarious position, she'd been curious about her. Well-dressed, confident, with a commanding presence. Tedesko had maintained a subservient silence when the woman had approached her. There was something almost repellent in the way the woman ran her gaze over her. Tedesko had refused to be intimidated as the woman sized her up, almost as if she were little more than a Thoroughbred horse being assessed before a race.

"Change her hair," the woman had ordered. "Make it blond. Ash. Emphasize the color of her eyes. She has good bone structure. Cleaned up she will be an asset. She needs some body toning. See to it, Nash."

"Where's she going?"

"Miami, of course. She will work well under DiFranco. He will find plenty for her to do."

The woman had moved closer, peering directly into Tedesko's eyes. After a moment, a hint of a smile curled her full lips.

"You want to pull out my hair by the roots. Don't you?"

Tedesko held back any response.

"Speak. I would love to hear what you are thinking right at this moment."

"I don't think you would."

The woman had laughed, then glanced at Nash.

"Leon DiFranco loves women with spirit. He has clients who enjoy a challenge." She turned back to Tedesko. "You will be making a lot of money in six months, little princess."

"Don't hold your breath."

"Oh, I like this one. Nash, make sure she gets the best. Give her a room on her own. Some comfort. I want her looking her best when she goes to Miami. Understand?"

Nash had simply nodded. The look in his eyes warning Tedesko he didn't like being ordered around, but he couldn't do a thing about it.

Later, when the woman had gone, Tedesko was moved from the cell block and pushed into a small room that held a bed and a television set.

"You might have impressed her," Nash had said, standing in the doorway. "You're still nothin' to me. Don't do anything to make me mad, bitch." He'd turned to go, then paused, grinning. "I like it when they fight, too. Gives me a fuckin' buzz. You ain't in Miami yet, so don't get lippy."

Tedesko had kept silent. She wasn't about to anger Nash. He had been the one who had beaten the unfortunate woman when she had resisted. She hadn't forgotten the bright gleam in his eyes when he had attacked the woman. He had enjoyed what he was doing, and it had showed.

The days passed routinely. The only difference for Tedesko had been the comfort her new room afforded her. She was provided with clean clothing and shoes. The quality of her food improved, and she was left alone for most of the time. The television in her room at least allowed her to finally identify where she was.

America.

She spent her time flicking through the channels, trying to take in the programs that filled the days. She understood English, so she could at least follow what was being said. Local news programs told her she was in Kansas. Her only reference to Kansas was the movie *The Wizard of Oz*. The character Dorothy had come from Kansas. According to the movie, it had a lot of tornadoes. Knowledge of where she was did little to help her while she was locked up in her room.

At night, trying to sleep, Kira was sometimes disturbed by the cries and the pleading that filtered through from the cell block. Sometimes they were simply the frightened sounds of the women lost and alone in a strange place. Other times the sounds were different. Muffled, agonized cries of pain that told her Nash and his men were in the cells. She felt relief that she was being spared the humiliation and at the same time guilty that she was being left alone while the others suffered.

Then today she'd heard a distant commotion.

Shooting.

Men shouting.

There was a crash of sound.

More gunshots.

Hard, vicious sounds that spoke of death and injury. She heard a new sound. The cries of pain coming from men. The door of her room was unlocked and thrown open. One of the lockdown operators stood there, a pistol in his hand. He'd lunged at her, grabbing her and pulling her in front of him.

"What are you doing?" she'd asked.

"Getting myself out of here, bitch. Now shut your mouth and let's move...."

"WE CAN TALK more later, Kira."

"Nash, the other men in the house, are they all...dead?"

"Should they be?"

Her head came up and she fixed him with a hard stare.

"If you knew what they have done to the women. Even while I have been here they have killed one of them. They beat the others, too. At night they came to these cells sometimes and...raped them."

She saw the hard shine in his eyes.

"They've paid," he said, quiet reassurance in his voice.

"You had better mean that."

"I don't lie." He looked over her shoulder at the room she had been imprisoned in. "Why were *you* on your own?"

"The woman who runs this place decided I

should go to a special client. When I talked to her she decided I was worth something better." Tedesko gave a little chuckle. "I wish I had her here right now. Then I could show her I *am* better than she will ever be."

NOW BOLAN LOOKED around the room of cells. He saw the place where the jailers had sat. He moved to the desk and saw keys in a bunch. He handed them to Tedesko and told her to unlock the cages and free the women. While she did this he kept watch in case there were some of the Suvarov crew he might have missed. He also spent time checking the desk drawers, scattering stuff he found useless. He picked up a cell phone and pocketed it. He found a fat manila envelope. When he opened it there were wads of cash. A great deal of cash. He pushed it into one of his blacksuit's deep pockets.

"Now what do we do?" Tedesko asked.

The freed women were standing in a silent group, close together for mutual protection. A number were holding on to each other. Every one of them looked lost and frightened. Bolan could understand that. Like Tedesko, they had been taken off the streets and transported thousands of miles to a strange country where they had been imprisoned, beaten and assaulted. They had a right to be scared. Bolan felt for them. He wondered how many others were in the same predicament, and how many would never be freed. Of the many illegal practices Bolan had encountered and fought against, this had to be one of the vilest. Denying these women their freedom and forcing them into lives of despair and sexual abuse had to be high on the scale of crimes in anyone's book.

Bolan took out his cell phone and tapped the speed dial that would connect him with Turrin.

"I'm at the lockdown. Situation under control. I have a number of females who were being held by Suvarov's people. They need taking care of. And I mean care. Not stuck in some holding facility and treated like suspects. Do this right, Leo."

"You have my word."

"That's all I need."

"Give me the location and I'll have a team in there soon as possible. You staying around?"

"Only as long as this takes to clear up."

"Pick up any leads?"

"Maybe. I need a cell phone checked out. Numbers called and messages coming in. Can I hand it over to one of your people? Get it sent to the Farm for analysis?"

"I'll see to it personally. You meet any resistance?"

"Some. They won't be needing care and attention."

"I didn't think so. We can handle that, too. Run IDs on them. Check fingerprints and see who they are and what affiliations they have—had. We might get lucky."

"The ones who need the luck are the women they had penned up here. It might pay to have a check made around the area. I was told one of the women was killed. She might be buried in the vicinity."

Turrin was silent for a moment. "Okay. I'll get it done. A search team can come in later and look for the body."

"One more thing," Bolan said. "One of the women met the woman who ran this setup. Even talked to her. It seems she was being groomed for something higher than the normal establishment. I need to talk to her on her own, away from this place. She'll stay with me when the others leave."

FOUR HOURS LATER Bolan was moving again, this time with Kira Tedesko at his side. He left behind the burned-out remains of the lockdown and the house that had been its cover. Turrin's team had flown in using a couple of large helicopters. From the moment they touched down they deferred to Bolan in every respect, obviously primed by Leo Turrin.

There had been no preamble. Bolan had the women ready and they were taken to one of the choppers and flown out within thirty minutes. Men from the second chopper went inside the lockdown and took fingerprints from the dead. They also took away anything that might provide information on the Suvarov organization. One of the men had mentioned the cell phone Bolan had located, and he handed it over.

After the departure of the second helicopter Bolan was left alone with Kira Tedesko. She sat in the SUV, watching as he vanished back inside the house, then the lockdown cellar, carrying with him a carry-all from the rear of the SUV. He reappeared after ten minutes and climbed in behind the wheel after depositing his weapons in the rear. As they pulled away she heard a soft *whoosh* and saw flame and smoke issuing from the windows of the farmhouse. Shortly after there was a similar burst of flame from the cellar. Even when they rejoined the main highway she could still see the high pall of smoke far behind them. She turned to glance across at Bolan. He hadn't looked back once.

"So, are you an American policeman?" she asked finally.

"No."

"Then you work for the government?"

"If it'll make you happy, then, yes, I work for the government."

Tedesko tested out that answer and wasn't satisfied. "No, you do not work for the government."

"How's that?"

"All you did was give me an answer to shut me up. I don't think I like that."

Bolan was forced to smile. "You're right, Kira. You deserve better. Let's say I do work for the government and myself, and I don't actually answer to anyone."

Now she was puzzled. "Are you one of these vigilantes I have heard about?"

"No."

"Then what?"

"I do what has to be done."

She made a soft sound. A gesture of understanding that was offered in the place of words. After a moment she twisted in the seat and studied Bolan's profile. There was something in the man's face that explained a great deal: his strength of character, determination. She recalled his telling her that he never lied, and she believed that. She was with one of that rare breed of men who lived by a simple code. It made them what they were without pretension, or having to parade a set of false virtues. This, and she came to a stop, this man without a name.

"What do I call you?"

"Matt Cooper."

"And this is your real name?"

Bolan smiled. She was checking him out on his honesty.

"Only while I work."

"And how can *I* help *you*, Cooper?"

"You said you had been picked for something special. What were you told?"

"Not a lot. Only that I would be sent to Miami. And I would be working for someone called Leon DiFranco. Does this mean anything to you?"

"Not right now, but I'm going to find out."

Bolan took out his cell phone and called Turrin.

"My contact would have been sent to Miami, to one Leon DiFranco."

"I'll check it out. The name's familiar. Be back to you."

Bolan cut the connection. He saw a sign up ahead, made a left turn at the next intersection and was back on the main highway. He checked his speed and settled in for the ride back to the motel that he had booked into on his arrival in Kansas. Glancing at his watch, he figured they would be there in just under an hour. Tedesko had fallen silent. When he turned to look at her, he saw that she was asleep. He didn't disturb her until he pulled into the parking spot outside his room. Bolan cut the engine. The silence and lack of motion alerted her. Kira came awake with a start, eyes wide with alarm. She sat upright, swiveling her head until she saw Bolan. Then she relaxed.

"I thought I was—"

"Take it easy, Kira. You're safe now."

"Safe?" Her face lost some of its tension. "That is a nice word to hear."

INSIDE THE MOTEL ROOM Kira Tedesko stared at the furnishings. The room was standard, nothing special, but as far as she was concerned it was a palace. She wandered around, inspecting the bed, putting on the bathroom light and standing looking at the shower. She returned to the room and sank into one of the chairs.

Bolan had busied himself with the carry-all he had brought from the SUV, checking his weapons and making sure they were all reloaded. It was a necessary procedure, and something he always did once he was on safe ground. His world was a dangerous place and confrontation was always close. He survived by staying ahead of the game.

Always watching. Always listening. Mistakes in Bolan's universe had fatal consequences. He had no intention of becoming one of those statistics. He completed his equipment check and put his weapons back in the carry-all.

"You hungry?" he asked.

She nodded.

"There's a diner close by," Bolan said. "We can go and get something."

She nodded, then stood, brushing at the clothes she was wearing, running fingers through her thick black hair.

"I would like to clean up first."

"Help yourself."

Tedesko vanished into the bathroom, closing the door behind her. After a short while Bolan heard the hiss of the shower. He used the time she was gone to get out of his blacksuit and change into civilian clothing. He donned the shoulder rig that carried the 93-R, pulling a sport jacket over it.

His cell phone rang. It was Turrin.

"Leon DiFranco is Miami-based, Suvarov's main man in Florida. He runs nightclubs, topless bars, the usual stuff. That's the front for the main business—drug distribution and escort agencies that do a lot more than provide just talk. He peddles porn, too. DiFranco is a real charmer, and has a bad rep with the ladies. He likes to knock them around, among other things. Miami P.D. has a thick file on him, but no convictions. He has a lawyer who could have sprung Adolf Hitler on a sympathy plea."

"Information like that could make it a busy time for me in Miami."

"You thinking of making a house call?"

"You never know."

"I'll have a location for you later."

"Okay."

"By the way, when my people moved in to look for the dead woman they reported back that the ranch site had burned down. You wouldn't happen to know anything about that?"

"It was me. After your first team checked it through I decided it needed cleaning out."

"I figured something like that. They did find her. Buried in a dry wash about a quarter mile away."

"Damn."

"They also found the remains of five other bodies. Preliminary CSI report has them all as young and female."

As Bolan ended the conversation, Tedesko emerged from the bathroom, toweling her hair.

She had brushed down her clothing and looked different from the disheveled woman who had gone into the bathroom.

"I just talked with my guy," Bolan said. "Not the best news. They found the dead woman. And the remains of others."

Tedesko sat on the edge of the bed, her shoulders slumping as she took the news in.

"What kind of a world do we live in, Cooper?"

"For the most part, a good one. If we don't hold that thought, we lose out to the killers and the monsters who exist alongside us. Kira, never lose sight of that. Give in to them and we end up losers ourselves."

Bolan went into the bathroom to freshen up himself, leaving the woman to her thoughts for the moment, giving her time to come to terms with the news he had just delivered. When he returned to the room she stood and crossed to him.

"Do you have a brush I could borrow?" she asked. "For my hair?"

Bolan located one in his bag and tossed it to her. She stood in front of the mirror, working on her thick black hair until she had it as she wanted. She turned finally and spread her arms as she faced Bolan.

"Thank you for what you said. I needed those

words." She gave him a warm smile. "So how do I look?"

"You look good."

He wasn't talking down to her. The young woman standing in front of him was beautiful. Her cap of black hair framed a sculptured face with large brown eyes and generous mouth. He was aware she had no makeup on and that only increased her appealing looks.

"And?" she asked, determined not to accept such a simple comment.

"And I would be honored to accompany you to the local diner."

The woman laughed. It was a nice sound, a release of the tension she had been holding inside her. Bolan knew there might be something more to come. Maybe tears as she fully accepted what had happened to her before he had shown up and freed her and the other women. Delayed reactions were common. They showed themselves in different ways from person to person. He wouldn't have been surprised if Kira Tedesko displayed something different. Despite the short time he had known this young woman, she had kept tight control over her emotions. She was a lot tougher than she appeared. Her actions back at the lockdown had exposed another side to her character.

They left the motel and walked the short distance to the diner. Tedesko stood on the sidewalk and studied the establishment, then glanced at Bolan, frowning at the slight grin edging his mouth.

"What is so funny, Cooper?" she demanded. When she was annoyed, her accent deepened, and Bolan found it pleasing to listen to.

"I take this place for granted. I suppose it's the first time you've ever seen one."

"In movies I have seen them. It is like every American only ever eats in a diner."

"Some do."

They went inside and Bolan chose a corner booth where he had something solid at his back and could see the entrance. A natural position for him. Always on the defensive, ready to pick up any challenge. As he had stepped inside his gaze had checked out the place, locating the opening behind the counter that led to the kitchen and the rear exit. As they sat down, Kira across from him, he saw that she was watching him intently.

"What?"

"Are you always so cautious? It is like watching a John Wayne movie. I suppose you sleep with your gun under your pillow?"

Bolan was unable to hold back a smile. This

was an extremely smart young woman. He was starting to be glad she was on his side.

"Not always," he answered. "Depends on the company I'm keeping."

Now her expression changed. The gleam in her eyes softened and she reached out to touch his hand where it rested on the table.

"So you do relax and enjoy yourself sometimes?"

"It has been known."

Not as much as he might have wanted, Bolan admitted to himself. His self-appointed distancing from the normal, everyday pleasures of life had become his norm. He would have been the first to admit times when he found himself observing the world around him. People, couples—families— going about their daily existence. Living their lives and shouldering the burdens that were part of that normality. He knew well enough that in these difficult days, with the world in turmoil, that even normal people faced the threats and demands of society. They weren't entirely free from the matters Bolan did his best to protect them from. He couldn't prevent tragedy from occurring, and there were times when people were caught on the firing line. He had seen them suffer, some die, and have their lives torn apart in a moment of pure terror. And he knew that their pain and grief was all the stronger because of the loss of loved ones. Of destroyed family groups. Yet he had seen these people pick themselves up, bear the pain and carry on. They rebuilt their lives. They survived. They moved on....

Whatever happened in his world, he was always alone, except for an occasional visit from his brother Johnny.

That was the unchanging definition of War Everlasting.

His was a lonely road. Behind him the ghosts of the dead. Ahead, the flickering shadows of battles yet to come.

In between the two was Mack Bolan, the eternal warrior who walked a predestined path. A stormy road to...where?

He felt the gentle touch of Tedesko's hand resting on his. And for the moment it was all that mattered, a caring touch from another human being, someone who made the difference, who showed him it was all worthwhile. No matter that it would be a short break in his enduring campaign. Like any true soldier Bolan took his breaks if and when they were offered.

"Let's order," he said.

His companion sat back and allowed him to order for them both. When the food arrived, she ate well, enjoying her first taste of American food. She had already dismissed the images of the slop they had fed her in the lockdown. This was real. This was now, and it was the present that was important.

She sat back, a fresh mug of coffee on the table in front of her.

"That was the best I have eaten for some time," she said. "I think I could get used to this."

"Now tell me about the woman who wanted to send you to DiFranco in Miami."

Tedesko told him everything she could. She described the woman, how she dressed, the way she commanded the men in the lockdown and the way they reacted to her demands.

"It was as if they were almost afraid to go against her. Like she was very important. Nash, the one in charge, he did not like what she ordered him to do. Especially about me. After she had gone he made threats against me. But nothing happened. It was as if he could not risk going against her."

"What about her accent. Was she American? Foreign?"

"She had an American accent but not a natural one. There was something else. I am pretty certain it was Russian. I wish I could tell you more. They never once spoke her name, so I can't even tell you that."

Bolan raised his coffee mug and drank. He

noticed Tedesko's sudden descent into a reflective silence. She was debating whether to tell him more, something she been keeping back until she had everything clear in her own mind, including the decision that she could trust him.

"I must make a confession. I am not exactly who you believe me to be."

"I was waiting for you to tell me."

"Oh?"

"The way you handled that guy back at the lockdown kind of gave you away."

"Kira Tedesko *is* my name. I work for a department of the Kosovo Civil Police. It is an undercover squad. Covert operations, I think you call it. I was on assignment. For months now we have been looking into the abduction of young women from within the city and surrounding area. Intelligence suggested they were being taken and sold into slavery. Sent to other parts of Europe and the United States where they would be forced into prostitution and pornography. From other intelligence sources we learned that many of these women were introduced to drugs, making them totally dependent, so that they would do anything to gain their next fix."

"Sounds familiar. And your assignment?"

"I went undercover on the streets of Pristina.

For two weeks nothing happened. I wasn't certain what I was looking for. These teams of men who go around snatching the women who did not work the red-light districts. They would snatch young women on their way home from work, after a night out. They went for fresh, attractive girls, not professionals. I took a temporary job at a law office, rented a flat that required I walk a distance home each evening."

"Did you have backup? A partner somewhere nearby who could watch you?"

Tedesko smiled.

"Cooper, I am talking about Pristina, not New York or Washington. We are a small department with extremely small resources. And my assignment was purely to observe. To see if I could pick up anything that might even guide us to these people. The last thing I expected was to become a victim myself."

"Didn't it occur to your superiors this *might* happen?"

"My superior is a fifty-five-year-old man who doesn't believe women should be in this kind of work. He is from an age that still considers us second-class citizens there to cook and wash and be available when the brain he keeps in his pants wants exercise."

"So he sends you out on your own?"

Tedesko shrugged. She picked up her coffee mug and drank. Bolan didn't fail to notice the slight tremble in her hand.

"Part of the reason we were asked to do this assignment was to appease the UN, which was concerned little was being done to protect these women. It was done to show our concern."

"Rough on you."

"I suspected as much, but I also admit there was a degree of bravado on my part when I was given the job. At least it got me out of the office and away from that idiot's wandering hands."

"Had the Suvarovs been mentioned?"

"Yes. Part of a report I read had them detailed a number of times. It was mostly hearsay. Nothing concrete. That was part of my assignment. To see if I could obtain solid evidence of their involvement." Her face suddenly broke into a wide smile. "At least I got that part right."

"I'd say so. How did it start, Kira?"

"Two of the women from my office and I went out one evening. To a concert. We were walking home together because they both lived in the same area as I did. It was a pleasant evening. I had almost forgotten why I was there in Pristina. It all happened before we could take it in. I think you call them 'panel' trucks? One suddenly pulled up beside us. Men jumped out. Grabbed us and we were thrown inside. There were other men inside. They held us down and we were injected with something that made us unconscious. It all happened so fast we had no chance to resist."

She paused, her gaze wandering around the diner. Bolan left her to the memories. She had been through a hard time and needed to sort things in her mind. He waited, patiently, and then saw the determined shine in her eyes again.

"Excuse me," she said.

"No need. You take your time."

She looked across the table at him, seeing a gentleness in his blue eyes that gave her comfort. She drew on his own inner strength.

"They must have kept injecting us during the journey. It was strange. A jumble of sounds and dark images. Sometimes I was half awake, half asleep. I do recall being on an airplane. I was fastened down in the seat, but I was able to turn my head and I saw blue sky and clouds. The plane must have been turning then because I saw water below. Green and blue, with the whitecaps of waves. Then I drifted off again and the next time I opened my eyes I was in a moving vehicle. We seemed to travel for a long time. And then we were at the place in Kansas."

"It wouldn't be much help to say welcome to America, would it?"

"Cooper, I have always wanted to come here. I expected to do it under more pleasant circumstances."

"Maybe we can turn it into something a little more profitable. You want to tell me everything you saw and heard at the lockdown?"

"I owe you that at least."

Tedesko had kept her eyes and ears open during her time of captivity. The young woman had a natural ability that enabled her to retain most of what she had been witness to.

She told Bolan about an earlier part of her investigations, prior to her Pristina assignment. Tedesko had visited Moscow where she had liaised with a unit based in the city.

"Moscow was very interested in what we were doing," she said. "The Suvarov Mob has plagued them for years. But they have never been able to gain enough solid evidence to lead to conviction."

"We have the same problem. Arkady Suvarov is in custody at the moment while the Justice Department tries to build a case. The trouble is, three protected witnesses have been killed and the Feds can't hold Suvarov indefinitely."

The woman nodded.

"Commander Seminov of the Moscow Organized Crime Department was desperate for anything he could use."

"Valentine Seminov?"

"You know him?"

"We have shared a few choice encounters together."

Tedesko smiled. "He made it clear he has little time for the Suvarovs. He is also aware they have influence. He told me there were people in high places who were taking Suvarov money."

"Maybe it's time to show them money doesn't buy everything."

She studied him closely. "But the Suvarovs have wealth, influence and many people working for them."

Bolan tapped the gun he wore beneath his coat.

"This is all *I* need, Kira. The Suvarovs understand a simple philosophy. Brute strength and intimidation. They have to be faced with some of that themselves."

"What about the law?"

"The law didn't prevent what happened to you and those other women. It didn't keep one of them safe and alive. I'm wondering how many others died at that place. The Suvarovs stepped around the law a long time ago. It doesn't mean a thing to them except when they use it to buy off trouble. They've put themselves above the law by what they do."

"So tell me, Matt Cooper, what do you do?"

"Me? I just bring them down. They accepted their guilt the moment they committed their first crime. I just close the book."

Tedesko caught her breath as she took a longer look at Bolan. She turned over old memories in her mind and when she had finished she allowed herself a gentle, acknowledging nod of her head.

"Yes," said softly, "now I understand."

Bolan caught her intonation and realized that this perceptive young woman did understand. She understood not just what he was, but *who* he was.

"Do you remember news reports about three months ago? A container coming off a freighter in Seattle? It was opened and there were dead bodies inside."

"I heard about it," Bolan said, recalling the photographs Turrin had shown him at the mission briefing.

"The dead were all young woman. Just like the ones at the lockdown. After the publicity died down, the U.S. Justice Department investigated, trying to trace the container back to its point of origin. They were only able to go back so far because everything about the container was falsified. The paperwork meant nothing. The only thing that came to light was the fact that it had come from Europe. It was the same old story. Bribes. Corruption in certain quarters that made it possible for that container to be loaded on the freighter. My department became involved because of a slight lead that came all the way to Pristina. We knew that the Suvarov Mob had people in the area. Again it was all basic intelligence without anything we could go to the authorities with. It was as if the Suvarovs were laughing in our faces. Like here in America they are untouchable. Their power and influence is staggering."

"How far have you gotten?" Bolan asked.

"A number of the dead women were finally identified as having come from Pristina itself. The others were from outlying areas."

The woman reached for her coffee mug, almost snatching it up off the table in her anger. There was a look in her eyes that spoke of her frustration, her rage at not being able to do more to help the victims. Bolan laid his hand on hers.

"We'll make sure they're not forgotten."

She looked into his eyes, finding comfort there.

"You saw how they treated the women back at the lockdown. How many have we missed? There must be dozens out there somewhere. Being treated like animals. Slaves. Made to work in those clubs and brothels. Why is nothing being done?"

The question was almost shouted. The moment she uttered the words she lowered her head, realizing she was calling attention to them both.

"Don't sweat it, Kira," Bolan said.

He glanced up and caught the stare of curious customers. The moment they realized he was looking at *them* they turned their heads away and went back to their own business.

"I won't apologize," she said. "Staying angry keeps me determined to follow this through. Cooper, I am still on assignment."

Bolan studied her and saw the hard core being the feminine exterior. He also realized he would have a hell of a fight on his hands of he tried to brush her aside.

"So how do you feel about a trip to Miami?"

"I CAN'T BELIEVE THIS," Valentina said, looking around the room. "How is it being allowed to happen? First, Lebowski has his shop burned down. By one man. Then our weapons shipment is hijacked. Again by a single man. And then to make things worse, he wipes out the people we send to kill him and Morey Jacklin."

She fell silent, gazing at the assembled faces. The only one who dared look directly at her was Nikolai Petrovsky. Valentina allowed the silence to drag on, and it would have seemed an eternity to the embarrassed gathering.

"No one has anything to say? No excuses? Lame, feeble excuses? Here we are at a critical time when we need to exploit our strength and we are allowing one man, one fucking man, to make fools of us. He has the legendary Suvarov organization standing by with its head up its ass so none of us can hear the world laughing at us."

"We weren't expecting anything like this," Lebowski protested. "When he hit my place, he just appeared out of nowhere."

Valentina's stare was scathing. "That's true enough. He was able to drive right up to your door, walk in and blow the place right from under you. Your first question should be why." She thrust a finger in Lebowski's direction. "I'll tell you why. Because you had no one standing watch. No security. Like most of the idiots in this room, you believed you were safe. No need to take precautions. In other words, you have become lazy. Soft. Life is too easy. And now we are paying the price for that laziness."

"That guy was crazy," Lebowski yelled, losing his control. "He wanted to kill us all."

"No, Gregori. If he had wanted to kill you all, he would have done so. He set out to cause problems for us and that is what he's doing. First you, then hijacking the guns. He is making a point. A good point. That no matter how big and strong we believe ourselves to be, we can still be open to attack."

"We should also be questioning his purpose," Petrovsky said. "Why is he doing this?"

"Is he from one of the other organizations?" someone asked. "Maybe Kirov is trying to make his mark now he's stepped into Kukor's shoes."

"Sitting here isn't going to answer any of your questions," Valentina said. "You want those answers? Get your people out on the streets. Talk to your informers. Buy information. Steal it. I don't care how you get it—just find me something we can deal with."

She watched them file out silently. If any of them had any comments, they were keeping them to themselves until she was out of earshot. Not one of them wanted to incur any more of her anger.

As the last of them left the room, Tibor Kureshenko appeared. He stepped into the office and closed the door. Valentina, watching from her seat behind the desk, saw his grim expression.

"Somehow I don't think I'm going to like what you have to say, Tibor."

"I seem to bring you nothing but bad news just lately. Apart from telling you we got that journalist, McKay."

"Something we managed to get right finally. We should have done it before. Not allow that idiot brother of mine try to handle it. Nikolai, a drink. I think I'm going to need one."

She waited until the tumbler of mellow whiskey was in her hand. Noticing the exchange of looks between Petrovsky and Kureshenko, she banged her free hand down on the desktop.

"Now, Tibor. Never mind the coy glances at Nikolai. Just tell me."

"I received news from Kansas. The farm has been hit. Our people are dead and the girls have been taken into some kind of protection by a team from Justice. The farm itself has been burned to the ground."

Valentina tapped the thick glass with the tip of a manicured nail. Her outer calm might have fooled a stranger but Petrovsky could sense the growing rage inside.

"Is there anything else, Tibor?" Petrovsky asked.

"The Feds unearthed some of the dead girls. One who died recently and others from a year or so back."

Valentina took a sip from her glass. She was saying something, almost under breath, and it took Petrovsky a moment to recognize, "It's getting better every day...."

He caught Kureshenko's puzzled expression and wagged his head in the direction of the door. The man took the hint and left, quietly closing the door behind him.

"Did I ever tell you when I was twelve I wanted to be a singer?" Valentina asked.

Petrovsky took her empty tumbler and refilled it.

"No," he said. "I don't think you would have enjoyed that kind of life."

She stared at him, curious. "Why not?"

"Too much traveling. Having to face the public all the time. It's an extremely transient occupation."

"So how do you see me, Nikolai?"

"More of a Mary Poppins figure. Creating peace and harmony from chaos. Reaching satisfactory conclusions to unsettled disputes."

"Really?"

"With the added refinement of an automatic pistol tucked under your coat."

Valentina turned the big chair so she could look out of the window and see the extensive grounds that surrounded the big house. It all looked so peaceful. Ordered and unchangeable. It was a pity, she decided, that life could not be the same.

CHAPTER SIX

Miami, Florida

"Leon DiFranco's headquarters," Bolan said.

They were sitting in the SUV across from the Bird House. The frontage, wide and low, was painted a vivid pink. The L-shaped building rose to an upper floor at the rear.

"This would be where I would have ended up working?" Tedesko asked.

Bolan picked up the disapproval in her tone.

"Not to your taste?"

She gave him a withering glance. "Are you serious, Cooper? Look at that color."

It was midmorning, hot and sultry. Even the palms dotted along the ocean side of the street were wilting. The Bird House was closed at that time of day, though there were a number of cars in the fenced-off parking lot at the side of the club.

What Bolan and Tedesko did see was a procession of young women coming and going, entering the club by a door at the far end of the parking lot. Most of them entered the building, stayed for around ten minutes, then left again.

"DiFranco's girls handing over last night's earnings," Bolan said. "Looks like it was busy."

"I could get angry at you, Cooper," Tedesko said suddenly.

"Me?"

"You are a man. If men were not so weak, there would not be a need for these women. DiFranco only supplies because men demand the services those women provide." She punched his arm in her frustration. "Why are you such pigs?"

"I don't have any defense for that, Kira. No excuses. But I'm not taking the blame for it, either."

She relented, her cheeks flushing at her outburst.

"You want to kick me out of the car? Send me away?"

Bolan grinned at her. "I might give it some

thought if you hit me again. You got some power there."

"I get angry when I think of what these men do to those women. The ones at the lockdown. Those who died in that container. All so that these damned gangsters can pile up their money. That is what it's all about, Cooper. Making money from the suffering of others. Shouldn't I get angry at that?"

"Get angry, Kira. Stay angry and remember when we make our move. But don't let it cloud your judgment. We need to stay sharp here." Bolan tapped the side of his head.

Tedesko leaned forward suddenly, staring through the windshield.

"Hey, who is that? I recognize his face from the computer files you showed me."

She was pointing at a lean man, dressed in a creased white suit and gaudy shirt, who had emerged from the club, crossed the parking lot and climbed into a white Thunderbird.

"Harry Tipping," Bolan said. "DiFranco's collector, according to the data. All he does is arrange pickups. Passes money, collects money. Could be on his way for a meet now."

"Why don't we follow him? Could be interesting to find out who he's seeing."

Bolan started the SUV. "And if he takes a delivery we can lift the worry off DiFranco's shoulders."

"Cooper, you have a weird sense of humor."

"It's one of the reasons people like me."

BOLAN TAILED Harry Tipping out of Miami, staying well behind the white Thunderbird as it cruised US-41 heading west, the green of the Everglades spreading out on either side, water glinting among the foliage.

After a run of twenty miles Tipping slowed and turned off the highway, rolling the Thunderbird down a rutted side road. Bolan drove on by, easing to a stop. He climbed out.

"Get off the road and into cover. If anyone shows and takes that side road, don't follow. Stay put until I show up again."

"But…"

"Kira, this only works if you do what I say. Okay?"

She nodded.

"Is this another of those reasons people like you?"

"Something like that," Bolan replied, then turned and was gone.

HARRY TIPPING WAS a nervous man. He sat in his car, wilting in the heat because the air conditioner had gone on the blink again. He'd had it back to the dealer twice already, and each time he turned it on it ran for a while then died. So today, of all days, when he needed to be cool, in every sense of the word, he was slowly dribbling away like an ice cube under a grill, and that just added to his unease.

He glanced at the dashboard clock. At least that was working. He double-checked by glancing at his watch. His contact was due any minute. Tipping felt under the jacket of his once-white suit. Now it was slightly soiled, and he could feel sweat soaking through the back. His shirt, all gaudy colors, had already become soaked. He wondered how it was that some people could sit out all day in the hot sun and not even break a sweat. He had to have some kind of imbalance. He only had to step outside and he started oozing moisture. He was beginning to realize that having a metabolism like his and moving to Florida hadn't been his best choice. On the other hand, there had been little choice left open to him. His earlier mistakes could have left him dead. He had been given the choice.

Move to Florida.

Work for us.

Or die right now.

It wasn't as if life out here was all that bad. He

made decent enough money, lived in a comfortable condo and the work wasn't too demanding.

Most of the time.

This day wasn't one of his better deals. Having to negotiate with Raul Manzanar wouldn't have been a choice Tipping would have made. The man was a pig. There was no other way to describe him. Manzanar always made Tipping feel uncomfortable. The guy had that effect on people. The strangest thing was, Tipping always felt lucky to be alive when a meeting with Manzanar ended.

The sound of a car approaching made Tipping break out in a fresh wave of perspiration. He glanced in his rearview mirror and recognized the gleaming silver Mercedes Manzanar always drove. He started to get jittery so he opened his door and stepped out, facing the oncoming car, his back to the Florida swamp that lay beyond the secluded parking lot. There was a closed diner at the edge of the lot, with bleached For Sale signs dotting the area. The property belonged to the Suvarovs. They had owned it for a couple of years now, having purchased the site through one of their subsidiary companies, and used it mainly for this kind of clandestine meeting.

Manzanar rolled in behind Tipping's vehicle and left the Mercedes running. He opened his door and stepped out, rising to his six-six height. He carried a black leather attaché case in his left hand. Clad in black from head to foot, wearing aviator shades, his dark hair gelled and brushed back, Manzanar exuded menace. He didn't have to do or to say anything to increase the suggestion. He *was* threatening.

"That time of month again," Tipping said. He never knew how to open a conversation with Manzanar.

The tall man didn't respond. He crossed to the trunk of Tipping's car and placed the case on it. He opened the case and showed the contents. Deep stacks of hundred-dollar bills, all neatly banded together.

"Three-quarters of a million dollars," he said. "I checked it myself. You want to count it?"

"That won't be necessary, Mr. Manzanar."

"That's what I thought. I'd hate to feel you didn't trust me."

"What's not to trust?"

Manzanar closed the attaché case and pushed it across the trunk.

"You have my payment. Collect my coke and let me know when to pick it up. Hang on to that money, Tipping. If you lose it, I'll have to take it out of your skinny hide," he said, then turned and walked away.

Tipping watched him drive off, leaving a pale

mist of dust in the air. He picked up the heavy attaché case. The sooner he delivered the money, the better he would feel. He turned to get back inside his car.

"Just put the case down, then place both hands on the roof."

The voice was deep, commanding, and it was emphasized by the nudge of a hard object that pressed into Tipping's spine.

A hundred wild and crazy and jumbled thoughts fought for space in Tipping's mind. Uppermost was Manzanar's last remark before he had left.

Don't lose it.

"You might as well kill me right now," Tipping said. "You take that money, I'm a dead man. You understand?"

"That's not my concern."

"What...?"

"You're in a dirty business, Tipping. Your employer is in a dirty business. Not a thing to get you off the hook. Play in the slime and you're bound to get soiled. Now put the case down."

"Yeah? So what if I don't? You going to kill me? Oh, hell, I forgot, you already did."

The gun muzzle pressed even harder into Tipping's spine. It was painful.

"Quit the whining, Harry. No one forced you to

work for the Suvarovs. You knew what they were into when you signed on. It's time to pay your dues."

Tipping turned about face, still clinging to the attaché case, and stared into Mack Bolan's ice-cold blue eyes.

"So who the hell are you?"

Bolan reached out with his free hand and took the attaché case. Tipping resisted for a second, then resigned himself to losing the money.

"You realize how much is in there? Three-quarters of a million bucks."

"And no small change."

"Jesus, this isn't funny, pal. You don't just walk in and steal from the Russian Mob. Or Raul Manzanar. They'll cut out your heart and let you watch it stop beating. You understand? These are seriously bad people."

"And you work for them, Harry."

"Look, I never claimed to be a saint. But I'm not a fuckin' idiot, either. They'll hunt you down. They'll wipe out anyone who knows you. Right down to your fuckin' housekeeper."

"*You* know me now, Harry."

"The hell I do."

"DiFranco won't see it that way. You lose his money, and you won't stay alive. I don't credit him with much savvy, but even DiFranco will add this up to you selling him out."

"No way you're pinning me with that."

"Not me, Harry. DiFranco will do the math."

Tipping visibly wilted against the side of the car.

"Jesus, this is turning into the crappiest day of my life."

"Want to trade, Harry?"

"What for what?"

"Tell me where the drop is and I let you walk. Give you a chance to get out."

"Oh, sure. I'll take the next NASA freighter to Mars. Even that won't be far enough."

"It's your only option, Harry. That or I make a call to Leon and let him know how you screwed him."

"He wouldn't…oh, shit, he would…why the hell would you want to do that to me?"

"If I had the time, Harry, I'd go through it all."

"Don't tell me you're one of those religious nuts."

Bolan moved the Beretta. "Does this suggest I'm about to give you a benediction, Harry?

"Putting a couple of those 9 mm slugs in me might be the kindest thing you could do."

"I'm not in a forgiving mood, either, Harry."

Bolan placed the attaché case on the hood of the car and opened the clasps. He reached inside and took out a couple of thick stacks of cash. Tipping watched as Bolan placed the money on the hood.

"How much do you think is there, Harry?"

"What?"

"Come on, Harry, I know you can count."

"I guess close to a hundred thousand."

"This is the deal, Harry. Give me the location of the drop and you can pick up the money and go. As far as you want, and take your chances."

Sweat was pouring down Tipping's red face now. He looked from the cash to Bolan and back to the money. The numbers were clicking away inside his head as he worked the odds.

Take the money and run, gambling that DiFranco was going to be so involved with this guy with the gun he would forget about Harry Tipping until it was too late.

Or DiFranco might figure what was going on and send out his icemen the minute he realized.

And there was Manzanar, too. He was a miserable piece of shit with a nasty temper, and he didn't like being screwed over.

Tipping weighed the balance.

He could get a long way with a hundred thousand dollars in his back pocket. Far enough to leave all this behind. Maybe set himself up in a little business somewhere up near the Canadian border in some little backwater town. The place didn't matter. As long as it was far enough away from Florida. And of course the promise of so much money helped to sway him. Tipping could never resist money. It had always been the one thing that led his major decisions in life. It had also got him into most of the problems he'd experienced, but there had to be a downside to everything.

He made his decision within the space of a half dozen heartbeats. He had reached fifty-six years of age without achieving greatness and, the way things had been going, that wasn't about to change. At least this time he had a chance. It was risky. But then climbing out of bed every morning brought a risk.

"What the hell, mister. I don't have much else going for me. Let's do it. You got a deal."

Everglades, Florida

THE LOCAL BOYS never learned, Bolan decided. They still used the eponymous, sprawling acres of the wetlands for their wheeling and dealing, figuring the endless stretches of plants and grass and reptile-infested water would offer them sanctuary. The drop was engineered via the Colombian main suppliers and Leon DiFranco's pickup team. With an attitude of either full confidence or unbending arrogance, those involved made their trade with blithe indifference to the possibility of being apprehended. Such was the power and influence of the drug dealers. The teams carrying out the hard physical effort, armed to the teeth and with cell phones holding speed-dial numbers direct to their legal advisers, hauled the solid, plastic-wrapped packs of cocaine from speedboat to truck in broad daylight. It was a little after 4:00 p.m.

Mack Bolan had been in position for a couple of hours, armed and ready for the drop to take place. He was clad in black, armed with a Beretta 93-R and Desert Eagle, plus a 5.56 mm M-4/M-203 combo rifle. He was also armed with a powerful radio, tuned in to the one that Kira Tedesko had beside her on the seat of the SUV. She was parked back off the main highway, the big vehicle deep in the thick greenery, waiting for him to contact her. It had taken Bolan some time to convince her that for this part of the operation it was better that she stay clear of the kill zone. He had been entirely open with her, making her realize that *kill* zone was not being overly dramatic. He knew from past experience that the participants in the drug trade were all branded with a violent and manic disposition when it came to being confronted. His intention was to take the consignment of drugs away from DiFranco's crew. He knew that his intention would precipitate a total refusal on their part to let him do it. So, he insisted, she had to stay clear. His promise to allow her to partner him on their follow-up strike on DiFranco himself placated the fiery young woman.

The shallow-drafted speedboat had made its way from the ocean, up through the winding channels, to make its rendezvous with the pickup crew from Miami. They were in a battered old Ford truck that carried a load of ripe melons. It was a less than sophisticated camouflage, but DiFranco's team had been using such devices on a regular basis and had been getting away with it. Once the Colombians had delivered their packages they would make the return trip to the coast, leaving the DiFranco crew to transport the cocaine back to Miami and its final destination—the unsuspecting Manzanar, who was still unaware that his payment had been taken away from Harry Tipping, said intermediary who was already on the first leg of his hastily planned disappearing act.

Standing apart from the truck were two cars that had brought the other members of the DiFranco crew.

At the actual time of the drug transfer the telephone in Tipping's condo was ringing off the wall as Leon DiFranco tried to make contact to find out why his three-quarters of a million dollars hadn't shown up yet.

Seven of DiFranco's soldiers were either standing watch or handling the consignment. Bolan had identified one of them. The crew chief was Alex Malinin, a bulky, broad-shouldered man who sported a white-blond crew cut. He stood to one side, his stocky figure draped in a light, powder-blue silk suit, under which he wore a white T-shirt. He carried a squat H&K SMG, suspended from his shoulder by a nylon strap.

Bolan waited until the last of the packages had been handed over before he raised the M-4/M-203 combo. He turned it in the direction of the speedboat and lobbed the HE grenade so that it dropped into the open hatch behind the wheelhouse. There was a moment of panic as realization struck. Men tried to clear the vessel before it blew. Only two of the four Colombians made it to dry land before the grenade blew. It erupted with a hard blast, tearing the boat wide open and creating a ball of fire that engulfed the two Colombians too slow to react. Their maimed, burning bodies were hurled overboard, following flame and debris into the water. The other pair were caught in the blast, singed and bloody as they were bounced across the ground.

In the following seconds, which had left the DiFranco crew briefly stunned, Bolan took the opportunity to strike. He moved out of cover, using the M-4 to cut a swathe through the crew. He put one man down with his first burst, then swung the muzzle across to hit another midthigh, pitching the yelling figure to the ground, following with a head shot that insured the man was permanently out of the deal. The remaining five scattered, throwing loose shots over their shoulders as they moved.

One of the Colombians regained his feet, hauling a heavy handgun from a hip holster. He opened fire, allowing anger and pain to direct his aim. His shots were way off the mark. Bolan engaged him even as he closed in on the truck, hitting the guy in the center of his chest, the impact knocking the Colombian backward. He fell from the edge of the bank and vanished in the swirling water that was still aflame with burning fuel from the wrecked speedboat.

Bolan hosed the area with a long burst from the M-4, forcing the gunners to keep their heads down long enough for him to move around to the driver's side of the truck. As Bolan reached the truck, yanking open the door, he caught movement near the rear. It was the surviving Colombian, his face and clothing scorched from the blast. The guy leaned around the rear of the vehicle, searching for a target. For a brief moment he and Bolan faced off. Then the M-4 spoke and the Colombian stumbled back, his head erupting blood as the 5.56 mm slugs blew his skull apart.

Bolan swung into the cab, reaching to hit the ignition. The moment the engine burst into life, he dropped the handbrake, shoved down the clutch and pushed the lever into first gear. He hit the gas and let out the clutch. As the truck lurched forward, Bolan felt the well-tuned power plant surge. The truck shuddered under the sudden pressure, but the wheels dug in and it moved off.

Bolan's hit had been swift and deadly, taking the unsuspecting crew by surprise, and by the time they were back in control the truck was speeding away from them, along the dusty trail that would lead to the main highway in a couple of miles.

Alex Malinin screamed orders to his men and they raced for their waiting cars to take up pursuit. Behind his bluster Malinin was trying to imagine DiFranco's reaction when he was told someone had hijacked his drugs.

BOLAN POWERED the swaying truck to the limits of its roaring engine, working his way through the gears in rapid succession until he could feel the vehicle vibrating. He held the wheel hard, watching the mirrors as he spotted the two crew cars behind him. Speed and maneuverability allowed them to catch up with the truck quickly.

Time was running out, but not for Mack Bolan. The pursuit team was doing exactly what he expected. They took up positions on either side of the track. Despite its narrow span, they were going to try to trap him between them. Bolan smiled as he imaged the fear driving them. Losing a valuable cocaine drop was like having a death sentence passed on them. They would go to any lengths to try to get it back.

The car on his right surged forward, growing larger in the mirror. It moved alongside, creeping in toward the cab, the outer side of the car flattening the tall grasses edging the trail. Now he could see a gunner leaning out of the rear window, angling a weapon into position. Bolan could read the minds of the car's occupants. They wanted to get into position so that the gunner had Bolan in target acquisition. He let the car surge forward a few more feet, then hauled on the wheel. The truck swung out and slammed into the car, tearing and rending bodywork, shattering window glass and crushing the upper body of the gunner leaning out the rear door. The guy let out a brief, terrified scream in the fleeting time he had left. Bolan pulled away for a second, then turned the truck again, risking a harder swerve. He felt the jarring impact as the truck struck the car, hung on to the wheel as he felt the bulk of the speeding truck shudder. Then he caught a glimpse of the car as it flipped, turning over on its side, then its roof, and began a bouncing, twisting cartwheel as its bulk and momentum hurled it along the trail. Dust spumed in its wake, pieces of metal flew in the air. The uneven edge of the trail caught the full impact as the heavy mass slammed into it, bouncing the car back across the road. A tail of fire trailed after it as the ruptured fuel tank allowed gas and vapor to escape. On its roof the stricken car spun, flame and smoke encircling it. The hurtling wreck blew in an incandescent ball of flame.

One down, one to go, Bolan thought.

The second car took a different approach, sneaking in around the rear of the truck. Bolan was unable to see it. But he heard the crackle of autofire. Bullets clanged off metal, then he heard a dull bang. The rear of the truck became unstable, and he knew they had blown a tire. He glanced in his mirror and saw dark chunks of the rubber flying out from the wheel. Bolan felt the wheel dragging against his hands. He pulled the truck back under partial control, realizing he wasn't going to get far if they did the same to... His fear was realized as more gunfire came and the other rear tire was blown off the rim. Now the truck was becoming a deadweight.

Bolan glanced ahead. The trail curved away to the left in the near distance. He held the wheel one-handed as he picked up the M-4, hanging it around his neck with the webbing strap. Then he gripped the wheel again and tramped hard on the gas pedal, feeling the tail-heavy truck pick up a degree of speed. He checked out the side of the trail as he approached the curve and saw brush and dirt edging the strip. He let the big vehicle drift as he went into the curve, crossing to the left side of the trail. The moment he started around the curve Bolan freed the door handle, pushing it open and dropping from the seat onto the metal step. With no one at the wheel, the truck started to wander. The Executioner leaned out, pushed hard and threw himself clear. He saw the thick grass coming up to meet him and curled into a ball. His momentum carried him along the edge of the trail, crashing through the grasses and raising a cloud of dust as he rolled.

The truck careered across the trail, hit the far edge and reared over, seeming to hang suspended in the air for long seconds before its own sheer weight brought it back to earth with a heavy crash.

There was a moment when it seemed the chase car might hit the truck. The driver managed to steer around the driverless vehicle, and as the driver fought to control his skidding vehicle, one of the rear seat gunners caught a glimpse of Bolan's rolling form. Then they were past him. The gunner yelled out a warning. Brakes locked and the car came to a shuddering halt. Before it came to rest the doors were flung open and the three-man crew piled out, spreading apart as they turned to search for their quarry.

Instead they walked into the crackling 3-round bursts from Bolan's M-4. He had regained his feet, clicking in a fresh magazine even as he straightened, turning to face his enemies as they hit the trail running, weapons up and seeking a target. His first volley hit the blond-haired man called Malinin. The 5.56 mm slugs ripped their hot way into his torso, splintering a number of ribs and chewing at his organs. Malinin stumbled and fell, dropping his weapon as he clutched at his body.

He slammed facedown on the trail, the coarse surface shredding the skin down one side of his face.

The second he saw Malinin go down Bolan sought a second target, firing as the running figure came into his field of fire. The short burst hit the guy in the upper chest, rising to hack into his shoulder and tear out a bloody wedge of muscle and flesh. One slug shattered the shoulder bone, spinning the target off balance. He fell to his knees, free hand gripping his ruined shoulder, and he was out of the fight for the moment.

Return fire reached Bolan's position but he had already moved, darting into the trail rather than for deep cover. His unexpected move made the remaining gunner pause to readjust his position. He was too slow. Bolan dropped to a crouch, turning side-on to narrow himself as a target, bringing the M-4 into full play. He hit the gunner head-on and the soldier dropped to the ground, hard hit. Bolan's finger stroked the trigger, sending twin bursts into the gunner before he was able to recover. His jerking form jetted bright blood onto the trail.

Bolan let the rifle/grenade launcher hang by its strap, reaching to free the Beretta as he stepped by the dead gunner. He picked up the sound of someone moving and turned to see the shoulder-hit guy struggling to raise the handgun he had freed from his waist holster. The guy was bloody, hurting, but still trying to make a fight of it. Bolan raised the 93-R and punched a triburst through the guy's skull, pitching him over backward, where he lay staring up at the sky.

Turning to the truck, Bolan loaded an incendiary grenade into the launcher. He triggered the weapon into the rear of the truck where the cocaine was stacked beneath the cargo of melons. He watched the first grenade start to burn, then followed with two more until the vehicle was a blazing mass. He crossed to the crew car and climbed in, moving off quickly, and cleared the area before the truck's gas tank blew, sending flame and smoke skyward.

AN HOUR LATER, driving back toward Miami beside Kira Tedesko in the SUV, he was on his cell phone talking to Turrin.

"I just picked up the report coming in through the Miami police net. Have I missed the start of something?"

"Could be WWIII," Bolan said.

"Oh, yeah."

"Hey, just remember who drafted me in on this."

"I'm not liable to ever forget. You need anything?"

"Wish me luck. I'm going clubbing tonight."

"Does Leon know yet?"

"It's going to be a surprise."

The Bird House

VASILY SUVAROV MADE his way along the corridor to Leon DiFranco's office. He was conscious of the heavy pistol tucked in the waistband of his pants. He had never been very comfortable with guns. With the current situation facing them, DiFranco had insisted everyone be fully armed at all times.

He could hear DiFranco even before he got close. The man was in a rage that had gotten worse as the evening had moved on. News of the theft of Manzanar's cash, then the hijack and destruction of the drug shipment had only served to enrage DiFranco even more. Added to that were the deaths of his people. He had taken Malinin's death badly. They had been together for a long time, and he had been one of a few people Leon DiFranco had really trusted.

As Vasily reached the office door, it was yanked open and one of the club's security men strode by. The man's face was deeply flushed and Vasily judged that he had been on the receiving end of Di-Franco's anger.

"Get your ass in here, Vass. Don't stand there like you just found your dick for the first time."

DiFranco had been calling him "Vass" from the day he had arrived. Vasily didn't like it but he had the good sense not to call attention to it, and especially right now.

"Have you heard any more from Manzanar?" he asked, closing the door behind him.

When DiFranco stood abruptly, throwing him a murderous glance, Vasily almost made a grab for the pistol to defend himself.

"Damn fuckin' right I have. He's been on the phone three times the last half hour. What does he think I did? Hijack the coke myself and then set fire to it?"

"We make it right? Yes?"

"Yes. My fault or not, there's no way I screw around with Manzanar. That mother is bad. Suvarov organization we may be, but we don't want to get on his wrong side. I got my people out there ready to shoot anything that moves in case it's one of Manzanar's boys coming for them."

"What do we do? Give him back his money or bring in another shipment?"

"Way that bastard is yelling blue friggin'

murder maybe we ought to do both." DiFranco banged a fist on his desktop. "What the hell is going on? Who the hell is doing this? To me. Don't they know who I am? Leon fuckin' DiFranco, that's who, and nobody jerks me off, especially not in my own backyard. I swear if I get my hands on who's doing this, I'll peel his fuckin' skin off in half-inch strips."

DiFranco crossed the office and poured himself a tall glass of Jack Daniel's whiskey. He stood and drained half the tumbler.

"Your people in N.Y. had any luck finding this guy who hit your operation?"

Vasily shook his head. "The way he operates, I think it has to be the same one."

"Yeah? But who pays his wages? Kukor's old Mob? Kirov's running it now, isn't he? We all know your old man and Kukor never hit it off. Maybe this is their time to try to run the Suvarovs out of town. With Arkady out of circulation, it must be hard keeping things together." DiFranco turned to peer across the office at Vasily. "That why you got sent down here? To keep you out of the way if the opposition starts a shooting war?"

"No," Vasily said a little too quickly, and he saw the way DiFranco's expression changed. "There isn't going to be any trouble. Val—"

He stopped, aware he might say too much. Before he had left, Valentina had made sure he understood she wanted nothing said about her move to the top position in the Suvarov organization.

"Val? Val who? You don't mean your sister?"

Vasily thought fast. It wasn't easy for him. He had never been very fast thinking on his feet.

"Valentina said Father had told her to pass on the message that there wouldn't be problems from Kirov."

He could feel himself starting to perspire. His shirt was clinging to his ribs.

DiFranco continued to stare at him until he became aware of the glass in his hand and took another drink. The whiskey seemed to clear his thoughts and he returned to his desk and sat.

"Get yourself a drink, Vass. Hell, get yourself two fuckin' drinks."

He opened a drawer and pulled out a large handgun, banging it on the desktop.

"If that mother wants to make a call here tonight, I'll be waiting. Let him see he isn't going to get the better of Leon DiFranco."

Vasily did get himself something to drink.

Despite the armed security crew and DiFranco's defiant mood, he sincerely hoped that the hitter had decided to call it a night.

He hoped.

But inside he somehow didn't feel as confident.

"KIRA, YOU DON'T have to come in with me."

"We talked about this before, Cooper."

"It's going to get bloody."

"And it isn't my first time under fire. My home beat is not a cozy one."

"Are all Tedesko women as stubborn as you?"

"My mother and two sisters? Yes. And you would never want to upset my grandmother."

"I can see that."

Bolan had parked well away from the club. When he had driven by twenty minutes earlier, he had spotted the dark figures close by the frontage. The Bird House stood at the end of the street, with its parking lot at the open side, bordered by a chain-link fence. There were a number of vehicles in the lot, which was illuminated by security lights on steel poles. The upper floor of the stuccoed building showed lights along the front and the side.

"The place is closed, but it looks like they're expecting company."

"Let us not disappoint them, Cooper."

BOLAN HAD ARMED Kira Tedesko from his weapon stash. She chose a standard 9 mm Beretta 92-F, adding a couple of extra magazines to the pocket of the flak jacket from the carry-all. Like Bolan, she was dressed in close-fitting black and carried a radio clipped to her belt.

"If we get separated, don't hesitate. Give me a call."

She nodded.

Bolan clipped a weighted belt around his waist. The belt pouches held a number of small, powerful explosive packs. Each one was fitted with a compact power pack that would detonate the charge from a signal transmitted by the control unit Bolan carried.

In addition to his handguns he slung a suppressed Uzi from his shoulder.

"You set? You sure you're okay with just the handgun?"

"I am sure and, yes, I am ready."

They exited the SUV. Bolan secured the vehicle, then led the way across the deserted street. They used the shadowed doorways of buildings to lead them in the direction of the club.

With only an empty lot separating them from the chain-link fence, Bolan studied the area. He watched as dark shapes moved back and forth in the parking lot. DiFranco's security. The strong lighting that flooded the lot also showed that the three men he saw weren't carrying any visible weapons, which meant they were probably armed with handguns under their jackets. That was more to avoid being seen showing SMGs in public than not being prepared. The heavy weapons would be inside the club building.

"You believe those guards are part of DiFranco's Mob?" Tedesko asked.

"Pretty sure."

"But not enough to kill them in cold blood?"

Bolan leaned against the wall and glanced at her.

"What does that tell you?"

"That you have compassion. That you would regret killing someone who did not deserve to die by mistake."

"I like to think it's the difference between us and them."

"Wait," Tedesko said, placing a cautionary hand on Bolan's arm.

He turned and followed her gaze, and saw the dark limousine cruise slowly along the street, then turn in at the club's parking lot. The car rolled up to the three men and came to a stop. The guards crowded around the vehicle as one of the rear doors opened. A tall figure stepped out, smoothing down the expensive suit he wore.

It was Raul Manzanar. Bolan had no problem recognizing the man. He watched as the dealer turned and beckoned to someone inside the car. A figure appeared from the vehicle, reaching back inside to drag out a second man. Manzanar was in discussion with DiFranco's guards. One of them was already using a transceiver to speak with someone inside the club.

The reluctant figure was roughly hauled out of the car and stumbled to his knees before being dragged upright. The once-white suit he wore was stained with dirt and darker patches that looked like blood.

Bolan knew this man, too.

Harry Tipping, the DiFranco man he had intercepted after Manzanar's money drop. Tipping should have been long gone from the Miami area by now, well on his way across country.

"Big guy in black is Manzanar," Bolan said.

"The one in the white suit is Harry Tipping."

"How did he end up here?" Bolan wondered.

"I thought he had left the area?"

"So did I."

They watched as Tipping was unceremoniously dragged across the parking lot by DiFranco's guards. He was struggling but without much success, and as the group around him reached the side door that had been opened, one of the guards started to hit him with the pistol he carried. By the time the group disappeared inside Tipping had to be carried as he hung limply in the grasp of his captors.

"I think we have confirmation who the bad guys are now. You think, Cooper?" Tedesko said.

Bolan's only response was a soft grunt that might have been an acknowledgment, or just as easily a rebuff against her slight sarcasm.

"Let's move," he said abruptly, and led the way from cover, angling swiftly across the final open space before he eased around the end of the chain-link fence onto the club parking lot, using the parked cars for cover.

He sensed rather than heard Tedesko close behind, and gave her credit for her silence.

Crouching at the rear of the limousine Manzanar had arrived in, Bolan peered in the direction of the single guard left behind after the others had vanished inside. This guy was standing beside the door the others had used. He had it slightly ajar, almost as if he was awaiting a summons to withdraw inside the building.

He leaned out from cover, bringing the Uzi to his shoulder and triggered a single, suppressed shot that took the guard in the face. The impact of the 9 mm slug slapped the man's head back against the wall. He slumped to his knees, a glistening dark red patch on the stucco, the pistol slipping from his nerveless fingers as he fell. He toppled forward onto his face.

"Go," Bolan snapped, and felt Tedesko rise from her knees.

She raced forward, stepping around the downed guard and hurrying through the door. Bolan was only seconds behind her. He bent to grab hold of the dead guard's jacket, using it to drag the man inside the club, then made a quick return outside to retrieve the discarded pistol. He handed it to Tedesko and she transferred it to her left hand. Bolan pulled the door shut, making sure it was secured on his side.

Steep stairs led to the upper floor. Before he moved Bolan took out one of the explosive packs and placed it in a shadowed corner beneath the stairs.

"Stay close," he said, and started upward, with Tedesko two steps behind.

The stairs came to an end on a wide gallery that stretched ahead of them. Beyond the railing to their right they were able to see down into the club's main area. It was in darkness now, with only a few subdued lights showing.

Somewhere ahead of them Bolan could hear voices, muffled behind closed doors, but he could also hear the unmistakable sound of someone being hit. The sounds were accompanied by the pained cry of whoever was on the receiving end.

Most likely Harry Tipping.

The man was paying for his mistakes, and knowing the way these people played, there would be little mercy for Tipping this night.

About halfway along the gallery a set of wooden stairs led down to the club floor. Bolan was almost level with them when he picked out a flitting shape moving up the stairs in his direction. There was little opportunity to avoid coming face-to-face with the newcomer. The gallery offered no cover, so Bolan took the only option open to him. He turned, dropping to a crouch, his left hand waving for Tedesko to get down, as well.

The armed guard reached the last few steps. Some instinct had to have warned him he wasn't alone. The SMG he was carrying came up in a reflexive defensive action, his upper body turning as he sensed Bolan's rising presence,

The Uzi ripped out its subdued chatter, the short

burst stitching across the guard's chest, spinning him away from Bolan. The man performed a half back flip, arms and legs windmilling as he lost co-ordination as well as balance, he fell across the stairs, the SMG dropping with a hard clatter.

"And there goes caution," Bolan muttered.

Even as he rose to his full height, his left hand was dropping another package of explosives in between two of the gallery railings.

Farther along the gallery double doors were hauled open and strong light spilled across the floor. Armed figures burst out, fanning left and right, weapons probing ahead of them

Bolan and Tedesko still held the advantage. They were out of the light spill, cloaked in the soft shadows.

His finger stroked the Uzi's trigger, sending hissing death into the restless group, 9 mm slugs punching in through soft flesh. The suppressed growl of the Uzi was accompanied by the harsher sound of Tedesko's handguns as she triggered single shots at the mob hardmen. The ferocity of their united fire took down the Suvarov hardmen like chaff before the storm. Bodies thumped to the floor, bloody and torn. The cries of alarm and pain were drowned by the chatter of gunfire.

"Kira, watch the stairs," Bolan snapped.

He had heard the crashing of doors below and the pounding of shoes on the stairs.

The young woman turned and leaned around one of the banister posts, picking out the trio of armed men already hitting the stairs. With surprising calmness she opened fire with her twin handguns, placing shot after shot into the exposed, vulnerable bodies. They were hard hit, broken and bloody after they had slithered back down the stairs.

Bolan had advanced to the wide-open doors, peering around the frame into the large, brightly lit office that served as Leon DiFranco's seat of power.

DiFranco was leaning against the edge of his desk, a large pistol clutched in one hand.

Raul Manzanar was several feet away, his tall, black-clad frame stiffly erect, his right hand in the act of pulling a heavy Magnum revolver from the holster he wore on his hip.

The bowed and bloody figure of Harry Tipping was slumped in a nearby chair. His face was a battered mask, strings of blood dripping from his slack mouth and nose. He was being held in place by a couple of DiFranco's and Manzanar's men.

Another figure stood off to one side, familiar to Bolan even in the split second before the scene went to hell.

Vasily Suvarov.

There was time for no more than a swift glance.

Manzanar caught a glimpse of Bolan as the black-clad warrior pushed the Uzi into view, his finger already against the trigger.

The handgun was pulled clear of the holster, Manzanar jabbing a finger in Bolan's direction.

"Hit that fuck…"

Bolan angled the muzzle of the Uzi in his direction and stopped Manzanar's outburst before he completed it. The short burst punched in through the dealer's chest, spinning him off balance and as he stumbled back, Manzanar's finger jerked against the revolver's trigger. The heavy boom of the Magnum round drowned the scream of pain from the closest soldier as the .357 slug exploded the side of his skull clear off. A splatter of bloody brains and bone misted the air as the guy went down.

Bolan went in through the open doors, dropping to a crouch, the Uzi still firing. He caught the second guy holding Tipping, the 9 mm slugs carving their way into the soldier's chest cavity. The guy flopped to his knees, clutching his chest, and felt warm blood starting to erupt from the wounds. Then the impact reached deep inside, the slugs shredding his lungs and heart. He retched up blood as he hit the office floor, his body jerking in response to the fatal damage.

Bolan had heard the Uzi lock on empty and dropped the weapon, his right hand hauling the Desert Eagle free, locking the muzzle on Leon DiFranco as the man snapped off a shot from his own handgun. The slug took a large wood chunk out of a chair to Bolan's left. The Desert Eagle boomed twice, the well-placed slugs taking out DiFranco's throat in a sudden explosion of bloody flesh. DiFranco tried to scream, but all that came out was a wet gurgle of sound. He slithered along the edge of his desk, trying to stay on his feet. He succeeded until Bolan hit him with two more shots from the Eagle, deliberately placing the slugs into DiFranco's chest, over the heart. DiFranco toppled backward across his desk, scattering everything on the top as he rolled over the edge and crashed to the floor on the far side.

Bolan pushed to his feet, the Desert Eagle swinging around to pick up the moving figure of Vasily Suvarov as the man made a try for the open doors. Vasily had his pistol in his hand, the weapon dangling loosely at his side.

Tedesko appeared in the doorway at that moment. She was directly in Vasily's path, and she hadn't pinpointed the moving figure as he raised his weapon in her direction.

Bolan didn't hesitate.

He raised the Desert Eagle, tracking in on Vasily's moving form. There was no hesitation in Bolan's action as he double tapped the pistol, the heavy booms of the close pair of shots hanging in the air.

The .44 shredders hit Vasily just above his right ear, blowing in through his skull and into his brain. The range was short and the driving force behind the twin slugs took them through and through, exploding from the far side of his skull, wrenching out a sizable chunk of bone and outer flesh. A dark gout of bloody mush followed. The pistol in Vasily's hand fired, the bullet ripping a piece out of the door frame as Tedesko stepped through. Vasily took a few more steps before his coordination went and he crashed to the floor in a quivering, shivering loose sprawl, the pistol flying from his dying hand. A widening spread of blood expanded from beneath his shattered head.

Bolan crossed the office, reaching out to sit Tipping upright. The man had almost slipped to the floor.

"Harry, you look like hell."

Tipping stared at him through slit eyes. *"You!* Every time I see you it means trouble."

"Harry, I don't have time to discuss our relationship. We don't get out of here soon, the cops will show up. Let's move."

Bolan hauled Tipping off the chair and guided him to the door. He slipped a number of the explosive packages from their pouches and handed them to Tedesko. She didn't need telling what to do, placing them in positions around the office and balcony as she followed Bolan out.

They reached the bottom of the stairs, Bolan having to support Tipping now. Before Tedesko opened the door she killed the lights outside by throwing the switch set in the wall. They emerged in near darkness, moving quickly across the parking lot, then back the way they had come in. They reached the SUV without being challenged. Once they were inside, with Tipping sprawled across the rear seat, Bolan and Tedesko took off their weapons and stowed them out of sight. The soldier started the SUV and turned it, then handed Tedesko the small remote control unit, activating it first.

"You want to do the honors?" he asked.

She took the neat box, nodding.

"I'll drive by."

As they drew level with the club, Bolan gave her the nod and Tedesko pressed the button. The multiple detonations weren't overly loud, muffled by the thick walls of the building, but a number of windows blew out and as Bolan pulled away, he could see the gleam of flame starting to rise.

At the end of the street he made a right turn, taking them quickly away from the vicinity. Bolan picked up the approaching wail of sirens. He eased the SUV to the side of the street, waiting until three police cruisers sped by, making enough sound to wake the dead, lights flashing.

"It's time we got out of here," Bolan said, and drove on.

CHAPTER SEVEN

The sleek silver-and-white Learjet took off from Newark airfield at precisely eight o'clock that evening. Valentina Suvarov retired to her cabin and went to bed, leaving Nikolai Petrovsky with a file of paperwork he had to clear. The flight was expected to be uneventful.

Two hours into the flight Petrovsky received a call. He sat back in his comfortable seat, recognizing Tibor Kureshenko's voice, then leaned forward when he became aware of how somber the man seemed.

"Tibor?"

"Is she there? Listening?"

"No. Tell me what's wrong."

"Where do I start? Miami is in a mess. Someone hijacked Manzanar's three-quarters of a million he paid for his drug shipment. Then the drop itself was hit. The Colombian couriers and DiFranco's team were wiped out. The shipment was fire-bombed into ashes. We had only just learned about this when reports came that the Bird Cage had been hit, too."

"DiFranco and his people?"

"Those who were at the club—all dead, Nikolai. Even Raul Manzanar."

There was a pause that left Petrovsky with a sense of dread at what was coming next. He knew because nothing had been mentioned concerning Vasily Suvarov.

"Tell me the rest, Tibor."

"Vasily, too. Dead like all the others."

Petrovsky's first thoughts were of Arkady. Of them all, he would be hurt the most by the death of his son. Weak and with little of the Suvarov ambition, Vasily had still been Arkady's son.

"It took time to find all this out. The club had been badly damaged by a number of explosions after the hit. A great deal of it burned. By the time we got people there to check, the whole area was under the control of the Feds and local cops. Our people had to call in favors to even get hold of information."

"Better tell them all to lie low. No vendettas,

Tibor. No tearing the town apart. This time we step back and close down the operations. This mess is going to be a godsend to the Feds. Let's not add to it by making waves. They will be waiting for us to do something stupid. Understand?"

"I already put out the word. Once it got around, the girls all scattered. Some went to the cops for protection. Suvarov business is shut down until further notice."

"As soon as possible see to Vasily's body being brought back to New York. If nothing else we can at least give him a Family funeral."

"A funeral for who?"

Valentina's voice came from directly behind Petrovsky.

"Tibor, I'll talk to you later. I have to go."

He put down the phone, pushing up out of his seat. Valentina was standing a few feet away, a thin cotton robe held tight against her body by her folded arms. Her dark hair was tousled from sleep, her face pale as she stared at him.

"Who needs a Family funeral, Nikolai? Tell me. Is it Dad?"

He moved to her, hands reaching out to hold her. In calm, measured words he repeated exactly what Kureshenko had told him. When he explained about Vasily he felt her lean into him, her head resting against his shoulder, and for some long seconds she stayed that way. Motionless, composing herself, and when she gently eased away from him Petrovsky found he was once again looking at Valentina Suvarov, head of the organization, and there wasn't a trace of a tear in her eyes.

"I expected a challenge, Nikolai. Not so quickly, or so hard, but we will come through this."

She turned and crossed the cabin to lower herself into the large leather seat her father had used so many times on business flights. She swiveled it around so she could face him.

"I would like a drink, Nikolai. A large one, please."

He brought it to her, watched her take a swallow.

"Did Tibor have any idea who was behind these Miami attacks?"

Petrovsky shook his head. "There was no one left alive to tell."

"I understand the reason for us to withdraw from activity in Miami for the time being, but I think we should have someone do some discreet checking. Nikolai, that man who worked the deal for the hijacked weapons? And the hit at the farm. Perhaps he's involved. The more I think about him and the way he handled himself when we sent those people in to deal with him and Jacklin, it's possible he's behind the Miami strike. Look how Jacklin vanished after the failed hit."

"An undercover cop? A Justice agent?"

"It's possible. Get a message to Bendix. If he's able to spot those hidden witnesses, maybe he can find out who this man is. If he is a Justice agent, Bendix should know about him. We pay him enough. Make him earn his money. That bomb he planted didn't work, so remind him he's on borrowed time himself if he doesn't get us answers." Valentina smiled. "Suggest our contract team might be getting a new assignment now that they've dealt with three of those witnesses—and one Fed. Put a scare into him, Nikolai. I want results. Fast results."

Petrovsky crossed to the other side of the cabin and picked up the phone. He punched in a long number that would be diverted through cutouts before connecting with the man he wanted to speak to. He had to wait for some time before the call was picked up.

"Time to put in some effort," Petrovsky said. "Your recent performance makes me wonder maybe I have been paying you too much. The results haven't been very encouraging."

"Haven't you heard what happened in Miami?

I've got to be careful. Everyone is all hyped up in the department. Jesus, things have been tightened to the limit since that bomb," Bendix told him.

"Since it failed to achieve its purpose, you still owe us. You've received a great deal of money. Just remember who you're dealing with. Lack of results upsets my principals. When they become upset, they have unpleasant ways to gain a settlement. Do you understand what I'm saying?"

"Yeah, yeah, I know you're a tough bunch. Right now I can't get too excited about all that macho shit because my ass is already on the block. Whatever happens, I can only die once. Do *you* understand that? So now we have the threats out of the way, what do you want?"

"We believe the strikes against us have been orchestrated by someone working undercover from within the Justice Department."

"You have proof?"

"No. That's where you come in. Do some checking. This man seems to be able to gain information very easily. He also seems to have spirited away Morey Jacklin since the failed hit on both their lives. Look into it. Look hard and don't let me down. *Macho shit* it may be, but you'll be knee-deep in it if I don't get results."

Valentina had been watching him closely

during the conversation. When Petrovsky ended it, he glanced across at her.

"He's losing his enthusiasm for the job. It showed in his voice. If he's getting scared, he won't be able to perform as he should."

"I don't trust him any longer, Nikolai," Valentina said. "Whether he gets what we want or not, he can become a liability. He knows too much about us."

"I think you're right."

"Make that other call. Offer our friends an additional contract. They can hold back on the witnesses for the moment. I'll feel safer with Bendix out of the way. With all that is happening at the moment we can do without the encumbrance of Vincent Bendix. End it now. We'll take our chances with the Justice Department once we return to the U.S."

"I will do it now."

Russia

THEY LANDED at a private field outside Moscow where a limousine was waiting. When Valentina stepped from the jet it was into a fall of icy rain. A sharp wind gusted across the tarmac, grabbing at her leather coat. She pulled it around her as she hurried to the waiting car, Petrovsky close behind.

As she sank into the soft leather seat, the door thudded shut behind her.

"Welcome home," Petrovsky said somberly.

She glanced across at him. "Thank you, Nikolai." As the car pulled away, she stared out at the gray landscape. "We have been pushed enough, Nikolai. I think it's time we started pushing back. Let's show our enemies the real Suvarovs."

LEO TURRIN TOSSED the file onto the table in front of Bolan.

"When you do some shaking, you go all out."

"What's this? Bills for damages?"

Turrin chuckled. "If it was, your insurance would have run out halfway down page one."

Turrin sank into a chair facing Bolan. He stared at his friend, noting the shadow of tiredness etched across the warrior's face.

"Kira has the right idea, Mack. You should be hitting the sack yourself. Getting some sleep."

"Time for that later, Leo. Bring me up to date."

"I figure you know as much as anyone. You've hit the Suvarov Mob where it hurts—the farm, Lebowski's car ring, and cut up their Miami operation. Reports filed by our teams say business is down, and Suvarov people are keeping their heads down. Our bonus has been witnesses opening up a little more now they see the big fish being chopped up."

"What about your leak? Anything there?"

Turrin shook his head. "Uh-uh. We'll get him though. Now here's something interesting from Kissinger. You remember he said he might have a line on that hit team? He thinks he might have it."

Turrin opened his file and took out papers. He handed them to Bolan. Cowboy Kissinger's report was succinct, direct and to the point:

The ammunition evidence reminded me of a couple guys I heard about few years back. They were in the military, a sniper team that did a lot of specialist work. Moved around a lot. Special detachments. They were in the first Gulf war, among other theaters. One was the shooter, the other the spotter. They quit the service after the Gulf and seemed to vanish from sight until rumors started to emerge they'd done some contract work for one of the East Coast Mobs. I heard about this at the DEA because there were suggestions they'd done work for some of the drug syndicates. This was hard to confirm or deny because these guys seemed to have pulled identity changes. Any checks on their previous IDs came up blank. I took interest because the weapon these guys used was the same as the one the sniper team used in the military, one that had been made for the shooter. It passed tests on military trials, and these guys were so good they kept the rifle. Had a special dispensation to have their own sniper rifle. Custom built, which is where my real interest got me hooked. You know me and weapons. The stuff you sent me jogged my memory, so I went back through records and there it was. Same oddball ammo. Sniper Boy makes his own, fired through this nonstandard configuration rifle.

I played a hunch and tracked down ballistic reports on the slugs they dug out of the drug victims. Same as the ones you sent me. I ran a comparison test and the database came up with at least a dozen more victims over the past few years. All crime-related victims. Our team has been busy working for the Mobs.

These are the same guys who did the drug killings. When I talked with Leo, a name came up—Raul Manzanar. Back in my DEA days Manzanar was suspected of paying for the shootings to get rid of some competitors. Bear tells me we have the now-late Manzanar linked to Leon DiFranco, who was part of the Suvarov Mob. Hell, I know it's a skinny link, but too much to be coincidence? Worth a look. Could be our sniper team have moved up the corporate ladder to work exclusive contracts for the Suvarovs. I'm going to continue to liaise with Bear to see if we can find any pictures if these guys fir you. There must be something on the Military Net. Even the Suvarov Mob doesn't have that much reach—or clout. Get back to you.

Bolan absorbed the information. If Kissinger could get a line on the sniper team, it would be worth following through on. The deaths of the protected witnesses and the innocent agent who had walked into a bullet had been the prime mover in starting this current mission. Bolan hadn't forgotten that, or his promise to take on the men responsible. His current strikes against the Suvarov Mob en masse had been fully encompassing. Now that he had created significant disruption there, it was time to look at this item on his agenda.

"Have you talked to Cowboy since he passed this along?"

Turrin shook his head. "Since that bomb blast I've been kind of taken up with relocating my department."

"I guess so, Leo. How bad was it?"

"My office is no more. The collateral damage wasn't so bad. Lucky for me the data on file was held within a central computer bank, so at least I haven't lost that. I got moved to another office down the hall. Not the same, but at least I get to look out on the street this time."

Bolan smiled. He stood and crossed to where the phone sat on a desk. He picked up the receiver and punched in a number that would, after rerouting, connect him to Stony Man. He listened to the soft clicks and electronic hums as the signal was sent. The actual connection didn't take all that long.

"I hear you've been a busy boy," Barbara Price said.

"Just doing a little tidying up."

"Really? On that basis I'd be interested in hearing your interpretation of mass destruction."

Bolan chuckled softly. "I need to talk to Cowboy."

He heard Price speaking to someone and the distant reply.

"He's here now. He came by to deliver some material for you. Hold on."

Kissinger's deep voice came on line moments later. "Hey, Striker, how goes it?"

"Better after reading that report you sent along. That's why I'm calling. Any results since?"

"I always figured you for a psychic. I just had the details come through. Bear is going to download it to Leo's laptop. You should be getting it in the next few minutes. Data and photographs. Listen up, those pictures will be a few years old so add that to what you see."

"Will do. What were these guys called back in the day?"

"Marvin Broderick. The dark-haired guy. He's the spotter. The backup part of the team. Leo Spavin, with the fair hair, was the shooter. A natural. The kind of sniper you only find once in a while. Kind of in your league, Striker. The way these guys fell off the world makes me think they'll be working under new IDs. Can't help you there yet."

"Thanks for what you did, Cowboy. It's going to help."

"Take it easy out there. You ever need any backup, just give me a yell. You hear?"

"Loud and clear."

Turrin had been on another phone, and he caught Bolan's eye as he crossed the room and sat facing his friend.

"Something on your mind?" Bolan asked.

"Might be nothing, but with the current situation I'm not taking chances. I just talked with my people. One of our most active field agents called in sick earlier. Said he needed time to get over some kind of virus."

"You not so sure it's genuine?"

"Maybe I'm touching paranoia here, but I've never known this guy to take time off for anything. Always struck me as dedicated to the job. Not married. Doesn't have much of an outside life from what I can gather."

"You know someone like that yourself," Bolan pointed out.

Turrin smiled. "Exceptions to every rule, Mack. You've got friends. A hell of a lot of them."

"Aren't we getting away from the point here?"

Turrin cleared his throat. "The agent's name is Vincent Bendix. He has an apartment in D.C."

"Okay. I'll go check him out."

"The bad part as far as I'm concerned is that I feel obliged to run some internal checks on the guy now."

"Give it to Aaron. Remember he can do it without having to compromise you. He has a free hand and doesn't need to worry about department protocols. And the guy is discreet."

Turrin nodded. "Let's hope all we find is that Bendix just has a cold."

ONE WAY OR ANOTHER, if he didn't do something fast, he'd be completely screwed.

Bendix knew that now. He had blown it with the department to the extent that he was an accessory to murder—not just of the witnesses under protective custody, but of a fellow agent. He felt bad about that. It had been preying on his mind since the day it had happened. That he had also known Walt Kershaw compounded his guilt. His feelings over the incident had festered away inside his head until it started to crowd in on everything else. Panic had gnawed at the edges of his thoughts. It had been a struggle to maintain a calm appearance each day, aware that as the department went about its investigation into Kershaw's death he was right there in the middle of it all. Off duty he had stayed pretty much isolated in his apartment, pacing the floor, drinking too much because he was accepting more and more that somewhere along the line it was all going to fall apart.

The demand that he plant the bomb in Leo Turrin's office had, oddly, been a distraction. He didn't like Turrin and would have been the first to admit they didn't get on. Turrin was too much of a professional for Bendix. He was no man's fool.

When Petrovsky contacted him and laid out the plan to get rid of Turrin, for once Bendix had had no difficulty with the suggestion. It would stop the man's investigation and distract the department from its ongoing search for a mole. But the planted bomb failed in its purpose, apart from causing some structural damage that wiped out Turrin's office. The man had received a warning to vacate his office with minutes to spare.

It changed Bendix's feelings once again. Turrin walked away from the planned explosion, and the very next day he was installed in another office, even more determined to complete the assignment that should have been at least thrown off track.

Bendix barely understood how he managed to get through the next few days. Things were starting to happen too fast. The Suvarov organization started to suffer from a number of hits against their business ventures. Bendix was in a position to be able to pick up and amass the information coming in from various sources because they were related to the Suvarov investigation.

First a hit against a car ringing operation in New Jersey, then the hijacking of a weapons shipment.

Hard on the heels of that came the attack of the farm in Kansas, with the Suvarov crew being taken down, too.

The worst scenario came with the destruction of an expensive drug shipment in Florida, compounded by the strike against DiFranco's club in

Miami and the almost surgical removal of Di-Franco himself, along with Raul Manzanar. The most devastating news came with the death of Vasily Suvarov who had been at the club during the attack.

It followed that Bendix received a call from Petrovsky. In itself it was scary enough. The man exuded civilized charm. He looked harmless in his expensive suits, always neat and dapper, with his calm visage and gentle manner. Bendix knew better. There was nothing civilized beneath the skin. Nikolai Petrovsky was a Suvarov through and through. Devoted to the Family and its cause, Petrovsky could order the death of a man with the same ease as he ordered a case of vodka.

When Petrovsky told Bendix what he wanted, the Fed had almost thrown up. He knew better than to refuse point-blank, because that would be signing his own death warrant. So he grudgingly agreed and after the call he stood with the phone in his hand, staring at it with the expectation it would suddenly strike at him like a fanged cobra.

Bendix knew then and there he couldn't do what they were asking. He was already operating on borrowed time, risking exposure with each passing day. From his position within the department, hearing the way the Suvarov Mob was being hit time and again, he began to experience a sense of foreboding. The Suvarovs were going down. Whoever this lone wolf was, he knew his way around, and if he was working in tandem with Turrin it wasn't going to be long before two and two added up to four. Once that happened, Bendix might suddenly find himself in the cell adjoining Arkady Suvarov's. The fleeting thought made Bendix smile, if only for a microsecond. He had no intention of spending time behind bars in a federal penitentiary.

He had noticed the tone in Petrovsky's voice, too. The man was only tolerating Bendix because he might still be of use to the organization. But the minute that usefulness evaporated, Bendix would be killed. He knew that as he knew the sun would rise in the morning. It was that inevitable. Once he was cast aside from the Suvarovs he would become a liability, having too much knowledge where they were concerned, so they would need to get rid of him. It was the way the Mob worked. It wouldn't be personal, they would say.

Just business.

SO, HIS NEXT MOVE would be to extricate himself from the whole damn mess. Clear out and make sure no one could find him. He had money salted away from his alliance with the Suvarovs, enough to keep him comfortable. His association had started well before the contract killings and, whatever else they might be, the Suvarovs were generous. They had always paid well and on time. He had a couple of accounts, in false names, with credit cards for each one so there would be no difficulty getting his hands on his money wherever he ended up. Bendix had always kept his eye on the ball and had been prepared for the day it dropped out of the box. He wasn't an overly ambitious man, and he had realized years ago that he was never going to end up in a high position. He would find himself a quiet spot and settle for a peaceful life away from both the department and the Suvarovs. As far as he was concerned, they could fight it out between themselves.

He had a couple of bags packed and stowed in his closet, enough clothing and accessories to keep him comfortable until he found his spot. Anything else he could buy as he went along.

Once he had his stuff ready, he changed into casual clothing, pulling a worn leather jacket over his cotton shirt. He had all his personal documents in one of the bags. Those would have to be destroyed once he was clear of the city. He took a second wallet he had prepared for such an eventuality. In it were documents in another identity. He had obtained these through contacts he had made while in the department—criminals who owed him favors, others who could be bought. He had a new driver's license, and a passport that he had used a few times to test out its authenticity, so it had exit and entry visa stamps on several pages. His credit cards were there, too, also in his new name. There was a substantial amount of cash in the wallet.

He left behind his department-issue gun. He had his own weapon, a 9 mm Beretta 92-S he had appropriated almost a year earlier after a drug-related bust. The weapon had been abandoned, almost brand-new. Bendix had confiscated the gun unnoticed and had kept it hidden in his apartment. Now he carried it in one of his carryalls.

He waited until early afternoon, after calling in sick that morning, then had a cab pick him up and drive him to a lockup facility on the north side of town. There he had kept the two-year-old Ford sedan he had bought six months earlier. It was in excellent condition, and he had kept it in good order, ready for such an eventuality, taking it out for runs at least once every couple of weeks. He kept it fully gassed up and had all the correct paperwork, including insurance, with him.

Bendix put his bags in the trunk, taking the Beretta and placing it in the glove box. He reversed out of the lockup and got out to close the doors before slipping back behind the wheel and moving off.

He eased his way through the traffic, intending to pick up Interstate 66 once he crossed the Roosevelt Municipal Bridge but along Constitution Avenue he had a minor collision with a wandering driver in a Toyota. There was little damage to either vehicle. Just a few paint scrapes, but the other guy started to make a fuss and before long a Washington P.D. cruiser rolled up behind them and Bendix felt his stomach roll. He watched the first cop step out and saunter along to see what was happening. Bendix played it cool, explaining what had happened, and made it clear he just wanted to exchange particulars and get on his way. The other guy decided to make an issue of the whole thing, which annoyed the cop. He called out his partner and suddenly a minor bump got messy. After he had handed over his license, registration and insurance papers Bendix stayed out of the argument, letting the other man talk himself in deeper with his belligerent attitude. In the end the cops told the guy if he didn't back off they'd take him into custody.

While the lead cop dealt with the guy, the other

came over and smiled almost apologetically at Bendix. He handed Bendix back his license and insurance slip.

"Sorry about this, sir."

Bendix shrugged. "Good thing I'm not trying to make an appointment."

"Okay, Hatcher, let's roll," the lead cop said as the other guy climbed back into his vehicle and pulled away. He puffed out his cheeks at Bendix. "You okay to go, sir?"

"Yes. Thanks, Officers."

The two cops watched Bendix climb back into his car and drive away.

The one called Hatcher watched the Ford disappear. He shook his head, then turned to follow his partner back to the cruiser. Hatcher was in the passenger seat. The moment he sat he leaned over and tapped details into the onboard computer.

"Problem?" his partner asked.

"I just feel I know that guy." Hatcher watched details spread across the small screen. He read the information. "According to this, his name is William Douglas. Driver's license and address all look legit. Photo matches, too. But I'm damn sure I know him as somebody else."

"Put it in the system," Dix, his partner, said. "Let it do the rounds. If he's not who he says he is, someone will flag it up. C'mon, it's time we took a coffee break. You can think about this guy while the caffeine kicks in."

Hatcher hit the keys and sent the accident detail to the P.D. mainframe.

BENDIX DROVE steadily for the next few miles, his thoughts on the incident that might have seemed small-time to a normal person. But he knew different. The details of the accident would be logged into the P.D. computer system and it would be there for anyone to see. His photograph from the license would be picked up by the department once he was reported absent from duty, because a routine search of databases would be carried out. Once his image came up, a deeper search would soon reveal that William Douglas didn't exist outside of bogus information. Establishment of that fact would initiate full-parameter searches, and his off-shore accounts would be located. The large amounts of money he had on deposit would set off alarm bells and before he knew it Bendix-Douglas would be the subject of a department manhunt.

He pulled off the main highway at the next exit and traveled some distance until he located a diner. He pulled in and parked in a corner, alongside a bulky semi-trailer. Bendix went inside the diner, found a vacant booth. He ordered coffee and sat waiting for it to arrive, watching the afternoon sky cloud over. A few minutes later it started to rain. The gloom matched his mood.

He had to do some reconfiguring of his position. The possibility of his being identified from the details the cops had taken was strong. He understood the way systems worked and the way different agencies were able to access other sources. There were times when it shouldn't have happened due to policy restrictions and the like, but in these days of terrorist threats and the growing alliance of national security, a lot of those barriers were being dropped. Cooperation was the watchword. It meant the likelihood of his deception would be revealed sooner rather than later. If he tried to run, to hide, he'd find himself a fugitive from both the police and his own people in the department.

Bendix was still deep in thought when the waitress came over and refilled his coffee cup. He thanked her absently, absorbed in his dilemma, staring out through the rain-dappled window.

So how *did* he resolve his current position?

No more flight. Not for the time being.

The only sensible thing he could do was to

return home, pick up his real identity and carry on, wait it out until matters settled down and he could make another move.

He would drive back into the city, return the Ford to the lockup, take a cab home and establish himself in his old routine. The William Douglas persona would be put on ice. If his image was picked up by the department computer system, he'd have to stonewall, making out that there had to be a double of him somewhere in the city. It would be tricky, but if he wanted to bluff it out, there wasn't much else he could do.

The situation regarding the Suvarovs was something else. He would have to string them along while he worked out what to do. Maybe he could feed them some information to keep them satisfied for a time. Their response was likely to be harsher than anything the department might come up with, but he had little choice now. He was caught in a trap of his own making. Getting himself out of it wasn't going to be easy. Even so, he had to try. The penalty for fouling it up was his life, followed closely by the loss of those large cash deposits in William Douglas's secret accounts.

If there was any way to save both, Bendix was going to make the attempt.

Stony Man Farm, Virginia

IT TOOK Aaron Kurtzman less than an hour to make the Vincent Bendix/William Douglas connection. With his Stony Man computer system, plus his dedicated team on hand, Kurtzman was able to throw everything he had into the search.

The William Douglas reference showed up within the first ten minutes. Carmen Delahunt, ex-FBI, had been running Bendix's image through all known databases, both national and local. The Washington P.D. string flashed up and she found herself looking at side-by-side images of Bendix and Douglas. She ran a ten-point facial comparison scan, and the computer came up with a hundred-percent match. She called for Kurtzman's attention and downloaded the information to his monitor.

The computer wizard studied the data. He tapped a few keys, increasing the definition on the screen, bringing the twin images into sharp relief.

"It's the same guy. No doubt about it. Akira, start digging into this guy William Douglas. If this is just an alias, somewhere along the line it has to end. Bendix is good but not that good, and I'm betting he wasn't expecting his work to have to come under such tight checking."

Kurtzman picked up one of his phones and put in a call to Leo Turrin.

THIRTY MINUTES LATER Mack Bolan was behind the wheel of his car, heading across Washington in the direction of Bendix's apartment building.

Bendix himself had arrived back at the apartment and was establishing himself in his normal existence, uncertain what the immediate future had in store for him, and also realizing he had little choice but to maintain his Justice Department persona until a more favorable time presented itself for his disappearance.

A DARK-BLUE DODGE SUV with tinted windows was also approaching the location. Inside were the two men previously known as Spavin and Broderick.

Driving was Marvin Broderick, his dark hair receding and worn cropped close to his skull. As he drove, he constantly checked his surroundings, ever watchful, the part of his job that had now become an essential of his life.

In the passenger seat, relaxed, seemingly oblivious to what went on around him, sat Leo Spavin. In contrast to Broderick's military cut, he wore his thick blond hair to his collar. It stood out against his tan. He wore expensive prescription sunglasses, and he owned three pairs. His eyesight was of prime importance. Being the shooter, he needed to have 20/20 vision and guarded his sight with near fanatical devotion.

Both men were dressed conservatively so they would not attract attention. There were times on a contract when they needed to blend in with a particular environment, so Broderick always checked things out ahead of time so they could create the correct impression. In the past they had dressed as utility employees, even as police officers, to get themselves into delicate areas without raising suspicion. Always careful, they had carried out contracts with unfailing success.

Which was why Broderick wasn't happy about this current assignment. He had been expressing his concerns since they had arrived in the city, and if Spavin had been the type to react to his partner's concerns, they might have been arguing by this time.

"Leo, you haven't said much."

"You're doing all the talking for us both, buddy."

"Am I making any sense?"

"I'm with you up to a point. But we had the same thing when we were in the service. Times are, the situation doesn't allow for planning. Something comes up that needs dealing with straight off. We handled those assignments before. So why not now?"

"Because now we can decide to do a job or not."

"Agreed. But there is also client satisfaction. Since we hooked up with the Suvarovs, we've made a mint and they keep coming up with new contracts. No point spoiling the relationship by getting all touchy over one job. Marv, look at what they're paying to get this done quick."

"Money isn't everything."

"Am I hearing you right?"

Despite himself, Broderick had to grin. "So I like money. I also prefer to stay alive and out of jail so I can make use of it."

"This will be over and done in a little while. We locate the target, make the hit, turn around and take the red-eye back to Palm Springs. Come lunchtime tomorrow you can be home, boning that dancer from Vegas. Now what could be better than that?"

"Same thing but doing it right now."

Spavin shook his head. "Lone Ranger had Tonto. Holmes had Watson. Who do I get? Sad Sack."

"Hey, you don't make fun of Sad Sack. I modeled my military career on that guy."

Spavin shook his head in despair. "I rest my case."

TEN MINUTES LATER Broderick eased the SUV to a stop, cutting the engine. He was checking out the street. It was almost full dark, and heavy clouds were sliding in from the east, threatening more rain.

"Okay, Hotshot," he said. "There's your building. Bendix's apartment is on the third floor. Number 36. Corner suite. Overlooks this street."

"Now how do you know that?"

Broderick tapped the side of his nose. "My job, remember? While you were cleaning your gun I was accessing the Internet and checking out D.C. city council databases. They have all kinds of details on file, including floor plans of apartment buildings listed under fire regulation applications."

"Keep this up and I might let you stay on."

"There's an alley that runs alongside the building that gives access to the service area at the rear. I can park there, and you can get in through the basement garage. Elevator or stairs will take you up to the third floor. Same way back down."

"With all this planning, you wouldn't happen to have a spare key for Apartment 36?"

"The trouble with you, Leo, is that you want it too easy."

Spavin reached in the attaché case at his feet and took out the pistol he had brought with him. It was a Heckler & Koch Mk.23, the civilian version of the .45 ACP chambered pistol developed for the U.S. SOCOM. The large, heavy pistol held a 10-round magazine and had a threaded tip on the extended barrel for the standard-issue Knight's Armament suppressor. The hard-hitting .45-caliber slugs provided better stopping power than the standard 9 mm, which was why Spavin had chosen the weapon for up-close-and-personal hits. His experience with the pistol during his service days had convinced him of its capabilities, and the suppressor kept the noise to a minimum. He wore a dual shoulder rig, with a holster for the pistol on the left and one for the tube suppressor under his right arm.

"Let's do it, Marv."

Broderick swung the SUV across the street and into the side alley. He drove to the end, using the service area to turn the vehicle around so it was ready to leave.

Spavin had checked the pistol, making sure the magazine was in place, with the first round in the breech. He eased it back into the holster and zipped up his light-brown leather jacket. He took out identical transceivers from the attaché case and checked the power, switching them on and handing one to his partner. The other set went into his pants' pocket.

"I'll check the garage to see if his car's there. If he isn't at home, we come back. You can see the garage from here. If his car shows up, give me a call."

"Hey, I've done this before, remember."

"Here, look after my glasses for me. And don't smear the lens."

"Yes, Momma."

Spavin went EVA and made his way along the alley until he reached the garage entrance. He took the down ramp and vanished from his partner's sight.

Broderick glanced at his watch.

It was ten after eight....

CHAPTER EIGHT

Bolan parked across the street and cut the engine. He checked his Beretta. Beside him Kira Tedesko did the same with her own weapon. There had been no contest when it came to her accompanying Bolan. The young woman's determination and her argument wore down his resistance, and there was no denying her performance at the nightclub in Miami.

"Take the alley," Bolan said. "The sign there indicates the garage is in the basement. If Bendix is home, his car should be parked there." Turrin had provided them with details on the department vehicle along with ID on Bendix.

"Is this an arrest?" Tedesko had asked as they'd driven in the direction of the apartment building.

Bolan hadn't taken his eyes from the road.

"That's up to Bendix. If he cooperates, we take him in. Leo needs answers to a lot of questions. If he resists, I don't want either of us getting hurt. Bendix is on the edge, so be careful. Understand?"

She nodded.

They checked the compact transceivers they each carried.

"Use it," Bolan said. "No heroics. Clear?"

"Yes, Cooper."

Hard spots of rain splattered against the windshield moments before they exited the car. Bolan turned up the collar of his jacket as he made his way across the street, Tedesko following then angling off toward the alley.

Bolan stepped under the entrance canopy seconds before the downpour began in earnest. He could hear it hitting the sidewalk behind him as he pushed in through the doors and crossed the lobby. He spotted the doors to the pair of elevators, then moved to the stairs and started to climb.

He had reached the first landing when his transceiver clicked.

"His car is here. Hood is still warm, so he hasn't been back long."

"Take the access stairs to the third floor. Keep your eyes open."

"What am I, Cooper? A novice?"

Bolan smiled at her taut reply.

He reached the third-floor landing and turned along the corridor, following the apartment number.

BRODERICK HAD SEEN the young woman enter the alley and turn in at the garage entrance. He sat there for a time, something telling him her appearance was unusual.

If she lived in the building, why enter the garage from the alley? Why walk down the alley, especially in the rain?

Broderick's role as spotter and troubleshooter for the team made him suspicious of anything that didn't quite fit.

And this didn't fit.

The more he thought about it, the more he was sure the woman shouldn't have been there. He revisited her image as she had moved down the alley. The way she had moved. Her stance. It had indicated someone aware of her position, alert, rather than a civilian simply entering the garage on her way to pick up her car.

A cop?

Maybe a federal agent?

Surveillance on Bendix?

Perhaps the man's cover had been blown and he was being brought in.

Broderick pushed open the door and stepped out, feeling the chill of the heavy downpour. He headed for the garage entrance, reaching under his jacket for the P-226 he carried. As he entered the garage, he paused to activate his transceiver.

"Heads up, Leo. We could have company. Might be cops heading to pick up Bendix."

SPAVIN ACKNOWLEDGED the call with a curt reply, then pushed the transceiver into his back pocket. He was already at the apartment door. Despite his partner's call, he remained calm, his concentration on the task ahead. No profit in letting panic distract him.

Take it one step at a time, Leo, he thought.

He paused at the door, taking a moment to press his ear against the panel. When he picked up movement inside, he nodded to himself, slipping the pistol from its holster. With practiced ease he took out the suppressor and threaded it onto the end of the barrel, then made sure the pistol was cocked and ready for use.

AS BOLAN REACHED the turn in the corridor that would lead him to Bendix's apartment, he caught movement in the subdued lighting ahead of him.

A lone figure paused at an apartment door.

Even as Bolan increased his pace the figure

raised his right foot and launched a solid blow at the door, just at the level of the lock. The door swung in and the figure followed through, light glinting off the metal of a pistol in his right hand.

THE CRACK OF THE DOOR being kicked open reached Bendix's ears as he stepped out of his bedroom into the living room. He turned in time to see a dark figure coming in through the door, a large handgun already tracking across the room.

"You son of a bitch," he snarled, turning to snatch up his own pistol lying on top of the unit by the bedroom door. His fingers had closed around the butt when he heard a low throaty sound, and a microsecond later he felt the hard punch of a slug bite into his upper chest, close to the shoulder. The caliber had to have been large, because the force spun him and he fell, striking the floor hard. He bounced across the smooth wood surface, the gun spilling from his fingers, and he was surprised at the suddenness of the pain that flowered around the wound. He hadn't even made any conscious thought about getting to his feet when he felt more slugs hit home. He felt numbing pain in his chest and his ravaged system reacted, nerves kicking back against the damage. Bendix had no idea what dying entailed, but all he knew in his final moments was hurt and fear and a desperate urge to stay alive. Whatever else went through his mind never registered as his killer fired two final shoots directly into his skull, blowing his brains out through the exit wound.

BOLAN REACHED the apartment's open door, hearing the subdued sounds of the suppressed gunfire.

He brought himself to a dead stop by throwing out his left hand to grip the edge of the door frame, the Beretta moving to cover the armed man standing over Bendix.

Spavin caught the slight sound Bolan made as he framed himself in the doorway.

He turned, swinging the big pistol around as he twisted his upper body, finger already taking up the pressure in the trigger.

IN THE SCANT SECOND before he fired, Bolan registered the face of the killer from the ID photographs.

Leo Spavin, the blond sniper.

His finger stroked the Beretta's trigger and it jacked out its 3-round burst. The 9 mm slugs hit Spavin in the chest, making him step back, surprise etched across his face as he realized he'd been hit. One of his heels caught against Bendix's outstretched left leg and he stumbled, throwing out his arms to regain his balance.

Bolan stepped inside the apartment, the Beretta following Spavin as he fell to his knees. He didn't hesitate. He never even registered the look in Spavin's eyes as he triggered the Beretta again, sending the next three 9 mm rounds into the assassin's skull. Spavin's head snapped back, dark flecks of bloody tissue erupting from the exit wounds. He arched stiffly in a final spasm and slumped back across Bendix.

Taking out his transceiver, Bolan hit the button.

"Kira, watch out for the partner. He might be close."

The transceiver clicked, and Tedesko's voice was slightly breathy.

"Yes, I understand. Hey, you know how many damn steps there..."

Bolan heard the rattle of shots in the instant before the transceiver fell silent.

TEDESKO HEARD THE SCUFF of footsteps on the concrete below her. She picked up the click of the transceiver as it acknowledged an incoming call and snatched it from her pocket to take Bolan's warning.

She caught a flickering shadow on the flight

below. The lean figure that came into view carried a handgun, and the moment he connected with her, seeing she was armed, he opened fire.

Tedesko dropped the transceiver as she pulled back from the railing. She heard the solid whack of the shots as they hit the wall over her head, showering her with concrete dust.

On her knees she dragged herself away from the rail, pressing against the angle of the wall. She could feel her heart pounding in her chest and experienced the rush of adrenaline mixed with the utter feeling of dread at what might happen to her. It scared and excited her at the same time.

Her ears picked up soft movement below, the sound closing as her assailant advanced. She leaned forward a few inches, not exposing her head but allowing her to see the steps below. She could now hear the gentle rustle of clothing. A shadow fell across the section of wall she could see, the outline of an arm, the hand holding a gun.

She didn't move. Her full attention was on that shadow as it extended to reveal the outline of a man's upper body.

Wait, wait, she told herself. Let him come to you.

Seconds seemed to stretch into an eternity. Kira held her breath, not daring to make even that gentle sound. The fingers of her right hand, gripping the butt of the pistol, began to ache, she was holding it so tight. The muzzle of the weapon was trained on the spot where he would show.

If she was right.

Unless he did something unexpected.

WHEN IT CAME, it lasted mere seconds. Nothing dragged out.

Broderick made his move with a rapid lunge that exposed him on the small landing that bridged the two flights. His weapon was tracking ahead of him, its muzzle probing like a dark, blind eye. As he turned his body, searching the steps above him, he caught a glimpse of the woman, pressed hard against the wall, her eyes wide with expectation, her own weapon aimed directly at him.

"Goddamn you bit—"

His finger was pressuring back on the trigger when he saw the brief burst of flame from the muzzle of her gun. He felt something strike his lower jaw, a wrenching, solid impact that jerked his head to one side, his gun firing in reflex, the slug hitting the ceiling high overhead. There was a rush of mixed sensations. He didn't see or hear his adversary firing again and again. He tried to yell, but his lower jaw had been torn and ruptured by her first shot and he choked on the surge of blood. The follow-up shots hit him in the chest, directly over his heart, and he fell back against the wall, dropping to his knees then toppling back down the steps he had just climbed, leaving a bloody trail in his wake.

TEDESKO STAYED where she was, her weapon trained on the spot where Broderick had been moments before. It was only when his pistol slipped from his slack fingers and clattered down the steps that she jerked to awareness. The sound of the shots had faded, returning the steps to their previous silence. She pushed to her feet.

Only now was she aware of the gritty dust from the wall tasting sour in her mouth. The sting of the gash in her cheek from a sliver of impacted concrete. And the insistent click of the transceiver on the step at her feet. She picked it up, keyed the button.

"...Kira, talk to me..."

She opened the channel.

"I'm here, Cooper. I'm safe. The other one followed me up the steps. He's dead."

"Get yourself up here." He paused, his voice dropping to a gentler tone. "You okay?"

"I will be fine."

BOLAN EXPERIENCED a surge of relief at the sound of Tedesko's voice. Something about her had gotten to him. Most likely it was her determination, the inner spirit that kept her pushing despite her recent experience at the hands of the Suvarovs. She was no quitter, that was for certain, and her irreverent attitude toward him had something to do with it.

Satisfied she was on her way up, Bolan turned to check out the apartment, easing his cell phone from his pocket as he did. He speed-dialed Turrin and when the man from Justice came on, Bolan drew him a swift picture of the incident.

"Better get your people here," Bolan said. "We need to secure the apartment and lock it down before the D.C. cops swarm in and take over."

"I'm on it. You think there might be information we can use?"

"I'll tell you that once I take a look around."

"How's Kira?" Turrin asked.

"Holding her own."

Finishing the call, Bolan began a slow walk through the apartment. He was still in the living room when Tedesko appeared. She took a long look at the two bodies before she put away her Beretta and closed the apartment door.

"Cooper?"

"I'm fine."

"What are we looking for?"

"Anything. The way I see it, Bendix was way in deep with the Suvarov Mob. He had information, they paid him for it. If he was any kind of agent, he'd understand the need for some kind of security. Something he could use against them in case his deal went sour. He was down and dirty, accessory to the murder of protected witnesses and one of his own. And he'd betrayed the trust of his department. A man like that would be looking after number one."

"Does he have a computer here?"

"Yeah, I just spotted it over there, on the desk by the far wall."

Tedesko crossed over and switched on the unit. As it flicked into life, she used the keyboard to access the stored documents and files. The way she ran through the various screens told Bolan she was well used to computers.

"This something else you picked up on the job?"

"Computers run our lives, Cooper. We have to be able to make them work for us."

Leaving her to it, Bolan carried on his search. On an impulse he knelt beside the bodies and went through the pockets. He found cell phones on both of them, and moved aside to check out the stored data.

THIRTY MINUTES LATER the apartment had been invaded by both Washington P.D. and a team from Justice, including Leo Turrin. The P.D. squad arrived seconds ahead of Justice, and there was a confrontation until Turrin took control, establishing Justice Department priority. The cop in charge, for whatever reason, played hardball until Turrin made a call, said his piece, then handed his cell phone to the cop. Turrin, now victorious, became the diplomat and took the cop aside, talking quietly, and by the time he'd finished the cop was nodding in gratitude. He marshaled his force and they left, bequeathing the apartment to Turrin and his team.

Bolan had observed this with silent amusement, still continuing his quiet search of the rooms.

Over at the computer Tedesko had carried on regardless of what was going on behind her. She never looked up once.

Turrin finally joined Bolan, locating him in the bedroom.

"Anything?"

Bolan had a leather travel bag on the bed and was laying out its contents. He indicated a thick wallet.

"Meet William Douglas. Passport, driver's license, insurance documents, credit cards. And a nice chunk of cash."

Turrin picked up the wallet, thumbing through

the contents. He opened the passport and found himself staring at the image of William Douglas a.k.a. Vincent Bendix.

"He had it all worked out," Turrin muttered.

Bolan found the Beretta and handed it over.

"I don't think that was ever issued to Bendix."

"This son of a bitch had a whole new life planned."

"Yes, and he was going to finance it with this," Tedesko said from the bedroom door. She held out a sheet she had printed off from the computer. "Bank accounts in the Cayman Islands. Took me a while to get through his firewall and codes. It wasn't too hard, though. He wasn't that clever at hiding things."

"Probably didn't figure he'd need to be," Turrin said as he checked out the information. He gave a low whistle. "I'm obviously in the wrong job. This makes his Justice Department salary look like change for coffee."

"You can say that again," Bolan remarked when Turrin handed him the sheet. "Kira, seeing as you're on a roll with the electronic snitch, how about sending me an e-mail?"

"Okay."

Bolan followed her through to the computer and under his instruction she typed his message and sent it to the innocent e-mail address that would transmit to Stony Man and Aaron Kurtzman.

"Some phone numbers I picked up from cells off Bendix and Spavin," Bolan explained to Turrin. "We might hit lucky and get something."

"When we leave I'll have my people take the computer," Turrin said. "They can dig deep and see if there's anything else Bendix might have in there."

"So where do we go from here?" Tedesko asked.

Turrin led the way to a corner of the room where they could sit and talk.

"What you've already achieved is to disrupt some of the Suvarov main operations, and remove some principal players from the scene."

"But not the main players," Bolan reminded his friend.

"Arkady Suvarov is out of the picture. Now so is Vasily."

"I'm thinking about Nikolai Petrovsky," Bolan said. "As long as he has his hands on the wheel, the business will still continue."

"I've been getting reports of movement on the streets. Other Families are starting to move on Suvarov turf. Once it got out that Suvarov operations were being hit, the idea took hold, and we seem to be having some minor skirmishes." Turrin held up his hands. "You've created a wave effect. The ripples are starting to spread."

"I don't want a ripple," Bolan said. "I want a tidal wave to wash them all away."

Turrin's cell phone rang. "Talk to me."

He listened to the information, then completed the call. "We just got the word. Things are happening in Moscow with the Suvarov organization. It seems there's been some kind of internal housecleaning. Sergei Denisov, one of the Suvarov bosses, and three of his close associates were found floating in a river. They had all been executed. Shots to the backs of their heads—after their tongues had been cut out and their throats slit. The word going around in Mob circles is that they were caught siphoning off Suvarov cash to bankroll a rival group."

"Not the best time for the Suvarovs," Bolan said.

"Something else for you to think about," Turrin added. "It seems our friend Petrovsky flew out of New Jersey on the Family Lear. Destination Moscow."

"Off to smooth the troubled waters," Tedesko said.

"He took a companion."

The way he said it made Bolan glance across at Turrin.

"It seems that Miss Valentina Suvarov went with him."

"Daddy's little girl? Why would she get herself involved?" Bolan recalled something Tedesko had said to him during their first meeting. "Kira, have you seen a photograph of Arkady's daughter?"

She shook her head.

"Maybe it's time you did."

A few minutes later they were in Bolan's car, Turrin in the rear, watching as Bolan opened the laptop and powered it up. Once he had the data files on the screen he opened the one that held images and scrolled through the photographs until he found what he was looking for.

"Same question, Kira," he said. "Do you know Valentina Suvarov?"

As he asked the question, Bolan turned the laptop so that Kira could see the image on the screen. She looked at the photograph of Valentina, leaning forward to fix the image in her mind. Bolan saw her purse her lips, a soft sound escaping, then she raised her eyes to look directly at him.

"It appears I do know her, Cooper."

"Someone feel like they want to tell *me*," Turrin said.

Tedesko glanced at him. "That is the woman who was at the lockdown. The one giving orders. The one who spoke to me and said I was to be delivered to Leon DiFranco in Miami."

Bolan nodded. "I'm getting the feeling we might be closer to finding who's really running the organization while Arkady's in jail. It never looked like it was Vasily. But it is starting to look like it could be the daughter."

CHAPTER NINE

Moscow, Russia

The man who stepped out of the car into the cold, slanting rain was big and solid. He was Commander Valentine Seminov, and he ran a section of the OCD, the Organized Crime Department. The man he had come to meet at this military airstrip had been associated with Seminov on previous assignments. Seminov stood and watched the civilian American aircraft as it taxied along the runway and came to a stop in front of one of the hangars close to where he was parked. The big Russian huddled in the folds of his heavy leather coat and watched the two passengers emerge from the aircraft, nodding slightly as he recognized the tall, commanding figure in the lead.

It was Mack Bolan, and he had just brought his war to Russia.

Bolan, followed by Kira Tedesko, crossed to the car, dropping his luggage into the trunk Seminov had opened for him. The woman placed her bags beside Bolan's.

"They tell me I have to call you Cooper now."

"Matt Cooper."

"Pah." Seminov shook his head. "Doesn't all this name changing confuse you?"

"*I* know who I am, Valentine."

"At least you still remember *my* name."

"How could I ever forget Commander Valentine Seminov?"

The Russian's face split into a wide, friendly grin. He leaned forward and threw his arms around Bolan, hugging him firmly.

"Good to see you, *tovarich*. I know that if you are here it will not be a quiet time."

"I don't do quiet."

"You need to remind me?"

Tedesko made an impatient sound to remind them she, too, was standing in the rain, and Seminov released Bolan and turned to her.

"Kira." He repeated his big bear hug, almost lifting her off her feet. "How did you get mixed up with this crazy American?"

"It's a complicated story, Valentine."

Seminov grunted. "Complicated should be his middle name."

Tedesko climbed into the rear of the big Mercedes sedan as Bolan took the passenger seat beside Seminov. The Russian closed his door and they drove across the tarmac in the direction of the exit gate. Seminov lowered his window and thrust his ID at the security man, then powered up the window again to shut out the rain. He spun the car away from the airstrip and along the feeder road to where it intersected with the ring road around Moscow. Seminov was concentrating hard, reaching up to wipe the condensation that kept forming on the windshield, then shaking his hand to get rid of the moisture.

"Damned heater is not working properly," the Russian grumbled. He threw a quick glance in Bolan's direction. "So this time it is the Suvarov Mob you are after."

"With your help."

"Whatever I can do. Those murderous bastards have been running criminal activities for too long and laughing at us all. When I spoke to your man in Justice, he told me how they are operating in the U.S. But now we have a chance to break them with Arkady Suvarov in jail. It won't be easy. They have power, influence and, most important, *too* much money. It makes them hard to touch."

"Not in my book, Valentine. I'm here to root them out and make them scatter like rats. I want to make them understand they don't have any kind of protection from me."

"Kira can tell you some of the things they get up to."

"We already covered that."

"Did you hear about the bodies that were found floating in the river?"

"We heard."

"Poetic, don't you think? Dead rats floating in the river. This would not have happened during Arkady Suvarov's time. Maybe the Mob is starting to fall apart. If so it's a good time to hit them. *Da?*"

"Works for me," Bolan replied.

"I heard from Justice that the son, Vasily, is dead."

"Yes."

"Your doing? I ask because this leaves a position open in the organization. We know that Petrovsky has arrived here. Probably to tidy up the mess left after the removal of Sergei Denisov and his partners."

"You know who came with him?"

"Cooper, I am OCD. I know everything."

Tedesko leaned forward to prod Bolan's shoulder. "Tell him."

"You could drive a man to desperate measures, Kira, you know that?"

He heard her soft chuckle as she sank back in her seat.

"We're working on the possibility that Valentina Suvarov has taken over from her father."

"What? Now I know you are crazy."

"I agree with Cooper," Tedesko said.

"You, too? Tell me why."

The woman related what had happened from the time she was snatched from the streets of Pristina, through her experiences at the Kansas lockdown, Bolan's intervention and the events that followed. She finished by telling Seminov that she had identified Valentina as the woman who had visited the lockdown.

Seminov was quiet for a while, his attention on his driving as he took the Mercedes through the rain-swept streets of the city. Traffic was thin and only a few pedestrians had ventured out on this cold, wet evening.

"If what you say is true, she will have a hard time making the hard-liners dance to her tune."

"Don't underestimate her just because she is a woman," Tedesko said.

"Cooper, this one here is stubborn. And she will chatter your ears off if you give her the opportunity."

"You're telling *me?* Since Kansas it would have been easier to shake off malaria."

Seminov's booming laughter filled the interior of the car. "Kira, he knows you well."

"Not *that* well," she riposted.

THE OCD HAD BEEN relocated in an anonymous warehouse that had been part of a now disused industrial complex. Following the bombing of their original base, the department had been left without accommodation. The warehouse had been offered as a temporary haven. Seminov had translated that as permanent. After their initial disappointment Seminov and his dedicated team had settled in well. Once they were established, the isolated building proved to be ideal for their operation. The basement provided parking for their assorted vehicles and the upper floor became the OCD nerve center.

"They haven't rehoused you?" Tedesko asked, memories of the place from her previous visit returning.

"*Nyet,*" Seminov said. "They say there are no new funds."

"Just like home," Bolan said as he emerged from the elevator cage.

"You mean, you live like this?" Tedesko asked, pushing by the tall American. She gave him a withering glance. "How sad."

"I think he is joking," Seminov said.

The Russian crossed over to where a number of desk were pushed together. The tops were heavy with computers and telephones, thick files and scattered mugs of cold tea and coffee. Seminov stood talking to two of his team. They were the only personnel in the place at the time. He rejoined Bolan and Tedesko after a couple of minutes.

"We are working on over a dozen cases right now," he said. "Crime is booming in Russia."

Seminov handed him a sheet of paper. "This came for you from your man at Justice."

Bolan scanned the information.

"The cell phones we took from Bendix and Spavin linked up with Nikolai Petrovsky. Both of them had spoken to him a number of times according to my source. They tracked calls, went through the cell providers and came up with a number tied in to Petrovsky."

"So we have our criminal connection," Seminov said.

"Isn't it careless of Petrovsky to let this happen?" Tedesko suggested.

"People like Petrovsky start to believe their own publicity," Bolan said. "They figure they've been doing it for so long they're above the law. Arrogance. They believe they are invincible. That's when they get clumsy."

"Come over here," Seminov said.

He took them to a corner of the area that had been furnished with chairs and a basic kitchen. A large cast-iron stove glowed with heat against the outer wall. A stack of chopped wood was on the floor beside it.

"Very cozy," Tedesko said. "No television?"

"It is being delivered next week. Kira, over there is a kettle and mugs for coffee. Would you, please."

Seminov crossed to the stove and fed in chunks of wood, speaking over his shoulder.

"The Suvarovs operate from a vodka distillery on the east side of the city. The business has been in the Family since early last century, passing from generation to generation. It is their cloak of respectability. Pah. The Suvarovs have bribed and murdered their way to where they are. Even before the collapse of the old regime the Suvarov brand of vodka was a favorite of the ruling party. Even then the Suvarovs were playing their crooked games."

Satisfied, the Russian turned away from the stove, rubbing his hands together, taking the steaming mug from Tedesko.

"Are they still buying favors?" Bolan asked.

"Of course. Now that we live in a democracy, there are many more hands taking their money and eyes looking in the opposite direction."

"Are you saying we can't trust anyone?" Kira asked.

"*Da*. Except me of course."

Bolan smiled. "The thought never crossed my mind."

"One day I will die from laughing at your jokes, Cooper."

Seminov's cell phone rang. He snatched it from his pocket, listened, interrupted, then listened again. He finally switched the phone off.

"One of my men. It seems you may have been right about the new head of the Suvarov organization. He has picked up information from one of his informants. There is to be a meeting at the Suvarov dacha outside Moscow tomorrow. Various members of the Mob have been summoned. Our informant is on the domestic staff at the dacha and he made it clear that all the orders are coming from the new mistress of the house. Valentina Suvarov."

Tedesko stared across the table at Bolan, her eyes gleaming with anticipation.

"This means we could have her."

"Only if we take it slow. If this is a Mob summit, the place will be sewn up tight. With everything that's been happening, they won't be offering an open-door policy."

"And I doubt we will receive invitations," Seminov said.

"That's the least of our worries," Bolan said. "We won't need invitations when we gate-crash. Valentine, what can you tell me about the dacha's layout?"

"Whatever you need. Like everything else, the Suvarov dacha is bigger and better than any you might have seen. You know what a dacha is? A family summer house for people to escape the city. The Suvarovs have built one like a damned palace. So big you could house half the city," the Russian cop said. "But first we eat. I will not let you go away saying Valentine Seminov didn't make you welcome to Moscow."

BOLAN AND KIRA LAY side by side in the damp grass, where tangled undergrowth fringed the dense forest spread around them along the eastern perimeter of the Suvarov dacha. Seminov hadn't been exaggerating. The house was large, the wooden structure imposing, set as it was in the forested area well away from the main highway leading to the city.

It was an hour after dawn. They had been in position for almost three hours, and during the past half hour they had observed a number of cars arriving and depositing passengers at the door to the sprawling house.

They lay concealed beneath a camouflaged waterproof sheet that afforded them protection from the chill rain that seemed to have become a permanent feature of their visit. Bolan had pointed out that despite the discomfort it presented it also diminished the visibility of the armed guards spaced around the dacha. The half dozen Mob soldiers, clad in weatherproof gear and carrying AK assault rifles, weren't the happiest individuals Bolan had ever seen. They made their patrols, tramping through the puddles and snapping at one another in passing.

Their uncomfortable situation would help Bolan when he made his move. The guards lacked the discipline instilled into professional soldiers. These men were nothing more than low-ranking mobsters, not experienced combat veterans. The hit-and-run methods employed by these Mob bullies didn't equip them for combat situations.

Mack Bolan had military experience instilled into his makeup. It was what allowed him to penetrate enemy positions, to confront and defeat his opponents by performing his duties to the extreme. For Bolan this was familiar territory. The battleground was his home. His chosen turf. It was where he belonged and he knew that without even having to give it room in his conscious thought.

The ability to wait patiently was something Mack Bolan took in his stride. He admitted surprise when he realized that the young woman at his side exhibited control over her own emotions on a level with his. During the long hours of their stakeout, Tedesko had never made any kind of complaint about the cold and wet. She followed his orders without comment, only speaking when necessary, asking a few pertinent questions. The rest of the time she maintained her watch, scanning the area with the field glasses she carried. The only reminder of her presence came when she moved and Bolan became aware of the press of a warm thigh against his.

They were both clad in combat blacksuits and boots, and wore black wool ski caps. Transceivers were clipped to the harnesses over the blacksuits, as were extra ammunition clips. Bolan carried a mix of grenades, and the Cold Steel Tanto knife was sheathed on his hip. The 93-R was in its shoulder holster, the big Desert Eagle packed in a high-ride holster on his right hip. They both carried 9 mm Uzis as their main assault weapon. The machine pistols were loaded with 32-round magazines. In extreme combat situations Bolan preferred familiar, reliable weapons and there were few more competent than the Israeli Uzi. It had served him well over the years and he retained an affection for the 9 mm SMG that wasn't about to fade. Bolan also had an additional weapon in the form of an M-79 grenade launcher. The elderly weapon was capable of delivering 40 mm grenades up to 400 meters at a muzzle velocity of 75 meters per second. Kissinger had surprised Bolan by producing one of the shotgun-like weapons. The warrior had a number of the 40 mm grenades clipped to the harness.

"Boris Yelenko," Tedesko announced as she followed the progress of yet another new arrival.

Bolan tracked his own glasses in and picked up the stocky, broad man just stepping inside the house, shadowed by his bodyguards. Both he and Tedesko had been furnished with data and photographs of Suvarov Mob members during their time at the OCD. Seminov had detailed files on the entire hierarchy: bosses, their bodyguards, local foot soldiers, names and images of their mistresses and in some cases, boyfriends.

Yelenko had charge of the Suvarov entertainment section, which meant he controlled the porn business. Theirs was an ever-growing market that spread all across Russia and well into Eastern Europe. The business was extremely lucrative, and there was a demand for fresh product, which in turn called for a constant supply of participants, willing or otherwise. Tedesko had a deep well of information on the subject. It had been part of her mission brief because the missing women she had been investigating often ended up in the porn trade. Bolan had an insight into the U.S. end of the market from the information Turrin had furnished him with, so he understood the global potential of the trade.

"Do you realize how many sites there are on the Internet alone?" Tedesko had asked as they discussed the problem at the OCD. "Thousands. And every one leads to another. They all need feeding with fresh material. Of every kind. From child porn to adults and beyond. And the Suvarovs are into this in a huge way. Cooper, they are making millions from it. On top of all their other business dealings."

"I understand," Bolan had said.

"Do you, Cooper? Do you see the faces of those young women on those videos? On the photographs? The self-disgust in their eyes when they are made to do those things. Do you *really* understand?"

Seminov, in the background, had been startled himself by Tedesko's impassioned outburst.

"Kira," he had said, "if you allow it to become too personal it'll distract you from what you are trying to do."

She had flopped back in her seat, calming down, her fierce stare fixed on Bolan's face.

"We'll do this together, Kira. I promise. And yes, I do understand."

A HALF DOZEN BLACK limousines were parked in front of the dacha now. Behind the house, in a clearing where the undergrowth had been cut back, stood a sleek blue-and-white AS-365 Dauphin helicopter.

"According to Seminov's list, that's the last of them," Bolan said.

"Going to be a lot of weapons in there," Tedesko pointed out.

"Getting cold feet?"

"You wish, Cooper. If my feet are cold, it's only because of this miserable Russian weather."

Bolan checked his watch. "Seminov's informant should have the domestic staff outside within the next five minutes. That was the arrangement."

"Those guards are moving around the house. Won't they be seen?"

"We can't avoid it. We give them a full thirty seconds after the deadline, then we go. You know what to do?"

"Shoot anything that isn't you?"

Bolan turned on his side and fed an HE round into the barrel of the M-79 then locked it into position, making certain the launcher was ready to fire.

"Pick a target," he said.

"Yelenko. The last one to arrive."

Bolan settled back on his front, studying the layout and the patrolling guards. He estimated the target distance to Yelenko's car at around 120 meters, well inside the M-79's range. If he scored a solid hit and the car blew, it would create a big diversion. He would follow with a few more strikes at the other parked vehicles.

"As soon as I drop the last HE, I want you moving around to the far side of the house. If you see the domestic staff, get them clear. I'll lay down a couple of smoke canisters to give you cover."

She nodded, her face pale now as she envisaged what lay ahead. Bolan had no doubts as to her ability. She had proved her worth at the DiFranco nightclub. Any caution she might exhibit now was in her favor. No one went into a combat situation unaware of the possibilities. If they did, plunging in with casual disregard, they were risking their lives, and those of their companions too casually.

"Kira?"

She turned at the sound of his strong, calm voice.

"I will be fine, Cooper."

"Damn right you will," he said with mock gruffness.

Bolan checked his watch. Time was almost up. If they were going, it had to be now. He hoped the staff had managed to exit the dacha and get themselves in the clear. Once the strike got under way, things might become a little unsettled.

He pushed up from beneath the camouflage sheet onto one knee and raised the M-79. He laid the sights on Yelenko's expensive limousine. His finger stroked the trigger and the launcher jerked as it fired the 40 mm grenade. Bolan saw its hazy line of travel as it cleaved the falling curtain of rain.

The explosion rocked the area. Yelenko's Mercedes was turned into a shattered tangle of blistered junk by the detonation, metal and plastic debris spinning through the air.

"Go," Bolan ordered, and out of the corner of his eye he saw Tedesko push to her feet, turn and fade into the trees behind them.

He reloaded and fired on a second, then third car. More explosions ripped through the target vehicles. A gas tank blew on one of them, spraying flaming fuel in a deadly rain. Heated glass shattered, tires burst.

Bolan slipped a smoke grenade into the launcher and fired it toward the corner of the dacha where Tedesko would be moving. He saw the thick white spumes start to rise. He put a second one down a little farther out, cast the M-79 aside and stood upright, bringing the Uzi online, then turned as he homed in on running figures moving around the burning cars, spreading across the area.

The guards.

The Mobs always had their gunners on tap, the foot soldiers who caught the flack for the bosses. Eager for advancement, they put themselves in the firing line, anxious to prove themselves in the endless struggle for supremacy. They were coming now, two-legged hyenas with the scent of the hunt in their nostrils. They called out to one another as they advanced on the tree line, dedication to their jobs making them less than cautious. They were all armed and hungry for the kill.

Bolan snapped back the Uzi's cocking bolt and brought the weapon into play, laying down a short burst that took out the closest gunner. The guy ran directly into the burst. The 9 mm slugs caught him midtorso, punching him off his feet and slamming him on the ground and into a world of pain that closed in and devoured him. Bolan had already swept the muzzle of the Uzi to its next target. He caught a pair of gunners moving almost parallel and hit them with a scything burst that shredded flesh and clothing, put them on the ground and removed them from the game.

The other gunners opened fire, drilling rounds into the shrubbery without finding a solid target. Their hard bursts tore at timber and foliage behind Bolan, filling the air with splinters and shredded leaves.

Bolan, already in a new position, tracked in and hit one guy in the side of his skull, the impact of the 9 mm slugs rendering the guy speechless from shock. He dropped to his knees, unaware of the sodden mass of bloody brain matter pumping from the gaping wound in his skull. He fell facedown, his body jerking in nervous reaction. The dying man's partner, lean and with a shock of black hair, swung around, pinpointing the source of Bolan's fire. He advanced on the position, finger curling around the trigger of his AK-47, eager to make his kill and be the one who brought down the intruder. His anticipation turned swiftly to short-lived disappointment as he became aware of a flitting shadow moving through the rain mist on his left. He twisted, panic rising as he realized he had walked into Bolan's fire zone. His last image was of a tall, grim-faced man dressed in black, leveling a 9 mm Uzi at him. The hardman continued to bring his own weapon online, even though he knew he would never make it. He saw a wink of flame erupt from the Uzi's muzzle, felt the impact of the bullets as they tore into his chest. He dropped hard, numb, and briefly heard the following crackle of Bolan's burst before his life closed down.

Five down—one to go.

Bolan saw the guy come around the end of the house, emerging from the smoke. He was sleeving the stinging smoke from his eyes, staring in alarm at the sight of the vehicle pyre. One of the remaining cars, burning from sprayed fuel, suddenly lost its own fuel tank. The rear of the limousine raised from the ground as the tank blew. A writhing ball of flame swelled out from beneath the vehicle, throwing long slivers of fire across the sodden ground.

Using the cover of the explosion, Bolan skirted the blazing tangle of vehicles, bringing himself around on the surviving guard's blind side. The guy was yelling into a lapel microphone, trying to get some guidance. He caught a glimpse of Bolan's dark figure as the big American emerged from behind the wall of fire.

AK-47 at the ready, the guy triggered the weapon hard and fast. Bolan saw the 7.62 mm slugs chop their way across the earth. He turned away from the line of fire, then double-handed the Uzi and locked on target, triggering a burst that caught the guard midthigh, traveled up into his torso and shattered his rib cage. The guard stumbled back, hitting the side of the house before he pitched to the ground facedown.

Bolan cut across toward the veranda that ran the length of the dacha, replacing the spent magazine and recocking the SMG. He hit the steps and went up onto the porch, raising a booted foot to drive the wooden front doors open.

As the doors flew inward, Bolan spotted a dark-suited figure moving rapidly toward the entrance, handgun already raised. The pistol began to fire, punching out shots that chewed wood splinters from the door frame above his head as he took a dive to the floor. Bolan slid across the smooth, polished wood of the hall, his forward motion taking him into the shooter. Twisting his body, the Executioner swept his right leg around, scything the guy off his feet. The man fell hard, his fingers still working the trigger of his weapon, slugs tearing into the walls, shattering glass in a window.

As Bolan pushed to his feet, he saw the other guy coming upright himself, turning his gun toward him. The big American didn't hesitate. He knew he couldn't get the Uzi on track in time, so he reached for the Cold Steel Tanto fighting knife, yanking it free with a swift action. He flipped the knife, held its tip for a heartbeat before launching it at the rising target. The blade struck just under the guy's jaw, piercing soft flesh and cleaving its way in deep. The target dropped his gun and clutched at the chill blade wedged in his throat. Blood began to pulse from the wound, welling through the guy's fingers as he tried in vain to remove the Tanto. He started to gargle, red froth erupting from his mouth, spilling down his chin. He was down on his knees when Bolan moved to stand over him, reaching down to grasp the hilt of the knife. The Executioner jerked the blade free, ignoring the surge of hot blood, and jammed it back in its sheath, already moving deeper into the house as the dying man fell facedown on the floor.

Bolan had picked up the noise coming from behind double doors to his left, turning as one of the doors was yanked open and armed men burst into view.

He recognized Boris Yelenko. The squat, broad-shouldered *mafiya* boss held a large pistol in one hand. His round face was suffused with rage, and he was screaming commands at the top of his voice. The moment he saw Bolan he yelled at his armed escorts, directing them at the American, then opened fire with his own weapon.

The Uzi in Bolan's hands barely moved. It rattled off a short burst that ravaged Yelenko's thick chest and drove him back through the door, his last words strangled off in a harsh squeal.

Bolan held his ground, an image that momentarily knocked Yelenko's shooters off guard. They had expected their intended target to back off, maybe even turn aside, and they held their fire until they knew which way he would move. When he didn't, they had to redirect their fire.

It was far too late.

Bolan's Uzi began to chatter, spitting out a volley of fire that stitched the hardmen in a zigzag pattern. Clothing and flesh was shredded. A fine, bloody mist clouded the air around the shooters as they shuddered in a grisly jig beneath the impact of Bolan's fusillade. The pair of shooters went down in a bloody heap, the brassy clink of 9 mm shell casings from Bolan's Uzi the last thing they heard.

Bolan yanked one of the incendiary grenades from his harness, pulled the pin with his teeth and tossed the canister to the far side of the hall. It skittered and rolled across the polished wood floor, coming to rest at the foot of the staircase. Bolan quickly followed it with a second, then clicked his transmit button.

"Kira?"

Her voice, breathless as she spoke on the move, came through briefly.

"I have them moving away from the house. Toward the trees."

Her words were cut off as the rattle of gunfire crackled through the radio.

The incendiary grenades detonated behind Bolan. He could smell the acrid rise of the fiercely burning chemicals as the canisters spilled their white-hot contents.

"Kira?"

He was moving toward the doors to the room Yelenko had stepped out of, and he could see movement beyond the doors. A weapon opened up, autofire chewing at the panels, splintering the expensive wood.

Bolan snatched a smoke canister from his harness and pulled the pin. He leaned toward the open doors and lobbed the canister, heard it strike the floor inside and roll. The soft thump of the igniting chemicals reached his ears. Smoke would be issuing in thick clouds from the canister, rolling across the floor in dense milky coils.

Behind him the incendiary devices were spreading fire across the hall, eating at the dry wood, devouring the layers of lacquer and varnish coating the timbers. Smoke was starting to rise, curling up into the rafters and across the ceiling.

A coughing figure raced out of the room. An expensive suit, shaved head, one hand wielding a stubby SMG. The guy was pawing at his streaming eyes, and he stumbled directly into Bolan. The Uzi swept around in a brutal arc, smashing against the man's skull, dropping him to his knees. Bolan hit him again, hard, spreading the guy flat on the floor. He kicked the dropped SMG across the hall, then turned his attention back in the direction of the doorway where thick smoke was starting to move into the hall.

More mobsters emerged from the smoke, firing as they came. Bolan moved aside, not quite fast enough, and felt the solid impact of a slug coring into his right side. He clenched his teeth against the burn of pain and pulled the Uzi back online as the advancing gunners closed on him. He got off a burst that took down one of the armed men, then felt the solid bulk of the other man strike him. The man was big, heavy, and his brute strength drove the breath from Bolan's body. He could feel blood flowing freely from the wound in his side, and the damage was enough to weaken his responses.

Other figures swam into view, hard fists pounding at his face and body. Blows landed against his wound, drawing gasps of pain from his lips. He was attacked from all sides, vicious blows rendering him semiconscious. He fought back, using everything he possessed to inflict damage on his enemies. He was driven to his knees by a savage blow to the back of his skull that turned the world dark. He felt a hand grasp his hair and yank his head back. Through misted eyes he saw a face swim into view and even in his dazed condition he recognized Valentina Suvarov.

"You have come a long way to fail," she said, and Bolan saw the ugliness behind the mask of beauty. "You and your bitch helper. I should be angry at what you have done here, but actually you have done me a favor. I was trying to decide how to get rid of that pig Yelenko. He didn't want to acknowledge me as the new head of the Suvarov organization."

"Enjoy it while you can," Bolan rasped through bloody lips. "It's going to be a short reign."

She laughed. "Still a sense of humor. We'll see how long you retain that. Let's get out of here before we all burn. Bring him and the girl. We keep them alive until I decide whether we can use them."

Bolan was dragged from the dacha, across the veranda and out into the sudden chill of the rain. His waning senses allowed him to acknowledge he was being taken around the house to the rear. He managed to raise his head and caught a glimpse of the waiting helicopter. Its rotors were starting to turn. He was bundled inside, strapped into one of the seats. His head rolled to one side and he saw Tedesko, unconscious, in another seat.

Valentina, turning from her own seat ahead of him, smiled as she said something to one of her people. Rain had plastered her thick hair to her skull, spider tendrils clinging to her finely sculptured cheeks.

"Now you can sleep. We have a long trip ahead of us, and I want you in better health when we arrive."

Bolan felt a hand grasp his arm, saw the glint of a thin needle before it was savagely stabbed into his flesh. He felt the spreading warmth invade his body, fought against it, but the glowing heat of the drug was too strong and it washed him gently into total oblivion....

"THEY WERE TAKEN away in Valentina's helicopter. That's all we know from what our informant said. The dacha was burned to the ground. Bodies were found inside, plus the six guards outside. Identification did not show Valentina or Petrovsky. So we assume they got away."

Leo Turrin sighed. "Valentine, thank you for calling. We'll follow through at this end. See what we can come up with. Damn, I hope they're still alive."

"If Valentina took them away, she had a reason. To me that suggests she will not kill them until she has what she wants."

"And what in hell is that?"

"I can think of one thing," Seminov said. "Revenge for what Cooper has done to her and the organization."

"I just knew you were going to say that."

CHAPTER TEN

Isla Blanca, Caribbean Sea

Valentina watched them filing into the room, quietly taking their places at the long table. No one spoke, either to the others or their own partners. The atmosphere was heavy with a mix of anticipation and not a little mistrust. The only one to make any acknowledgment was Oleg Kirov. The new head of the Kukor organization caught her eye and gave a knowing nod of recognition, which Valentina didn't respond to.

Kirov was flanked by Berin and Chekhov, the men who had always been at his side and who were now elevated themselves.

She gazed around the table, noting each guest, their organizations and rank.

Facing Kirov was the neat, well-dressed figure of Iguchi Katana, Yakuza boss from the Tiger Red clan. The California Yakuza clan had great influence in the West Coast area, with ties reaching across the Pacific. Katana had his own bodyguards with him, two impassive figures dressed in black, save for the scarlet Tiger Red ties. Both were skilled martial-arts masters, ruthlessly devoted to their master.

Farther along the table, at the same side as the Japanese, was a delegation from two other New York *mafiya* Families, Malekov and Solezin, each with their minders. They were minor players compared to the Suvarov and Kukor Mobs, but important in the territory they controlled.

When they were all seated, Nikolai Petrovsky moved to stand behind the empty chair at the head of the table. This was where Arkady Suvarov would have sat.

Valentina waited until all eyes were on him before she crossed to stand beside him.

"As you are all aware, my father is unable to be here, which is why this gathering has been arranged. In my father's absence I welcome you all to Isla Blanca."

Iguchi Katana turned to face her. He offered a precise bow of his head. "If Arkady Suvarov is not present, who stands in his place?"

Petrovsky rested his hands on the carved back of the empty chair.

"Gentlemen, I appreciate your curiosity, which will be satisfied in the next few moments. However, there is a matter I must clarify for you. You will all be aware, and it would be foolish of me not to raise the point, that the Suvarov organization has been subjected to a series of offensive strikes."

Kirov sat forward, his eyes bright with ill-concealed amusement.

"To be honest, Nikolai Petrovsky, you have been badly hurt. Both in the U.S. and Russia. Everyone here is aware of that. Many of your operations have been destroyed. People killed. Including Vasily Suvarov."

"We accept—"

"The Suvarov organization is on its knees," Kirov crowed. "Second now to my organization."

There was a moment of hushed surprise at Kirov's open hostility.

Petrovsky's fingers gripped the back of the chair, and only Valentina heard the sharp intake of breath.

"Oleg Kirov, you forget your manners."

"No," Valentina said, her voice surprisingly loud in the room, and every eye was fixed on her. "To forget manners, one must first have them."

Kirov rose to his feet, almost overturning his chair, his face darkening from the insult.

"Do I have to listen to this...*woman*."

"You were pleased enough to listen to me at Kukor's funeral when you thought I was succumbing to your clumsy charms."

Kirov made a halfhearted attempt at saving face. He sneered at Valentina, raising a hand to jab a thick finger at her.

"You..."

If he had been intending any further action, it was curtailed as Tibor Kureshenko stepped up quietly behind him, laying a hand on Kirov's shoulder. Kureshenko leaned forward and said something in the man's ear. After a moment Kirov sat, his hands flat on the table, still looking directly at Valentina.

"Mr. Kirov has assumed that because I'm a woman I have no right to express an opinion. He's wrong. We've moved on from his dinosaur days. This is the twenty-first century. So accept it." Valentina gazed around the table. Of them all it was only Iguchi Katana who maintained eye contact, a wisp of a smile touching his lips in anticipatory understanding. "We are *not* on our knees. Yes, there have been problems, which we are addressing. At this very moment the man who engineered the strikes against us is locked away in a cell on this very island. It would appear he is some kind of covert agent working for the American Justice Department."

"I congratulate you," Katana said. "May we then move on to resolve the matter that I know will be uppermost in all our minds."

"That being who will take control of the Suvarov organization in place of my father?"

"Of course."

"I will accede to Mr. Kirov's accusation of being a woman. But let me add that I am not just a woman. I am a *Suvarov* woman and as such, being the only surviving relative of Arkady Suvarov, *I* assume the position of head of the Family concerns."

Ignoring the whisper of sound that ran around the table, Valentina moved forward and took her place at the head of the table.

Kirov was unable to contain himself. He burst out laughing, slapping a hand on the table.

"*She* is going to be boss of the Suvarovs? This girl? *Ha,* all I can think, then, is that Arkady Suvarov isn't in a prison. He must be in a lunatic asylum to allow this to happen."

Valentina's eyes moved imperceptibly. Only Kureshenko received her glance. He leaned forward and circled his right arm around Kirov's neck, placed his left hand at the back of the man's head and applied tremendous pressure. Kirov struggled, his face contorting, his eyes wide in alarm. He threw up his hands to try to ward off the attack, but it happened so quickly that even his bodyguards, sitting beside him, were unable to do anything. That and the fact that one of Kureshenko's soldiers had a pistol aimed at them.

Valentina lowered her gaze, fixing it on Kirov as the realization dawned on him that he wasn't going to survive. Her expression didn't waver as she watched him die, his face darkening, his tongue protruding thickly between his lips.

Across the table Iguchi Katana was observing Valentina. His face was devoid of any expression as he saw the intensity in her eyes, the almost clinical way she studied Kirov's death. Here, he thought, was a woman with inner strength. A woman capable of anything. One who deserved respect.

Kirov's final moments were played out in a near silent pantomime of terror. His body wrenched and twisted, trying to break himself free, yet all his struggles achieved was to hasten his demise. Kureshenko's grip was unrelenting. No one around the table moved or spoke. They were absorbed watching Kirov's death. Every one of them had been involved in violence of one sort or another throughout their criminal lives. It was a tool of their trade, whether done close up, or from a distance, so they were far from squeamish. In this instance there was a certain pleasure to be derived from the man's death. He had never been a popular man when he had been Vash Kukor's second in command. Since he had moved to the number-one spot, his manner had become distinctly untenable. He was an arrogant man, flaunting his new position with open crudity. He wouldn't be missed.

Kureshenko released his grip and Kirov slumped back in his chair. The Suvarov enforcer motioned and two of his people moved in quickly to remove the body from the room.

Waiting until the door closed behind them, Valentina turned back to face the meeting.

"I detest boorish behavior."

Iguchi Katana rose to his feet and faced her. "May I be the first to congratulate Miss Suvarov on her accession to head of the organization."

"Thank you, Master Katana. I hope today will mark a new opening in the history of both of our groups."

There was a flurry of acquiescence as the others around the table added their congratulations.

"I would be interested in seeing this man you have locked up," Katana said as he resumed his seat. "He intrigues me."

"It will be my pleasure to introduce you, Master Katana.' Valentina considered her next words. "This man has a partner. A young woman of exceptional character. I believe you might also be interested in her. For your own amusement, shall we say." She saw the flicker of interest. She leaned in close, her words only for him. "I understand you are a connoisseur of a certain type of female. If this woman pleases you, I will present her as a token of my respect."

Katana inclined his head. "Thank you," he said softly.

Valentina turned her attention to the gathering.

"Now, gentlemen, down to business. Tibor will distribute an agenda we can discuss. I hope you find my proposals interesting. If we can agree on them, I envisage us all making a great deal of money and strengthening our combined power and influence."

"THREE DAYS, Cooper. When are we getting out of here?"

"Doesn't the accommodation suit? Or is it the company?"

"Cooper, you don't smell all that fresh any longer."

"And they keep telling me romance isn't dead."

Bolan climbed to his feet and crossed the stone floor of the underground cell to the barred opening in the outer wall. Below the window was a sheer rocky fall of about 150 feet that ended where the waves of the Caribbean crashed against the base of the cliff.

He leaned against the rough stone and pressed skin against the cool metal grille. His face was still sore from the treatment he had received back at the Suvarov dacha. The only good to follow that was the later realization that someone had dug the bullet out of his side during one of the long spells of unconsciousness that had followed. The wound was still sore, the flesh tender, but at least he could move around.

Bolan and Tedesko had finally awakened from the drug-induced sleep to find themselves locked away in the dismal, fetid cell. It had taken time for the full effects of the drug to wear off. Though alone for a great deal of that time, Bolan and Tedesko had been visited on a few occasions.

Not surprisingly one of their visitors was Valentina Suvarov. Dressed in a cool white cotton pantsuit, she had given the appearance of having stepped off the cover of a glossy lifestyle magazine. The only glaring note had been the armed guards who accompanied her on her visits.

"Welcome to Isla Blanca," she had said. "Sorry I had to put you down here. All the guest rooms are taken."

Bolan, squatting at the base of the wall, had raised his head and looked her over.

"Your price would be too high. And my money isn't dirty enough."

For a moment her well-groomed look was shadowed by the bleak, violent expression in her eyes.

"Make fun while you can. When I am ready I'll make you pay. For everything."

"Even getting Vasily off your back?" he asked. "No bonus points for that?"

A flick of her hand and Bolan had received a stunning kick to his ribs that drove him to the floor. The armed guard drew back, then lashed out again, catching Bolan across the side of the face.

"Consider that a form of thanks."

Tedesko had knelt beside Bolan, cupping her hand over his bleeding cheek.

"Just what was the point bringing us here?" she asked.

Valentina glanced at her. "Don't you remember

what I promised you in Kansas? That you would earn me a great deal of money? In a slightly different way, you will still do that. I have a new plan for you."

She turned to go, then looked down at Bolan. "Nothing else to say, Cooper?"

"I save my words for the living."

She remained staring at him, the superior expression in her eyes flickering with uncertainty for a moment. Then she regained her composure and walked out of the cell. The door had slammed shut behind her, bolts snapped into place.

"Now I know I don't like her," Tedesko said.

"Took you long enough to decide."

"I don't make snap decisions."

"You liked me right from the start."

"Oh, you think so?"

"THEY WON'T BE HAPPY until we're dead."

Bolan turned from the barred opening. "Are you trying to say something?"

She stared at him, shaking her head.

"Cooper, I'm being serious."

"I know. Just because they want it doesn't mean it's bound to happen."

"Oh, Lord, stop being enigmatic."

"Kira, they want to kill us—we don't let them. Simple enough?"

"Easily said."

"I didn't say it was going to be easy."

Tedesko crossed the cell, standing close to him. Without warning she reached out to hold him and kissed him hard and long. When it was over she stepped back, breathing fast.

"Now, that was easy. The hard part was stopping. Starting something with these people is the easy part. Stopping it won't be so simple. It will go on. They'll come at you with everything they have. Men and weapons. And on this island there's no backup. No place to run."

"That's what I'm counting on," Bolan told her.

"Damn it, Cooper, I meant for *you*."

Bolan actually smiled and it looked strange coming from someone with a bruised, battered and bloody face. It countenanced an almost brutal expression.

"No, Kira, I was thinking of *them*."

She heard his words, saw the look in his ice-blue eyes, and offered a brief and silent prayer in thanks for being on his side.

BOLAN WAS ABOUT to move from the opening when he felt the stronger motion of the breeze. He turned to stare farther out across the blue expanse of water and saw shadows dancing over the surface. Raising his eyes, he saw low, dark clouds gathering, moving in toward Isla Blanca. He could feel the sudden rise of the wind against his face, then the chill slap of rain.

"A storm on its way. Could be our chance if we can get out of this cell."

She joined him and studied the clouds. "Big storm?"

"The way it's shaping up, I'd say yes."

"So, how do we do it? Get out of here, I mean."

"If it happens, it'll go hard from the get-go. We get one chance. No debates. No compromises. Us, or them."

"Understood."

"Kira, be certain you do understand. Hold back for a second and you're dead. It's that simple."

"Okay, Cooper, if you wanted to scare me, you did."

"Kira Tedesko, you are some lady."

"I bet you tell that to all the girls."

"Only the ones who earn it."

She glanced over her shoulder at the sound of someone outside the cell door.

"Room service," she said.

"If we get the chance, follow my lead," Bolan stated.

He faced the door, in a submissive stance, and watched as the door was pushed open to allow the armed Russian to enter, followed by the his partner who carried a tray holding bowls of hot soup and mugs of water.

"No spoons again?" Bolan asked, staring at the tray.

The armed guard shrugged. "We don't want you hurting yourselves. The boss wants to do that to you herself."

"By the way," Tedesko asked, "how is the bitch queen today? Still ordering you *men* around?"

The taunt stung and the guy with the AK turned an angry face in her direction.

"Maybe we will have to..."

Bolan lunged forward, fast, and as he moved by the guy holding the tray, he used his left hand to push it into the man's face. The hot soup splashed his face, drawing an agonized yell from his lips. The guard pawed at the slick layer stinging his flesh. Bolan had continued his forward motion, closing on the guard with the AK and striking him full-on before the guy was able to turn away from Tedesko. The force of Bolan's contact drove the guy against the wall, drawing a stunned gasp from him.

As the guard turned to retaliate, Bolan slammed the palm of his hand under the man's chin. The impact closed the guard's mouth with a snap and smacked the back of his skull against the stone wall. Following up, the Executioner drove his right knee into the guard's groin. The guard grunted, sagging a degree and Bolan used the moment to close both hands around the Kalashnikov. He wrenched it from the guard's grip, snapping the finger that was curled around the trigger.

Swiveling on his feet, Bolan brought the AK on track, the muzzle settling on the figure of the tray carrier as the man, still wiping soup from his eyes, used his free hand to yank out the pistol tucked in his belt. Bolan didn't give him any leeway. He triggered the AK, hitting the guy with a short burst of 7.62 mm slugs. The impact drove the man to his knees and he caught Bolan's second burst through the back of his skull, pitching facedown on the stone flags. Without pause the Executioner took two steps forward, turned and fired another burst that put the first guard down.

"Kira, get the handgun and see if he's got a spare mag."

Bolan frisked the AK owner. There was no spare ammo.

"Let's go," he snapped harshly because Tedesko was staring at him, the pistol in one hand, an extra magazine in the other. "Move!"

He grabbed her shoulder and shoved her hard at the door.

The crude passage stretched ahead of them, lit only by a few bare bulbs.

"You think anyone heard the shooting?"

"We'll soon find out."

Someone called out from the top of the steps that led up from cellar. The Russian's voice was concerned.

Bolan called out in reply. His Russian was passable and in this instance it brought the other man down the steps. He didn't see the American until it was too late. The Executioner's AK crackled briefly, the hits toppling the *mafiya* hardman to the foot of the steps, his weapon spilling from his hands.

"Get his rifle," Bolan said.

Tedesko did as she was told. She jammed the pistol in one of the blacksuit's pockets, pausing to check the Kalashnikov. Bending over the dead man, she located a spare magazine for the AK and tossed it to Bolan. He dropped it into one of the blacksuit pockets.

"Let's move, Kira, I don't want to get cornered down here."

He moved up the steps, the AK tracking ahead. He reached the top without any more interference.

If there were any hostile guns waiting, they'd be well back from the steps, using whatever cover they could find.

Bolan stepped to one side, pressing himself against the wall, peering around the edge to take in the area ahead.

He could make out a wide, expansive, covered building; silent, rusting machinery; overhead gantries; the sweet smell of decay. He was looking at some kind of processing plant, a building that had been here on the island long before the Suvarovs purchased it and turned it into their private retreat. On the main island of Puerto Rico one of the main products was sugarcane. There was a whole industry geared toward the processing of the product. Perhaps Isla Blanca had been part of that enterprise.

Some twenty feet away a large opening showed a wooden loading platform. Beyond he could see an exposed area fringed by trees and thick undergrowth. He could also see the storm had hit the island fully. Torrential rain was slanting in across the open ground, bouncing off the glistening planks of the loading platform.

"Anything?" Tedesko asked, crowding the steps behind him.

Bolan shook his head.

"Somebody had to have heard the shots, Cooper."

"Maybe not. We don't know how far we are from the main house. And the storm just hit pretty hard. It could have blocked the noise."

"So why are we sitting here waiting for someone to come?"

"Because there might be additional guns we can't see."

Tedesko muttered something to herself.

"Say what?"

"I said we could grow old and die on these steps."

A smile ghosted Bolan's lips.

"Okay. First thing is to get out of this place. Off to the right there's a big door that seems to lead onto a loading platform. That's where we'll head, okay?"

She took a quick look, nodding, then checked her weapon again.

"Trust me?" Bolan asked.

"Yes."

"I'll cover you. Head for the door and make yourself a hard target. Stay focused. Remember there might be others outside."

She ran her hand through her tangle of dark hair. "I enjoyed our stay down there. Not the best accommodation, but the company was entertaining."

"Kira, shut up and go."

She eased by him and located the door opening. Two quick breaths and she was moving, her long legs carrying her across the open expanse of concrete.

Off to Bolan's left a gunner emerged from behind the cover of machinery, raising an assault rifle. Bolan leaned out, his own Kalashnikov tracking the would-be shooter. He held his aim, squeezed the trigger and saw the single 7.62 mm slug hit dead center in the target's chest. The guy went down with a solid thump. A second shooter opened up, sending a burst of autofire in Bolan's direction, the slugs chipping at the edge of the concrete wall. The Executioner pulled back briefly, not fast enough to avoid the side of his face catching the bite of concrete fragments. As the shooting ceased for a second, he emerged from cover, turning his attention to the spot where the shots had come from. He spotted the shooter, his weapon moving as he sought his target.

The moment he was clear of the steps Bolan ducked low, moving to the additional cover of machinery a few feet away. He caught the crackle of shots and heard the whine and clang as the volley impacted against metal. Down on his stomach, peering through the support struts, Bolan made out the figure moving himself, turning his attention to

Tedesko. She was close to the door opening, zig-zagging as she ran.

The shooter swung his rifle in her direction.

Bolan pushed to his feet, leaning over the top of the machine, and triggered the AK, pulling the trigger with deliberate intent. His first shot cored into the target's right shoulder, blowing out the rear and spinning the shooter off balance. His weapon discharged, the short burst losing itself in the rafters. Dust sifted down from the shadowed metalwork. Bolan triggered another volley, this time aiming at his adversary's torso. He saw the impact. The shooter dropped hard.

Bolan glanced in Tedesko's direction and saw her race through the door and out onto the loading platform. He followed, sprinting in the direction of the door.

She had come to a stop at the edge of the platform, weapon up and ready, turning as something caught her attention.

An armed hardman stepped out from the outer wall, pistol in his hand.

"Kira."

In the long moment that followed he saw Tedesko step back, her own weapon firing as she faced the armed man. Her shots went wild. The pistol returned fire and the woman gave a startled yell, losing her balance and vanishing over the edge of the platform.

Bolan had no time to fire. He was on the shooter. He struck the man head-on, the momentum taking them both across the loading platform and over the edge, following in Tedesko's wake.

They dropped to the sodden ground below, the abrupt landing jarring weapons from their grip, each trying to gain the upper hand. They swung wild, unrepentant blows at the other, some landing, others sliding by without doing any damage. They fought with deadly intent, knowing the end of this struggle was going to mean death for one of them. Flesh tore, blood flowed, neither man giving an inch as he tried for supremacy over the other. They breathed hard, sucking in the precious oxygen that fueled their rage. The *mafiya* soldier struck the first solid blow, raking a bony-knuckled fist across Bolan's jaw. The Executioner jerked his head back as the fist landed. The pain only added to his own anger and he struck back, hammering his fist down onto the Russian's face. Bone snapped. The guy's nose blossomed like a red flower, blood streaming in bright runnels. He gasped at the sudden pain, arching his body and throwing a wild backhand that clouted Bolan across the side of his head.

The American leaned away from his opponent's fists, driving a hard knee into the other's exposed groin. This time the guy howled in agony, his body trying to double up against the pain. Despite his hurt he saw an opening and swung a booted foot that struck Bolan in the side, toppling him away. The Russian struggled to gain his feet, slipping awkwardly on the wet ground, desperately attempting to get a grip on his pistol where it lay a few feet away.

Bolan didn't allow him any leeway. Recovering from the kick, he rose to his feet, taking a single step forward and launching a powerhouse punch that came from deep inside his very being. It connected with the Russian's jaw, snapping his head back, mouth open wide, blood spraying in a crimson flood. He was slammed back against the wall of the loading dock, the breath driven from his body by the impact. He fell to his knees. Bolan followed through, lunging at the man, his right knee smashing hard into the guy's chest. His hand palmed itself across the Russian's bloody face and he drove his head into the wall with every ounce of strength remaining. This time the Russian made no sound as his skull was crushed against the unyielding concrete. His features went slack and he slipped to the base of the wall, first on his side, then over onto his face. Faint air bubbles erupted from the soft mud that engulfed his features. The pouring rain washed away the glistening blood oozing from his shattered skull.

Bolan leaned against the wall, supporting himself as he sucked air into his lungs, turning his bloody, battered face to the skies and the tumbling rain. He remained there for a brief time, aware that time wasn't on his side. Reaching down, he picked up his Kalashnikov.

He turned, looking for Tedesko, and spotted her a few feet away, hunched against the concrete wall, her left hand pressed to her upper right arm. Blood was spilling from between her fingers.

"That hurt," she said.

"We need to get you under cover somewhere."

"Cooper, they are not going to sit and wait until my arm gets better. Get the hell out of here and do what you need to. I have the pistol and rifle."

He knew she was right. The alert could be raised at any moment, and once it was, all considerations went out the window. He had to make his strike now. Fast. Before he lost any advantage.

"Go, Cooper." Rain was streaming down her pale face. "I'll be fine."

Bolan turned then, not saying another word. He picked up the pistol the dead Russian had been carrying and went through the man's pockets, locating a spare clip. He also found a compact transceiver clipped to his belt, the transmit button open. Not good news, he thought.

He pushed to his feet and saw Tedesko watching him. He showed her the transceiver.

"Ouch," was all she said.

He tossed the item into her lap. "Listen out for me. If I find a way, I'll contact you."

She glanced down to pick it up, clicking off the transmit button. When she looked up again Bolan had already left.

CHAPTER ELEVEN

Valentina shook her head in disbelief at the news. She stared at Nikolai Petrovsky, and it was as if she was unable to take it in for a moment.

"They got out?"

He nodded. "No details yet, but they did. We got a brief message from Tupov, then he seemed to get into some kind of struggle. I heard shots before that. Now we can't pick him up at all."

They were alone in the room that served as Valentina's office. The meeting had broken up so everyone could absorb and discuss her proposals over drinks and food. Valentina felt she needed something strong herself as she crossed to the small wet bar and poured herself a large tumbler full of whiskey.

"And before you say anything, Nikolai, I damn well need this."

He didn't say a word, but the look in his eyes annoyed Valentina even more.

"Am I drinking too much these days? Is that what you mean to say?"

"That is none of my business."

"No, it isn't and yes I am. It helps me, Nikolai." She frowned at him. "Did Dad drink a lot?"

"Sometimes when he was—"

"Under stress? You see, I am like him."

"Shouldn't we discuss this at a less problematic time?"

She waved her tumbler at him. "Of course. Is Tibor managing this matter?"

"He has every spare man on it. They're moving out now. We'll find Cooper and the woman."

"Nikolai, this island is eleven miles long by seven wide. Apart from where we are, it's wild terrain. Trees, undergrowth, ravines. That makes a big difference when you are looking for one man and woman. And don't forget who we are dealing with. Don't underestimate this man. He's good. And I *should* have killed him back in Russia when I had the chance."

"No point worrying about that now."

The distant crackle of gunfire reached them,

cutting through the rising wind and the hammer of the rain on the windows.

"I get the distinct feeling he's coming this way," Valentina said, "looking for us."

She drained the whiskey and placed the tumbler on the desk. Moving around it, she opened a drawer and took out a compact SIG-Sauer P-228 pistol. She freed the magazine, checked the loads and returned it. Petrovsky watched her cock the weapon. Her face was flushed, her eyes bright, but he couldn't tell whether from the drink or the current situation. Either way, he was starting to become concerned.

"Perhaps we should leave," he suggested, immediately regretting his lame remark.

"Nikolai, are you nervous?"

"I've felt better. How do we explain this to our guests? First we tell them there's nothing to be concerned about, that we have our recent problems under control. Now we have the cause of those problems running loose on the island. Not exactly the best way to inspire confidence in the Suvarov name."

"So let's deal with it, Nikolai. Not stand around twittering like a bunch of old ladies."

Valentina pushed past him, making for the door. She left Petrovsky alone and deflated. He realized she was under stress because she never spoke to him in such a way. As he turned from the desk, he saw the empty tumbler. That was part of her problem, he decided. She was taking to the whiskey too well and too often.

A sudden rise in the force of the storm threw heavy rain against the window. He crossed to stare through the glass. The rain was sweeping in from the sea, laying a gray mist over the island, bending the fringe of trees.

Despite Valentina's response, Petrovsky still felt it would have been advisable to get off the island and leave the capture of Cooper and the woman to the team under the command of Tibor Kureshenko.

VALENTINA HAD REJOINED the rest of the gathering, explaining what had happened. She crossed to speak with Katana.

"My sources tell me you are a man who enjoys a challenge," Valentina said.

Katana simply inclined his head. Of them all, the L.A. Yakuza boss had exhibited little agitation at the news of Bolan's escape. Whatever his personal thoughts, the Japanese kept them to himself. Now he simply topped up his coffee cup, taking his time before venturing a response.

"I hope you are not about to tell me you arranged this for my amusement."

"That would be an insult to both of us, Master Katana. My fervent wish right now is to accomplish the death of this man Cooper."

"Better to capture and recruit him. A man of his obvious skill would be an asset."

"Somehow I fail to see that as an option. He has proved himself resourceful, I agree, but he is, sad to say, on the *other* side."

"A pity." Katana indicated his own bodyguards. "I myself have no illusions. These men are mine alone. They are bound to me by a code of loyalty that transcends money or deceit. If I asked either of them right now to sacrifice himself, it would be done without hesitation."

"I envy you that degree of devotion. It only serves to show the great divide between our two cultures. Such absolute loyalty would be hard to find within the ranks of my own people. The only one who would come close is Kureshenko."

"Yet this man—Cooper—exhibits strong convictions. He persists where others might have given up long ago. He is single-minded. He does not veer from his path, nor does he allow himself the luxury of a momentary lapse. Do you know anything of his background?"

"Only that he appears to have some tenuous connection to the Justice Department. Little else has been forthcoming."

Katana spoke to his bodyguards. Valentina was unable to understand his rapid Japanese. He finally appeared satisfied.

"*Hai.*" He turned back to Valentina. "There was an American a few years ago who waged his own war against the American Mafia. He did great damage to them. Destroyed their enterprises and killed many of their people."

"The point being?"

"That he waged a war of attrition against the Mafia. He struck here. There. Took down pieces at a time. Caused confusion and unrest within the Mafia hierarchy. I am struck at the similarity between this Bolan and your man Cooper."

"That he might be the same man?"

"A thought."

"Personally, I don't give damn what his name is. Just as long as we can take him down."

"Knowing your enemy and the way he thinks can aid in combating him."

"I understand your philosophy, Master Katana. I just want an end to this so we can continue our agenda." Valentina glanced around the room.

"Gentlemen, I think we should all get out there and put ourselves at Tibor's disposal. The sooner we deal with this man, the better."

BOLAN HEADED for the high ground. Behind the derelict plant the landscape merged into heavy undergrowth and trees, with the terrain rising in a series of hills forming as ragged line that ran east to west. Gaining a high elevation would allow him to scope the area and give him direction.

The strong wind and torrential rain made it hard going. He worried less about that than he did the opposing force. Since arriving on the island, Bolan and Tedesko had been held in virtual isolation and it had been a calculated guess on his part that they had been transported to the Suvarov island. Once Bolan had been able to view the exterior, through the barred window in the cell, it had become apparent they were far from Russia. The blue swell of the ocean beyond the island and the climate had confirmed Bolan's suspicions they were on Isla Blanca. Now he was out of the confines of the cell and able to study the plant and tree life, Bolan knew they were on the island, that according to Turrin's data, lay some thirty miles off Puerto Rico. Which might as well have been thirty thousand under the present circumstances. Bolan didn't dwell on that fact. He was, as usual, fighting this war on his own terms now. And that meant single-handed, utilizing whatever he could obtained from the enemy. In this instance, taking their weapons and using them on their former owners.

He pushed through the dripping foliage, ignoring the discomfort. His blacksuit was soaked through, his battered body aching, but the burning resolve fueling his trek only increased as the way became harder.

The low foothills gave way to steeper slopes. Bolan pushed on, concentrating on his climb but not letting his guard slip because he knew damn well that the Suvarov crew would be out looking for him and Tedesko.

His thoughts returned to the young woman. He hoped she had managed to find somewhere safe to hide. Having seen her in action and the way she handled herself, he figured she wasn't the kind of person to simply sit back and let things overtake her. She was a fighter, and if the Suvarov soldiers came up against her they would know it.

He paused after a half hour, leaning against the trunk of a tree and peering back down through the driving rain. To his left he could see the outline of the plant, standing at the extreme edge of the island. Making a slow sweep, he tracked right and picked up distant movement. A number of vehicles were roaming back and forth across the uneven terrain. From his position Bolan made out the squat shape of the civilian version of the military Hummer, certainly the right kind of vehicle for the island's rugged landscape. He extended his range of vision and stopped when he finally saw what he was looking for.

The main house.

It was a sprawling mansion, two-storied, painted white with a dark red slate roof. A number of smaller outbuildings lay behind the house. At the rear there was also a concrete circle, painted with red stripes—a helicopter pad, with a medium-size chopper resting on the pad.

Bolan saw figures moving around the house. Some of the enemy was staying close to base.

He panned out from the house, picking up the small natural harbor that lay just below. A large oceangoing motor vessel rode at anchor out in the harbor.

The constant drum of the rain on the foliage almost deadened the sound of someone approaching. Bolan had filtered out the sound of the storm, his keen hearing listening for anything apart from the natural sounds. As it was, he almost missed the conversation between people approaching his position. Bolan immediately sank to the ground and eased into the overhanging greenery. He laid the AK on the grass beside him and took out the handgun. It was a solid SIG-Sauer P-226. He had checked the magazine earlier. The weapon was cocked and ready.

He saw their booted feet first, tramping through the wet grass, the soaked legs of their pants brushing aside the dense foliage. Both men were armed with Kalashnikovs and carried pistols in holsters on their hips. They wore thick waterproof coats and long-billed baseball caps. Bolan didn't fail to notice the transceivers clipped to their coats. They were in deep conversation as they walked past his place of concealment, scanning their surroundings.

He waited until they had moved on by, rising to his feet, a black-clad figure streaming water, his battered features set as the P-226 tracked on and chose its first target.

"SHOTS," the voice said through Kureshenko's handset.

"Where?"

"North. High ground."

"Get up there, check it out. Who's up that way?"

"Karl and Roskov."

Kureshenko gestured for his driver to stop the Hummer. He raised his transceiver and put out a call for the two men. There was no response. The handsets were dead.

It had to be Cooper. He would go high first to locate his position and check out the lay of the land. The man was no beginner. He knew his way around a battlefield. Kureshenko didn't fool himself. Battlefield was exactly the name for where they were right now. The American had extended his war against the Suvarovs organization to cover the island. They had brought him here, and he had made it his new war zone.

"Let's check the plant to see if the woman's still there," he instructed his driver. He was about to call the rest of his crew but stopped short of switching his handset to transmit. If Cooper had taken out Karl and Roskov, which he most likely had, then he would have their transceivers. He'd be able to listen in to any conversations. If Kureshenko ordered his men back to the house, he would simply be warning Cooper. They would have to protect themselves if they went after the American.

THE FIRST OF the searchers found the missing hardmen. They were both dead from shots to the head. Although their AKs lay beside the bodies, they were missing their magazines, and when the bodies were checked, the spare magazines were also gone, as was the extra ammunition for the handguns they had carried. Only one transceiver was located.

"Damn," one of the men said. He clicked his handset to transmit and send out the message. "Karl and Roskov are dead. The bastard took their spare ammunition and one of the transceivers."

He got no response, but he knew his message would have reached the ears of the other searchers.

It also told Kira Tedesko exactly what Bolan was doing. And decided her own next move.

VALENTINA SUVAROV leaned her face against the cool glass of the window, watching the rain streaming across the pane, the heavy pistol hanging loosely at her side, whiskey glass in her right hand. Her thoughts were tumbling over themselves as she tried to make sense of what was happening. How could it all have started to fall apart so quickly? It seemed such a short time ago she was in full control, her ambitions driving her forward, command of the Suvarov organization in her grip and her plans for the future rising in front of her. Now there was dark shadow threatening to destroy it all, a shadow wielding a destructive power that was cutting into the structure of the organization and breaking it apart piece by piece.

Cooper.

That damned man. Waging his war against her and tearing apart the Suvarov empire. His relentless dedication frightened and excited her. Despite her hatred of him, she had to admit that his way was effective. He obviously had good intelligence because he knew exactly where to go and what to take out.

The woman stepped back from the window, staring at the rippled reflections in the glass, and for a moment she could see faces. Her father, his eyes deep-set and reproachful. Then Vasily, a crooked smile on his face that said, "I knew you'd screw it up." She drained her glass, shuddering as the strong liquor coursed down her throat and settled in her stomach. For once it failed to console her. It left a sour aftertaste in her mouth.

She jerked herself back to awareness, realizing she was allowing current events to erode her resolve.

No way was she going to let this man ruin everything. She was a Suvarov, not a pitiful, weak woman. This had to be settled today, here, now, on this island. Her island. She wasn't going to capitulate and let one man defeat her.

She had her men out looking for him. The other *mafiya* guests, as well. Katana and his bodyguards were at the rear of the house. They would get him.

They had to get him this time.

She spun, hurling the glass across the room. It hit the far wall and bounced off, falling to the floor where it rolled across the carpet.

Valentina watched it come to rest, a lopsided grin curling her lips. You and me both, she told herself. We don't break so easily.

IT WAS TIME to keep the momentum, to gain as much advantage as he could before the enemy had time to gather itself and work out just where he was.

Bolan, well armed now with the extra ammunition, cut his way along the ridgeback hills, moving in toward the house. When he had looked out beyond the island, he saw that the storm front was still strong. The wind and rain showed no sign of abating, and that was in his favor. Adverse weather inhibited his adversaries, especially the Suvarov crew. They were city mobsters more suited to urban surroundings, not the rugged terrain the island presented, and that made them easier targets. Not that he dismissed them completely. Bolan wasn't into diminishing any enemy capacity for fighting back. That was arrogant and led to mistakes. He hadn't survived for so long by treating his enemies with contempt. He simply judged them against his own skills. Mack Bolan had fought in many different locations, including jungle battlegrounds. He was as at home out here as he might be within a building complex or a trash-strewed back alley. The current weather conditions did little to hamper him and he used the terrain and the natural foliage for cover and concealment.

He paused briefly, crouching in cover, to look down on the house. He had traversed the hill ridges, bringing him to close proximity to his intended kill zone, and he was more than ready to take on whatever Valentina Suvarov threw at him.

He heard a yell as someone raised the alarm.

Bolan followed the sound and saw armed hardmen moving to cut him off. He had expected there would be a concentration of defenders surrounding the house, and he was well prepared.

He let them get within range. The advance team had already opened fire, slugs chunking the sodden hillside well short of Bolan. The Suvarov gunners were firing on the move, weapons on full-auto. Pushing up on one knee, Bolan leveled the AK, butt to his shoulder, and began to jack out single shots, placing each one with well-targeted accuracy.

The lead hardman went down with a grunt, a 7.62 mm slug lodged deep in his chest. His body had barely hit the ground before Bolan triggered more shots, placing high-impact projectiles into exposed bodies. He put three more down before the remaining pair scattered, desperately seeking cover.

Bolan allowed them no quarter. They had shown themselves willing to take him down without any consideration, and in his eyes that made them fair game.

He strode across the hill slope, past the bloody corpses of those who had already tried to take him down. He turned and caught one of the survivors as the guy let fly from his position some yards down the slope. Bolan's short burst hit the soldier in the chest and throat, kicking him back and sending him spinning down the hill, arms and legs flailing as he gained momentum, finally coming to a dead stop at the base of the slope.

"Hey, I quit," the remaining hardman yelled, stepping into view. "I'm out of it."

Bolan dropped him with a shot to the head that laid the man flat on his back, his blood streaking the wet grass.

"Now you're out of it," Bolan said.

He took a moment to reload the AK before he

started on down the slope, cutting across to a thin stand of windswept trees. From this vantage point the Executioner studied the rear of the house, seeing the scattered and armed hardmen staring up the slope. He checked out the helicopter pad and the chopper resting there, and a slight smile edged his lips.

He used a jutting branch to steady the rifle and zeroed in on the aircraft. It was an American-built Sikorsky S-76, built for civilian use, and could carry up to fourteen passengers. This one was white with a red-and-black stripe along the fuselage. Bolan sighted in on the pilot canopy and began to fire, laying his shots farther back each time. He hit the engine compartment, then the fuel tanks, pumping in the remainder of the magazine. His shots caught the attention of the armed men below and they began to fire back, but they had to fire up the angle of the slope, into the sweep of rain, and Bolan was a much smaller target than the chopper. He simply pulled back and reloaded, then took up his stance again, blowing the tires on the landing gear, then concentrating on the tail rotor. On the far side of the landing area stood a wheeled fuel tank. The Executioner shifted his aim and laid half a magazine into the aluminum tank until aviation fuel began to spill out.

He shifted his aim to the steel framework supporting the tank, his shots clanging off the metal, and after a number of well-placed slugs he achieved his goal. One of the ricocheting bullets created a few sparks, which were enough to ignite the rising fuel vapor. There was a soft *whoosh* as the flames took hold, expanding with frightening speed across the concrete pad, following the flow of the released fuel. It seemed to pause for a moment, and then the area was engulfed by the violent flare as flame boiled across the pad, merging with the spill from the chopper's ruptured tanks.

Bolan saw men spreading out, racing for the base of the slope, heading his way. He watched them for a few seconds, attempting to gain the slope while keeping a watchful eye out for the hidden marksman. It was an impossible task. Clicking in a fresh magazine, he selected full-auto fire and began to lay down short bursts into the advancing hardmen. They took a number of hits before the remainder retreated, falling back in the direction of the house.

The burning helicopter and fuel tank blew within seconds of each other, throwing fiery debris in all direction, accompanied by a massive fireball that caught a couple of the scattering gunners before they could avoid it. Men became running torches, screaming out their lives before the superheated flames burned their vocal cords and seared their lungs. They tumbled to the wet earth, kicking out their final moments in silent agony.

Bolan watched the fireball as it began to shrink, the wind and rain reducing it to a twisting cloud of heavy smoke that drifted across the foot of the slope, cutting off his view of the house. It also hid him from the hardmen below, and he took the opportunity to clear his position and get to level ground, half upright, half sliding down the sodden slope.

"THERE," Kureshenko's driver said.

He had rolled the Hummer to a stop just yards from the loading platform.

On the ground at the base of the wall lay the hardman Bolan had killed. A few feet to one side, the body of a woman lay on its side.

Kureshenko eased himself out of the vehicle, his assault rifle in his left hand. He checked out the area, ignoring the heavy rain lashing at him. His driver climbed out and crossed to stand beside him.

"Now we know he's on his own, boss."

Kureshenko only grunted. He was still checking the area.

"Go and see if she's dead."

The driver walked over and crouched beside the motionless form, eyeing the curves beneath the sodden clothing. He saw the bullet tear in the right arm.

"She took a bullet," he called over his shoulder.

"Is she *dead?*"

The driver reached out to roll the woman onto her back. As he did, her left hand came into view, clutching the pistol she had acquired.

"Dead? Not hardly," she muttered, and thrust the muzzle against the driver's chest. She pulled the trigger three times, sending the 9 mm slugs coring in through tissue and bone into the man's heart. He gave a stunned gasp as the slugs blew out between his shoulders.

TEDESKO HAULED HERSELF into a sitting position as the dead man fell away from her, her pistol tracking in on Tibor Kureshenko as the Suvarov hardman turned toward her. He was already bringing his Kalashnikov online when she fired again, and kept firing. Her first shot caught him in the left shoulder, shattering the bone and chunking out a wedge of bloody muscle. Kureshenko kept moving, trying to bring the AK on track. Kira's 9 mm slugs kept jacking out, each one a hit, punching holes in his chest.

KURESHENKO STUMBLED back, hit the side of the Hummer and hung there, coughing blood and trying to rationalize the fact that he had been duped by a woman. No, a mere slip of a girl, and he was still coming to terms with the fact when she put her last shot into his skull, turning him off to one side and pitching him facedown in the mud.

TEDESKO CROSSED to the Hummer, slipping a fresh clip into the pistol. She picked up the AK the Russian had dropped and threw it on the passenger seat as she climbed in. She sat for a few moments as a wave of nausea swept over her. She could feel blood running down her arm from the open wound.

"Dead? Not hardly," she repeated, starting the engine so she could turn the Hummer around and head back the way it had come.

BOLAN LANDED HARD at the base of the slope. He was aching from the hard descent. His blacksuit was ripped and bloody from the scrapes and tears he had sustained on his way down.

Thick smoke from the burning chopper and fuel tank obscured his view of the house. There were a number of bodies on the ground close by. A couple were charred and blackened from being caught in the fireball. Others showed gaping wounds, the result of Bolan's long-distance shooting.

He pushed to his feet, clicked in a fresh magazine, cocked the AK and cut off through the smoke. He knew the house was on the far side, some distance from the pad. He took a breath before he hit the smoke, not wanting to suck in any of the harsh fumes. There was still a strong swell of heat coming from the burning mass of the chopper. He made a wide sweep and began to emerge from the fog with the hazy outline of the house ahead and to his right.

Bolan caught sight of armed hardmen moving in his general direction. They hadn't spotted him yet and he had no intention of allowing them any kind of warning. He knew he was well in range and leveled the AK, catching the first pair as they sprinted forward, hunched over against the heavy rainfall. The Executioner triggered the assault rifle, the bursts putting down the gunners hard, bouncing their ravaged bodies off the sodden ground. The moment he fired, Bolan turned aside, changing his direction and emerging from the smoke to the rear of hardmen still staring at their downed colleagues. He hit these with the same ferocity, slugs chewing at flesh and bone, putting the Suvarov men into the dirt in a spray of bloody debris.

The house lay twenty feet ahead.

A door crashed open and Bolan saw two men rush out, moving in his direction. They were Japanese, in dark suits and shirts, scarlet ties. Tiger Red Yakuza. One of them pulled a large handgun from beneath his coat and opened fire. Bolan felt slugs burn the air. He dropped to one knee, diminishing his body shape, and shouldered the AK. He risked precious seconds before he fired and saw his burst strike the shooter in the chest. The Japanese stumbled to his knees. His shirt and coat blossomed red as he toppled over onto his back, legs kicking in reflex.

The second Japanese altered his approach, crouching and coming at Bolan in a zigzag run. He was surprisingly swift for someone of his considerable bulk.

Bolan swept the AK in the man's direction, stroking the trigger. The AK's pin hit a dead cartridge. Bolan made no attempt to clear the jam. He had no time. The big Yakuza hardman was on him. His right hand swept around, the cold steel of a Tanto knife flashing as it cut in at Bolan. He hauled himself back, losing his balance, felt the sharp burn as the razor blade sliced across his side.

He hit the ground, his mind overriding the pain from the knife slash as he fought to stay in control. The Japanese swept his knife hand in a back slash, clipping Bolan's left cheek. In the microsecond that followed, the big American threw out his right leg, slamming the sole of his boot against the other's knee. He put all of his considerable strength into the kick and was rewarded by the crunch of collapsing bone. The Japanese made a low hissing sound. His injured limb gave way under him and he stumbled forward.

As the Yakuza's head came in range, Bolan slammed his right fist forward, the heel of his palm impacting with the guy's nose. Cartilage crunched. Blood spurted. Bolan twisted to one side as the man hit the ground, caught his balance and reached around to grab for the knife hand. The wrist was thick and muscular. The Japanese tried to pull free. Bolan rolled so he was straddling the guy's broad back. He laid his left hand on the back of the man's head and shoved hard, pushing his face into the soft earth. The Japanese struggled as he sucked in soft mud, starting to choke. Bolan, aware that he had no time to prolong this struggle, rammed the man's face deeper into the mud. At the same time he worked on the hand holding the knife and broke the guy's weakened grip. As the knife slipped clear, the Executioner snatched it up and rammed it into the exposed flesh of the man's neck at the base of his skull. He felt the keen blade cleave its way through, felt the slight resistance as it encountered bone, then it slid in up to the handle. The Japanese arched up in a moment of pure agony before his movements were reduced to a shuddering spasm. Blood welled up around the knife as Bolan pulled it out.

He lurched to his feet, aware of the keening pulse of pain in his slashed side and cheek. He could feel the blood streaming from the wounds. He turned his face to the cold rain and let it wash over him as he stood for a moment, the Tanto knife in his left hand, his right freeing the SIG from his blacksuit.

He made his way to the rear door of the house, stumbling as his feet dragged in the muddy earth.

THE HUMMER CAME barreling along the narrow approach to the house. It bumped over muddy ridges and through the streaming rivers of rain washed down from the low hills at the rear.

Kira Tedesko drove with one hand, her pistol clutched in her left as she surveyed the chaos of bodies sprawled on the ground. The smoldering wreckage on the helicopter pad. Greasy swirls of smoke, dissipated by the wind-driven rain, still rose from the pyre.

She jammed on the brakes well short of the house and sat studying the structure. There didn't seem to be any movement.

She knew Cooper was around. The bodies at the rear of the house proved that.

But where was he now?

Almost on cue she heard the rattle of shots coming from inside the house, answering her silent question.

BOLAN HAD ONLY taken a few steps inside the kitchen area when he was confronted by the figure of Iguchi Katana. The Yakuza boss, dressed in his expensive, handmade suit, held a poised Samurai sword in his right hand. His face was impassive, but the fury in his cold stare told Bolan the Tiger Red boss had witnessed the deaths of his two bodyguards.

"I was informed of your skills. Impressive. Now you must allow me to satisfy my honor for you killing my faithful servants."

Bolan raised his bloody face and stared the Japanese full-on.

"Honor? You don't know the meaning of the word."

He raised the P-226 before Katana could respond and put three slugs in the mobster's skull.

"THAT WAS inside the house," Petrovsky said.

Valentina only smiled at his reaction. "So it was. I have a feeling we're on our own, Nikolai. Everyone else seems to have gone hunting our elusive Mr. Cooper. And do you know what? I think he's outwitted them all and now *he's* hunting us."

"Katana?"

Valentina ignored him, reaching once again for the bottle of whiskey to refill her glass.

"For God's sake, Valentina."

"A little late for blasphemy, Nikolai. If I were you, I'd put more faith in that gun you hold like a limp dick."

"I'm not a killer like—"

She rounded on him. "Like *me?* True. It's easy to just pick up a phone and get someone to do it for you."

Petrovsky stared at her as if she had suddenly become a stranger he failed to recognize. Not the woman he had known since she was a child. This was a different Valentina Suvarov.

And one he wasn't sure he liked.

"I don't understand."

"Then get out of my way, Nikolai, because I have a job to finish."

She pushed by him, a bitter expression on her beautiful face. Despite his misgivings, Petrovsky followed her. They emerged in the spacious entrance lobby.

Valentina turned as movement from the rear of the house caught her eye.

Mack Bolan moved into view. He held a pistol in one hand and a knife in the other. He looked as though he had been dragged through hell and back. The blacksuit he wore was ripped. Blood was soaking his side from a long knife slash and from the reopened wound he had suffered back in Russia. A cut on his cheek was dripping blood. The expression in his eyes was unpleasant to see.

Petrovsky stepped by Valentina, standing between her and the man they knew as Cooper.

"Do you realize what you have done?" Petrovsky said.

"Ridding the world of a pack of vermin fits the box nicely."

"The Suvarovs are—"

"The Suvarovs are dead in the water," Bolan told him. "Finished. Your day is over."

"*No.*" Petrovsky screamed, and raised his weapon.

Bolan's P-226 thundered in the confines of the lobby, the sound magnified as he triggered three fast shots. The 9 mm slugs plowed into Petrovsky's chest, the impact knocking him backward. He slid across the polished floor until his legs gave way and he fell hard, the pistol dropping from his slack hand.

Valentina swept her own weapon up from her side, directing her anger at Bolan as she leveled the weapon, her finger already against the trigger.

Bolan moved his hand a fraction, lining up his shot.

Behind Valentina the main house door opened, swinging back against the wall. She ignored it, her concentration on the target in her sights, feeling the pressure of the trigger against her finger.

Bolan had his shot, free and clear, but he hesitated. Something deep inside held him back, a discipline that paused his own trigger finger, confronted as he was by this beautiful young woman. It was a split-second hesitation, but it was enough to allow Valentina to fire first. The slug hit Bolan in the chest, coring in to miss his lung and lodge in muscle. He stepped back, fighting the urge to fall, and he brought up the SIG again.

The second shot came hard on the heels of the first. This time Bolan felt nothing.

Standing in the open, Kira Tedesko fired a second and a third time, her shots driving Valentina Suvarov to the floor. She had placed her trio of shots between Valentina's shoulders, the slugs coring in deep. Valentina fell facedown, her eyes wide with shock, feeling the pain starting to invade her body, and the last thing she saw was Bolan staring down at her.

Tedesko moved into the house, stepping over the bloody body and reaching Bolan as he leaned against the wall.

"Why didn't you shoot?" Tedesko's eyes brimmed with tears. "Damn you, Cooper, why didn't you shoot?" Bolan raised his heavy head and stared at her. "Cooper, you chose a hell of a time to get saintly."

He slid to the floor. "You need to contact Leo," he said slowly. "There has to be some communication setup in this place somewhere. Do it through Puerto Rico."

"Hey, I'll figure something out." She placed a hand over the bloody hole in his chest. "Jesus, Cooper, you stay still. I'll have the damned U.S. Marines swarming all over this place before you know it. Just don't you do anything silly like dying on me."

Bolan only nodded. He felt tired and bloody, and all he really wanted to do was to rest. For a while. Just for a while....

EPILOGUE

The battle for Isla Blanca ended just as quickly as it had begun. The few survivors took to the moored motor vessel and fled. They were stopped three hours later by a Puerto Rico Coast Guard cutter and taken into custody.

By the time this happened Mack Bolan was in the U.S. military hospital in Puerto Rico, undergoing surgery to remove the bullet from his chest. In an adjoining operating room, Kira Tedesko had the bullet taken from her arm. Because of the numerous injuries they had each sustained earlier, they were both to be confined to bed for a week. They weren't good patients and the only way the hospital eventually got them to quiet down was to put them in a room together, in separate beds.

Leo Turrin arrived early the morning after the

firefight. He looked in on Bolan, who was still unconscious, before going to see Kira Tedesko. She was in a slightly better condition.

"Once you're feeling up to it, we need to clear up some details."

Tedesko heard him speaking, but her mind was on other matters.

"Is he always like this? Setting the world on fire to bring these people down?"

"He's a man who doesn't compromise, Kira. He can't. It drives him to do what he does."

"Something must have started him on this. What was it?"

Turrin smiled. She had insight, this Kira Tedesko, the knack to see deep into someone's soul and to figure out they had a special reason why they did what they did.

"You'll have to ask him that."

"You think I won't?"

"I know you will."

"Out there, there were times he scared me. I saw a look in his eyes that made me wonder if I was with a different person. Then he changed and I knew *I* was safe with him."

Turrin knew what she meant. He related a story in the media about the former head of the fragmented Suvarov Mob. Arkady Suvarov had been found dead in his cell. Somehow he had managed to smuggle a sliver of glass in with him. During the night he had slashed both his wrists, quietly bleeding to death in his bunk. By the time he was found he had been dead for hours.

ON A CHILL autumn morning Leo Turrin stood beside the grave of Federal Agent Walter Kershaw. He was accompanied by Kira Tedesko, who was in the process of transferring to the Justice Department, a personal request Turrin had been only too happy to sponsor, as was Mack Bolan.

"Just to let you know, Walt," Turrin said. "We got them. Damned if we didn't."

"God keep, soldier," Bolan said softly.

He still wasn't fully fit but had insisted on accompanying Turrin and Tedesko. For him it was a way of closing the mission. This particular mission, because for Mack Bolan, it was far from the end of his own personal war.